Best wishes

from

John

ALL FOR BLOOD

By John Pendleton

Table of Contents

To Wendy and Trudi for their help

Chapter One

A Sense of Family

DENSE mist hung like a shroud above the lonely drain in the Lincolnshire Fens.

It was a dark, still night, dank and drear.

A road bridge carried a narrow lane across the water and, at right angles to the lane, a mud track with grass growing up the middle led along the drainside. A high grass bank separated the track from the drain which travelled ramrod straight through the flat, almost featureless, countryside.

Even in daylight there was no human habitation to be seen from this isolated spot. Surprisingly, though, at the road-end of the track were two wheelie bins and a delapidated wooden post box, which had become detached from its metal frame and sat half-submerged by the grass, looking forlorn. This suggested that there must be a dwelling somewhere at the end of the track. In the daytime a handful of trees could be seen on the horizon, which might have provided just enough cover for a small dwelling. But anyone living there must surely have been a hermit – or in hiding.

On this particular night the eery silence of this remote location was gently broken by the rolling sound of an approaching motor vehicle. The wheelie bins were picked out by its headlights.

A long black estate car stopped and pulled into the track. Two men, clad in black, emerged from the car. They quietly opened the tailgate and bundled out a heavy load contained in a black bin liner. The men lifted one end of the package each and then scaled the drain bank, slipping and sliding as they struggled up the wet grass, but not exchanging a word. They disappeared for a few seconds and then repeated the exercise with a second similar parcel. One of the men returned to the car, took a wooden oar from the boot and clambered back over the bank with it. Both men returned a couple of minutes later and re-entered their vehicle, which was driven steadily away.

***

Two naked bodies writhed on the prickly office carpet of Dunsill's Properties Ltd.

***

It was the afternoon of Christmas Eve, 1974, and the small office had just been closed for the Christmas period.

Edward Dunsill was a smart 23-year-old, never normally to be seen in the office without a perfectly tailored suit, precisely ironed shirt and neat matching tie. He was every inch the successful young businessman.

But today was Christmas party day and the firm's tiny workforce of three was allowed to dress accordingly. Edward, tall, slim, dark and handsome, was in blue jeans and grey polo-necked sweater. Even in these casual clothes he managed to look well-groomed and affluent.

His PA, an attractive leggy blonde in her late-twenties called Shula, was wearing a black pencil-thin calf-length dress with black meshed tights.

Marilyn, the recently-recruited receptionist, had clearly made a big effort to impress at her first Christmas party. The pale-skinned, 17-year-old beauty had curled her shoulder-length raven-coloured hair into immaculate ringlets. Her "little black dress" had a plunging neckline revealing luscious ample breasts and was just long enough to preserve some semblance of modesty. She was about 5ft 10in tall - not as tall as Shula - and oozing sensuality.

When the threesome closed the office they walked for a quarter of an hour before reaching Toby's sea front bar where they planned to enjoy an afternoon drinking session.

The pub was packed with customers, many of them from local offices, shops and factories celebrating the start of their Christmas shutdowns. And holding court at the bar was the hotel's ebullient owner, a blunt but hospitable Yorkshireman who had swapped coal mining for catering in his middle years.

He was dispensing free champagne and trays of refreshments to all those who came into the bright modern lounge bar. Most of the customers, including the trio from Dunsill's Properties, were taking full advantage of his generosity.

Pop music was blaring out of the bar's sound system and, as the afternoon progressed and people were getting "merry", some customers turned the central area of the bar into a dance floor. Despite his good looks and stylish appearance Edward Dunsill was by no means an extrovert. He had a reserved, slightly aloof manner but liked a drink and was able to "let his hair down" when stimulated by a few beers. His favourite tipple, though, was champagne and on this particular afternoon he liberally imbibed the free bubbly.

Shula took him on to the dance floor and they bopped away energetically for several minutes until they were joined by a well-oiled Marilyn. They danced together off and on for the next three hours. Then, at around 5pm, Shula, who had a live-in fiance, said she had to go home to prepare an evening meal. They left the dance floor to say their goodbyes but then Marilyn took Edward by the hand and coaxed him to jig along to The Rolling Stones' "Satisfaction".

After a few more Sixties' classics had been played the music slowed down and the romantic strains of Barry White were introduced. Marilyn put her arms around Edward and closed up to him. She fondled his bottom and he returned the compliment, noting that she was wearing no knickers. Marilyn noticed a bulge in Edward's trousers and she secretly let a finger slide along his erection. She looked up at him and smiled cheekily. He smiled back and she repeated her move several times. Edward pulled her even closer so that now they were dancing crotch to crotch in rhythmic motion.

Marilyn took his hand once more and mouthed "Come with me".

She led him off the dance floor and over to a secluded part of the bar which was in darkness. They secreted themselves behind one of the thick pillars that supported the roof. They kissed passionately as Marilyn continued to do everything she knew to excite him. He gently stroked her right breast and, finding no opposition to this move, slipped his hand inside her black bra, tweaking her nipple and then fondly cupping the comely breast in his hand.

At that moment the landlord walked by, looked at the couple, smirked and said nothing.

"We need to go somewhere else," said Marilyn.

"Where?" asked Edward.

"Back to the office?" asked Marilyn.

"Okay. Let's go."

They left the bar quickly and hurried along the road back to the office.

The shutters were already down so the reception area offered a private if uncomfortable location for love-making. As soon as they were through the front door they stripped each other off and lowered themselves down on the floor – the one with a very prickly carpet.

When their passions had been enjoyably satisfied they rose and started to dress.

Edward started to laugh.

"What's the matter with you?" asked Marilyn, looking quizzical.

"It's your bottom," said Edward. "It looks as if it's been sandpapered."

"Oh my god," said Marilyn. "That carpet's so rough. I'd better not show my bum to my boyfriend for a few nights!"

"Boyfriend?" said Edward, looking a little worried. "I didn't know you had a boyfriend."

"Oh. Didn't you know? He's a professional boxer."

"Oh, great!" said Edward.

Marilyn giggled: "I was teasing you. He's actually a schoolboy. Huge tall lad, but a big softy. You don't need to bother about him. I'll probably chuck him in a week or two anyway. Anyway I must go now."

She kissed him gently.

"See you back at work after Christmas," she said, moving towards the front door.

"Yes. Have a lovely Christmas," said Edward.

"I will. Same to you."

"I've had a lovely Christmas already," said Edward.

Marilyn smiled and left.

***

It is 42 years later. Edward arrives in his Range Rover at the Marshyard cemetery car park, three miles from his home in the east coast resort of Sanderholme. He opens his boot lid and takes out two sprays of mixed flowers

14

wrapped in cellophane, a large pair of scissors, a piece of cloth and a plastic bottle full of water.

Ashen-faced, he walks towards the graveyard's white wicket gate and opens it. Along a gravelled drive in front of him is Marshyard's All Saints Church, a beautiful towered church built in greenstone and dating from the 14th century. Scaffolding at the front of the church and a "Danger – Falling Masonry" sign indicate that the building has seen better days.

The graveyard itself, particularly the newest section, is kept in an immaculate condition, with grass regularly mown and the kerbs of the graves neatly strimmed. Mature oak and elm trees provide shade and help to produce an atmosphere of ancient peace.

It is a beautiful summer's day. The sun is shining and the birds are singing. Pleasant smells of cow parsley and wild garlic greet the visitor. It is a scene which might uplift the spirits even of those whose bereavement is raw and recent.

It is eighteen months since Edward lost Elizabeth, his wife of almost 40 years. Tears still blur his vision each time he tends her grave. She had died unexpectedly of a heart attack, leaving a large hole in the lives of her husband, their 35-year-old daughter, Julia, and grandchildren Eve and Samantha. Elizabeth had been the rock of the family, loving, uncomplaining, and, outwardly at least, seemingly always cheerful. She was practical and resourceful, a perfect complement to Edward, who, although worldly and sensible most of the time, could sometimes lose himself in an academic haze.

Theirs had been a highly successful marriage, their love undimmed by time, and Edward had felt Elizabeth's loss tremendously. His way of coping was to throw himself into his many interests and hobbies with a passionate intensity.

Edward marches across the recently mown area to much longer grass in an older part of the graveyard. There, under a large overhanging holly tree, are two graves, one with a new white headstone, and, cheek by jowl, another much older stone, covered in green algae, moss and lichens. The new grave is Elizabeth's, the older one that of her parents.

Edward begins the rather painful task of removing fallen spiky holly leaves which choke both graves. Here and there a new holly bush has started to sprout through the concrete kerbs. These have to be yanked out of the ground. He removes dead blooms from the flowerpots and then uses a cloth and water from his bottle to clean the headstones and surrounds. Having tidied up the site to his satisfaction he unwraps the new flowers and carefully arranges a spray in each of the pots, using the scissors to cut the stalks to the right size. Then he rises from his knees, walks across the grass and disappears around the back of the church. He reappears a minute or so later carrying a metal watering can, which he uses to water the flowers.

He retraces his steps through the longer grass with a view to returning the watering can to the tap at the rear of the church. While tending the graves he has felt stiff and tense, trying desperately to hold in his emotions. Now, having accomplished what he came to do, he is more relaxed.

Being something of an amateur historian, Edward has always been fascinated by old churchyards and the family stories which the memorials can point to. As he walks through this old part of the Marshyard cemetery he takes leisure to read some of the inscriptions on the gravestones. His attention is particularly drawn to one grave, which he has never noticed before. Its stone is green and mildewed, ravaged by time and neglect, and its inscription has been almost totally obscured by fallen leaves. But, incongruously, its flowerpot has been very recently filled with fresh blooms.

Edward is intrigued. He bends down and pushes aside some leaves which are hiding the flat stone at the head of a grave. He can see odd letters of an inscription, but most of the letters are covered in dust and soil. He brushes the stone with his hand until the whole wording can be read.

What he sees sends a shiver of surprise through his body: "Gabriel Dunsill, aged 41, died March 1st, 1976. Beloved father of Anthony. Rest in Peace."

Gabriel is a new name to Edward. Dunsill is an uncommon name and he feels that this man must have been some forgotten relative.

He examines the pot of flowers and notices a card tied to the stems with string. The card has been laminated and embossed gold lettering on it reads: "To my dear Dad. From your ever-loving son, Anthony."

Anthony Dunsill is another name entirely unknown to Edward.

When he leaves the churchyard his brain is in overdrive.

***

Generations of the Dunsills had been farmers in Nottinghamshire. But in the mid-19th century William Dunsill, Edward's great great grandfather, bought a mixed arable and livestock farm on the outskirts of Sanderholme and moved to the Lincolnshire coast with his family.

The family still kept its Nottinghamshire land and connections and Edward's grandfather, John, met and married Fanny, daughter of rich Mansfield foundry owners. They moved into the spacious Sanderholme farmhouse and produced Bertram, their only child. Bertram later married Margaret, known as Peggy, and they too had one child, Edward.

After John's premature death of cancer in his late forties, Bertram, Peggy and their son continued to live with Granny Fanny, a formidable force of nature who reigned supreme over the household.

Granny Fanny had always been used to getting her own way. She was a curious mixture of ambitious snobbery and down-to-earth Midlands commonsense. Depending on her mood and inclination she could be Lady of the Manor or Grandma Giles from the famous Daily Express cartoons.

In her first guise, she insisted on all her family being educated privately so as not to mix with "the rough children from the council houses". They all had to have music lessons and she bought each of them "posh" cars as soon as they were able to drive. There were standards to uphold.

In "Grandma Giles" mode she was obsessed with doing the football pools and woe betide anyone who spoke during the Saturday teatime results programme. She poured scorn on ITV's Saturday afternoon wrestling with Kent Walton. But she secretly loved the sport. She would pretend to read her copy of The Daily Express while peering over the top of it to watch the grapplers at work.

She voted Conservative, while praising the Communist Manifesto and being first in the queue to collect her "divi" from the local Co-op. She avidly watched the Remembrance Sunday service at the Cenotaph on television while refusing to let any of her family join the Armed Forces where they might have to mix with "common soldiers". She insisted on every family member wearing their Poppy. Each poppy had been bought only once and had been taken out of a jar on the mantelpiece every year from time immemorial. Recycling is far from a new phenomenon.

She baked every day until her death, produced wonderful Christmas puddings, cracked nuts with her teeth, collected horse manure off the road for her garden and declared war on rats, wasps and ants, employing various methods of torture against them.

Granny Fanny was "a character". For all her faults, inconsistencies and domineering ways she was loved by everyone. For what she possessed was a zest for life, an indomitable spirit and, above all, a fierce loyalty to family and friends.

In her mid-seventies Fanny began to have bouts of illness - bronchitis, neuralgia, shingles and heart palpitations were among the ailments which laid her low. By the age of 79 she seemed to have rallied and be more like her old ebullient self. Then one night she spent an evening watching television, particularly enjoying a variety show featuring stand-up comedian Ken Dodd. She went to bed laughing at his jokes. Her daughter-in-law, Peggy, was awakened half an hour later by the sound of giggling from Fanny's bedroom and went in to see what was happening.

Fanny was still convulsed with laughter.

"That man's so funny," she gasped. "We will see him on telly again, won't we?"

"Yes," Peggy assured her.

Fanny gave way to another spasm of laughter and then slumped back on to her pillow. She died instantly – a massive heart attack.

Throughout his life Edward would declare to friends: "Ken Dodd killed my granny!"

As well as having inherited her late husband's estate Granny Fanny was wealthy in her own right. When she died a considerable fortune in land and money passed to Bertram. He was able to buy additional farmland on the edge of town, for which he eventually received planning permission for lucrative housing developments. This meant his son Edward had a good start in life. He attended a local preparatory school and then Repton School, an ancient independent school in Derbyshire. On leaving school at 18 he gained a Property and Land Management Degree and later joined the family business of Dunsill's Properties Ltd.

Edward was confident, shrewd, smart and, potentially at least, wealthy.

He was not the most mercenary person in the world but he did agree wholeheartedly with the sentiments expressed by Anthony Trollope's memorable character Archdeacon Grantly: "If honest men did not squabble for money, in this wicked world of ours, the dishonest would get it all; and I do not see that the course of virtue would be much improved."

Edward, though, also had a reflective, introspective side. At school he had been deeply interested in the Classics, English literature, history and philosophy. He was an avid reader of an eclectic range of subjects. He was equally at ease socialising in the pub or sitting quietly hunched over a book at the local library.

Before his marriage to Elizabeth he had spent rather too much time in the pub and not so much time with his books. But after he settled down to relative domesticity there was far more time for his academic pursuits.

***

After visiting the Marshyard cemetery Edward returned home.

Home was a spacious four-bedroomed detached house with large gardens and a mature orchard in Marshlands, a suburb of Sanderholme where the wealthiest members of the community resided. To Edward it was an empty home since Julia had left to get married and Elizabeth had died so unexpectedly.

After a simple microwaved tea, he went to a drawer in his study and pulled out a folder labelled "Family History". In this was a variety of old photographs, newspaper cuttings, family letters and farm account books, some going as far back as the Nottinghamshire Dunsills of the 17th century. In fact there was far more material about the family in the 17th, 18th and 19th centuries than there was about more recent times.

Edward was keen to find out something about Gabriel Dunsill, whose grave he had just discovered. But there was nothing in the folder which even acknowledged his existence. Then, working until the early hours of the next morning, he tried Google and various ancestry websites. All to no avail. Gabriel was, it appeared, something of a mystery man.

For Edward, his recent interest in the family tree was far more than the purely academic fancy of someone who described himself as an amateur historian. He was, in fact, in the grip of something which, since his wife's death, was becoming an obsession.

It had become apparent to Edward that when he died his branch of the Dunsill family would die out with him. He had no son to succeed him and his grandchildren would have the surname of his son-in-law – Jones.

Edward had a keen sense of continuity, family inheritance and the passing of both names and genes to subsequent generations. He was proud of the

Dunsills' history as landowners, farmers and pillars of the community and recoiled from the idea that all this would stop with him. It would not be so bad, he felt, if he had had any nephews or even male cousins with the Dunsill name to keep the bloodline going. But he had found none. The family had been surprisingly bad at producing children and male heirs in particular.

Edward had always been fascinated by the Nature v Nurture debate: whether human behaviour and psychology was largely inherited through the genes or was substantially the result of upbringing and social and environmental factors.

He had read enough and was intelligent enough to appreciate that both Nature and Nurture had a big role to play. But his personal observation of people had convinced him that Nature – genes inherited from previous generations – was the major driving force behind human thoughts and actions.

He noted how closely people resembled their parents, both physically and in their beliefs.

He was not himself a vain or conceited man, but he had such a strong sense of tradition and of family bonding that he was appalled by the prospect that the Dunsill family should become obsolete.

In most areas of life he was rational and moderate, but his fervent desire to continue the family line was always now at the forefront of his mind.

He was also a strong believer in the often overlooked Darwinian theory of sexual selection, which urges not only the survival of the fittest, but also the reproduction of the fittest. The Dunsills were a successful family and had been for generations. They *were* the fittest. They *were* the type of people who should reproduce as much as possible. At least that was what Edward had come to believe.

He never once shared these beliefs with anyone else because he did not wish to appear big-headed, or even worse, delusional. But his belief that the Dunsills were special, a family rooted in the soil of England, of the finest and most independent Anglo-Saxon stock, had become the mainspring of his life's aspirations. The Dunsills were The Yeomen of England, the type of worthies immortalised in the comic opera Merrie England.

Edward always told people that he took "a biological view of human nature". He believed that biological instinct – a kind of programming aimed at prolonging the future of the species – was the driving force behind most of life's emotions and activities.

He had a splendid daughter and she and her husband were perfectly content that they had produced two girls. But Edward desperately wanted a son to carry on the family's genes, its landowning tradition – and its name.

Elizabeth had suffered complications when giving birth to Julia, so she had been unable to have more children. Edward had given up the idea of having a son. In the privacy of his own mind he had recently decided to settle for something second best - to find the closest male relative who bore the Dunsill name.

He had given much thought as to what he would do when he found such a relative. He would make sure the lucky fellow would receive as much land and money as was necessary to ensure that future Dunsills would continue to prosper and fulfil their responsibilities as custodians of the landowning tradition. He knew that he risked upsetting Julia by passing wealth on to some as yet unknown kinsman. This was a bridge he had yet to come to and so he put it out of his mind. After all, such a relative might never be found. Even if he were found, he might be found wanting.

Notwithstanding these reservations, Edward knew it was his duty to ensure that not only the Dunsill bloodline continued but its name too.

He appreciated that duty was an unfashionable concept in the 21st century, but fashion had never interested him. He agreed with US General George S. Patton, who opined that: "Duty is the essence of manhood."

Chapter Two

Great Aunt Olivia

When Edward first discovered the grave of Gabriel Dunsill he was shocked. Dunsills were a rarity outside Nottinghamshire. Some of that name were recorded in the Nottinghamshire archives, which Edward had thoroughly researched, and he had discovered other Dunsills in the English speaking diaspora, mainly in Canada, the USA and the Antipodes.

But how could it be that there was a Dunsill buried just three miles from Sanderholme of whom he had never heard?

After shock came excitement. Gabriel definitely had a son and might well have other male relations. What if they were near enough in blood to Edward for him to "adopt" one of them as his male heir?

Edward pondered his next course of action. His mother and father had recently died within just a year of each other, taking to the crematorium any knowledge of Gabriel they may have had. So he decided to visit a distant cousin who happened to be Sanderholme's unofficial local historian and who was also said to be an expert on the Dunsill family and its connections.

The cousin, Harry Greensmith, was born the only child of Thomas and Charity Greensmith, nee Dunsill. His father was a respected gentlemen's tailor and his mother a gifted seamstress.

At the time of Harry's birth the family home of 5 Danish Terrace, Sanderholme, was a stylish ground floor flat in a terrace of six fine Edwardian town houses. These flats were much sought after, being close to the town centre and in a respectable area.

They remained like this until the property fell into the hands of a mercenary landlord. Gradually the flats deteriorated and the character of the most recent tenants became less salubrious. As tenants left, larger flats were divided into bedsits and the premises were officially designated HMOs – Houses in Multiple Occupation.

The Greensmiths' flat was left as an island of respectability in a sea of barbarity.

When Harry, an intelligent but unambitious young man, came of age he went to work as a clerk in the Sanderholme solicitors' firm of Hart Gamble and Lees – a position he held until retiring at 65.

When Harry was 25 his father died and the young man had devoted himself to the task of looking after his ailing mother. It was a task which lasted until the year he retired.

Now he was a dapper and sprightly 85-year-old, grey-haired and slightly built. He always carried a walking stick, but more to give himself a jaunty air when he promenaded than for any support needed for his legs. He loved to raise his cane in a gentlemanly manner to all the ladies he met in the street. And the ladies appreciated the gesture's old world charm.

Harry was notably well-dressed. His father, the tailor, guided him well in his choice of clothes. He invariably wore a small tasteful bloom as a buttonhole.

He was a true gentleman. The ladies loved him and he loved the ladies. In earlier years he managed to have at least one night out a week socially and he became an adept and graceful ballroom dancer.

He had also been an above average tennis player, a credit to his local club in his immaculately creased whites.

There was never any shortage of either dance or tennis partners and his name was linked to several eligible spinsters in his younger days and to a number of eligible widows in his latter years.

But his commitment to his mother held him back. He never married and most of his relationships with women remained sexually unconsummated.

Harry remained neat in his appearance, clean in his habits, and tidy around the house into his eighties and lived a reasonably content, if now somewhat lonely, existence.

When Edward arrived to see him Harry was watering his window boxes, his pride and joy and one of the few saving graces outside the now desolate row of buildings where he lived.

"Good afternoon, Edward," he said. "It is a pleasure to see you. It's been such a long time. Do come inside."

Edward was led into a neat and airy sitting room, lined with antique furniture and bookshelves full of tantalisingly ancient tomes. He was invited to sit down in an august but exceedingly comfortable leather armchair.

"Will you have a cup of tea or coffee?" asked the old gentleman. "I can soon pop the kettle on."

Edward declined. He was anxious to get on with the business he was there for.

He related to Harry the discovery of Gabriel Dunsill's grave and asked if the old man could place that name on the family tree.

"I believe I can," said Harry. "But I'm afraid it's all to do with something of a family scandal involving your great-aunt Olivia."

Edward started backwards and gave Harry an incredulous look: "Aunt Olivia? I've never heard of any scandal involving Aunt Olivia."

Harry smiled and replied: "I'm afraid it's a bit of a skeleton in the family cupboard. Everyone has always been very hush-hush about it. I remember that your grandmother, Fanny, was very sniffy about it all. She probably would have forbidden your mother and father from talking of it."

"But you know the story?"

"Oh, yes. I know. It was quite the talk of the town for a time, I recall."

"Can you tell me what you know?"

"Well, ok then. It will probably have Fanny turning in her grave. But I suppose I'm safe enough!" joked Harry. "Well, here goes..."

***

The great-aunt, Mrs Olivia Toucan, was sister of Edward's grandfather, John, and sister-in-law to the redoubtable Fanny, who saw her as more of a rival for John's attention than as a family member to be cherished.

Olivia was one of those formidable people who was more feared than loved, more loathed than respected.

In her early years she had thrived through running her own millinery business, building up a tidy amount of capital.

Then she met Bill Toucan, a red-faced pot-bellied publican who had moved to Sanderholme to take over the Stag's Head, then the town's busiest commercial hotel.

Olivia married Bill, a good-hearted and amiable man, and sold her shop to help him run the hotel.

There she ruled the roost. She would perch herself on a high stool in the men-only smoke room each night and do her knitting. She would cast icy stares of disapproval towards any fellow who might dare to use a swear word.

In 1933, Bill, who had become fatter, rounder and redder through his colossal intake of beer, passed away – leaving Olivia, then in her mid-thirties, to a very long widowhood.

She sold the hotel and used the proceeds from that and the millinery business to start a mini property empire in the town. At the peak of her prosperity she rented out 20 dwellings.

Her widowhood – at least at the beginning – was not entirely without romantic incident.

Olivia was a tall woman with a trim figure and a commanding presence. She had a bossy sort of charm, which meant she invariably got her own way, and which was not without its charismatic effect on the opposite sex.

One night the new owners of the Stag's Head invited Olivia to have dinner with them, and, not one to shirk attendance at a social get-together, she readily accepted. It was the first of several meals they shared.

The new hosts, Frank and Connie Simpson, had come from London where they had run an East End dockland hotel.

At one of the dinners with Olivia they introduced her to a friend they had made in the capital.

Albert Clarkson was a dapper 45-year-old, later always described by Olivia's family as "black as the ace of spades". He was a smiling, fit looking man of slim build, but with a well-lived-in lined face and badly nicotine-stained fingers.

Olivia was a chain smoker, so the two immediately had something in common as they lit up for each other during the dinner party.

Albert was clearly well travelled and described in vivid detail the fights he had had with a variety of wild animals, and even wilder drug dealers, in Africa, the West Indies and the Far East.

He described himself as the director of an African tobacco-importing company and boasted of having owned a fleet of Bentleys in his native Nigeria.

But what really excited Olivia, and added intensely to his exotic charm, was his revelation that he was a Prince – Prince of the Botwali tribe which owned many square miles of mineral-rich countryside in Nigeria.

Albert had been a regular at Frank and Connie's East End pub. In fact he had spent most of every day and every night in there.

He was a popular customer with the locals, always having a cheery word for everyone and full of anecdotes both of his own derring-do and of his ancestors' exploits. He claimed that some of those ancestors had been cannibals before a Christian missionary converted them.

For a while Albert had lived with a widow, Elspeth, whose late husband had reputedly been "big" in the diamond mining industry in South Africa. Their common interest in Africa had been the spark which had brought Albert and Elspeth together.

But one day when he walked into the pub Albert was clearly distressed and trying hard to hold back his tears.

"What possibly can have happened?" asked the concerned landlady.

"It's Elspeth," he said. "She passed away last night – had a massive heart attack. I will miss her so much, you know. She was a super lady."

For the next few weeks Albert had kept up his usual routine of visiting the pub on a daily basis. Then came some news that added to his sadness - Frank and Connie had sold up the pub and were taking over a large commercial hotel in Sanderholme.

"Where's Sanderholme?" asked a disconsolate Albert. "I've never heard of that place."

"It's a holiday resort on the east coast – Lincolnshire," said Frank in his broad Cockney accent. "It's a bustling little town with some marvellous beaches. We think it's got a great future. You will have to come down and visit us when we've got settled in."

"I surely will," said Albert. He paused, and added: "You know, if I like it, I might even stay!"

He supped at his pint, deep in thought.

"In fact, I think a change of scene would do me the world of good. I might as well make a break and come with you to Lincolnshire."

Frank had always been curious as to how Albert made his living, as he always seemed to be in the pub. Albert had told him he did his business on the docks. He had lots of contacts and the deals he cut kept the board of his company happy. Now he talked of staying in Sanderholme, Frank wondered how he would be able to keep up those contacts.

"It would be great if you could come," he said to Albert.

In the back of his mind he felt that a black Prince full of exciting tales could be just the sort of interesting customer who might appeal to the hotel's regulars.

During his brief trips to Sanderholme Frank had several times mentioned to Connie that, compared with docklands, there was little or no racial variety in the town's people. Most either spoke with Midlands or Yorkshire accents or had the rural dialect native to the Fens agricultural area surrounding the resort.

A black man with a big personality could be an exotic attraction in such a place, thought Frank, much like the two-headed sheep and the five-legged cow he had seen in the sideshow under Sanderholme pier.

Frank kept such thoughts to himself and was successful in encouraging the Black Prince to "up sticks" and live in Lincolnshire. He remained curious as to how Albert could continue to make a living in the tobacco importing business in such a remote location. But Albert assured him that by making judicious telephone calls and occasional journeys back to London he could manage his affairs quite satisfactorily.

He seemed eager to make the move as soon as possible, telling Frank and Connie effusively that he would feel lonely and bereft when they left the East End.

It was arranged that Frank and Connie would have a couple of weeks to settle in at the Stag's Head and then Albert would travel to Sanderholme and take up permanent residence in one of their hotel's letting rooms.

Frank and Connie were skilled "mine hosts" and wherever they went perfected the art of what would nowadays be called networking. They would cultivate good customers by offering them the odd free dinner or a round of drinks. When Albert arrived what better, they thought, than to introduce him to Olivia, who had been quite lonely since the loss of her husband?

So the dinner party was duly arranged.

Albert and Olivia hit it off immediately. They had lots in common, aside from chain smoking. Both had travelled the world extensively and both liked to drink rivers of best Scottish malt whisky.

Olivia, normally full of stories herself, sat back quietly in her chair at the dinner table captivated by Albert's amazing tales - of piracy, cannibalism, struggles with evil drugs barons and his adventures as a mercenary in Mozambique.

They were stories of violence and crime, but Albert had always been on the side of right and justice.

Some people who told such stories would have been dismissed by right-thinking company as boring charlatans, but Albert told his tales with such lightness of touch and humour that all his hearers were immensely charmed.

The first dinner party invitation led to many more. As time went on Olivia would invite Albert for "a nightcap" at her plush town centre flat, and well, shall we say, "things developed".

After a couple of months Albert announced to Frank and Connie that, regretfully, he would be leaving his room in the hotel and moving in with Olivia.

The publicans were sorry to lose a paying guest but wished Albert well, satisfied that he and Olivia would continue to be very good bar customers.

Olivia was in proverbial seventh heaven. She was completely in love with her Prince Charming.

They even talked of marriage - a traditional African wedding back in Nigeria, which, bearing in mind his princely status, would be a lavish affair attended by all the important political dignitaries and tribal chiefs of that country.

This state of affairs was scandalous to Olivia's strongly Christian family. They thoroughly disapproved from a variety of angles - Olivia and Albert were living in sin, they suspected he might be sponging off her, and, by far the worst of his faults, he was black.

The family's experience of black people heretofore had been largely limited to visiting a freak show called The African Jungle in the local amusement park, where exotic scenes from the tropical jungle were acted out by real African natives - and some blacked-up ones - covered in war paint, wearing grass skirts and brandishing spears.

It might also be mentioned that the Dunsills' favourite recording artist was a gentleman called G. H. Eliot, the Chocolate Coloured Coon, but he too was a white man blacked up! These days their attitudes would be alarmingly non-PC, but in the early and middle twentieth century they were merely commonplace.

Olivia was well provided for and did not ask Albert for any money towards housekeeping or his accommodation, a fact which both annoyed and worried her family.

Then, unexpectedly, The African Jungle mentioned above came up for sale and Albert sensed a good business opportunity. He needed money quickly for the purchase and so he asked Olivia for a temporary loan. She willingly obliged.

However, a few months later, following a series of disputes with the badly paid workers, the business flopped, leaving Albert with large debts. Again Olivia helped out.

Albert became increasingly reliant on his lover's generosity. Eventually even he declared that this state of affairs was unsatisfactory and that he could not countenance being a leech living off Olivia's rent monies. He would make monthly contributions to their living expenses, but in order to do so would have to make more trips to London to earn extra commission from his tobacco imports. To achieve that, though, Albert would need to be more mobile than he currently was. At one time, he said, he could have had one of his Bentleys imported into the country. But he had had to sell them all before coming to Sanderholme to pay for a niece's extravagant "royal wedding" in Nigeria.

He explained to Olivia that his funds were inextricably bound up in the company at that time, so he could not immediately get hold of enough cash to buy a car in England. Train journeys between Sanderholme and London were at awkward uncivilised times.

Albert told Olivia he would have to give some further thought to his predicament.

Then one morning he was awakened early - at 11 o'clock - by Olivia striding into their bedroom and tugging excitedly at his arm.

"Come downstairs this instant," she demanded.

"What is it, my bright-plumaged oiseau?" asked Albert.

"Don't ask. Just come downstairs - now!"

Albert moaned a little, stretched, and did as he was told.

He followed Olivia downstairs and she flung open the front door of the flat.

"There! Do you like it?" she exclaimed.

"What is this??" asked Albert, staring at a gleaming silver Bentley parked in the street.

"It's your new car. I've bought it for you. Now you can get to London."

"I don't believe it, hen. You can't spoil me so!"

"I can. I have. So shut up. I love you."

Albert did an excited little dance and then clasped Olivia to him, passionately kissing her all over her face and neck.

When the Dunsill family found out about the car they were horrified.

"She's heading for such a big fall," declared Fanny to John. "And you're not to go running to pick her up."

"Of course I won't," pledged John.

But this was a lie: families like the Dunsills always stick together in the end.

Albert drove off to London in the Bentley that very day to transact some business. Olivia never saw him again. A box of rent money from the bedroom of her flat was likewise never seen again.

Olivia was absolutely distraught, although she never let her family see it. The family, in turn – even Fanny - tried not to gloat over her distress or say "We told you so". They were too basically good-natured to do that. They did all they could, without ever specifically saying so, to ameliorate her condition.

Then, a week or so after Albert's departure, came the bombshell - Olivia was pregnant. To begin with the family assumed that the baby was Albert's and they contemplated with utter dread the prospect that it would be half-caste. But then Olivia admitted that the pregnancy was the result of a drink-induced one night stand with a travelling salesman who had stayed at the hotel. She had been unable to contact him since, presumably because he had signed into the hotel under a false name. Olivia explained that the Bentley she bought for Albert had been to sugar the pill of the news she had to tell him about the baby.

As she always did when she was in trouble, she immediately sought the support and advice of her brother John.

In the Shire counties, pre-Second World War, illegitimacy still had a large stigma attached to it. Olivia had already scandalised the family within the respectable community of Sanderholme through her affair with Albert. Her pregnancy was the last straw. John's advice, strongly urged upon him by Fanny, was that the birth should be concealed and the offspring spirited away.

John hit upon an idea. His brother, Joseph, was a wealthy farmer in Woldsby, a village some 25 miles away in Lincolnshire's hilly area. He and his wife, Myrtle, had unsuccessfully tried for years to have a family of their own.

John approached his brother with the suggestion that Olivia should live at Woldsby for the duration of her pregnancy and then hand over the baby to Joseph and Myrtle for them to bring up as their own. The couple agreed with alacrity. Olivia, who ostensibly had little in the way of maternal instincts, initially showed some reluctance to giving up her baby. But after some persuasion from John, and not a little bullying from Fanny, she endorsed the arrangement.

And so it was that little Gabriel came into the world and was given the name Dunsill. His adoptive parents were indulgent of him. He was spoilt. When he became a man it was clear that the farming life had no attraction for him. He became a drifter, guilt-ridden largesse secretly showered upon him by his real mother giving him the means to travel the world. There was some irregular contact with his mother and with Joseph and Myrtle, who in later life had sold their farm and down-sized to a modest bungalow at Marshyard.

But he was lost forever to the wider family, who conjectured that they were kept in the dark because of some misbehaviour on Gabriel's part.

For Olivia, the hurt of giving up a child had been deeper than anyone realised. The gregarious Aunt Olivia drastically changed her lifestyle. For the last 35 years of her life she buried herself in her flat, rarely going out.

When invited to family gatherings she would arrive late and refuse to take off her trademark blue straw hat with a pheasant feather sticking out of it and a vicious looking hatpin, which more resembled an offensive weapon than a fashion adornment.

Keeping on her hat was Olivia's way of signifying that she would not be staying very long. As soon as it was polite to do so she would make excuses and leave. No, in truth, that's not entirely correct. She would leave before everyone thought it was polite to do so - and the rest of the family would spend the remainder of the occasion decrying her decision to go so soon.

Inevitably one or two of the elder family members would whisper darkly: "She's never been the same since she went with that African!"

At home Olivia's daily routine would be to rise early, at 6am, do her housework and go to bed early. With the exception of one individual, visitors were excluded after 3.30pm.

One regular guest, whom she expected to attend for a weekly audience, was the Rector.

Olivia had become a strong supporter of the church, although a mystery illness prevented her from attending any services.

These weekly visits from the Rector, though, kept her up to date with current church affairs. The priest probably thought them an imposition on his valuable time, but the pill was sweetened by her frequent generous donations to the local church and various overseas missions it was supporting.

Two other routine visitors were her niece by marriage, Peggy, and a neighbour called Martin. Peggy and Martin were useful to Olivia. She would treat them like servants, Peggy helping with domestic chores and shopping and Martin carrying out various DIY jobs.

They both found Olivia incredibly patronising, but relationships were oiled with occasional gifts of money.

Olivia's second floor town centre flat was, from the outside, unprepossessing and faintly forbidding. But inside it was luxuriously furnished, with a huge plush suite, antique dining table and chairs, and many exotic ornaments, notably the impressive range of huge carved ebony elephants with real ivory tusks.

After the usual 3.30pm watershed she normally took herself off to a comfortable, warm bed, plied herself with chocolates, brandy and whisky and watched television until she finally dozed off at about midnight.

Although she was a physically self-indulgent woman Olivia was by no means a mindless hedonist.

Her brain was as sharp as a tack. She was an avid reader on a wide range of subjects and watched all the educational television programmes.

Physically she was confined to her flat 99 per cent of the time. But mentally she roamed throughout the whole of the known universe. She was as knowledgeable about the head hunters of Borneo, the Lapps who lived within the Arctic Circle and the planets of the Solar System as she was well versed in the history and principles of the Church of England. Had she lived in the age of home computers she would probably have spent most of her time surfing the net.

As we have noted, one visitor was allowed to break the 3.30pm curfew. This was Olivia's great-nephew, Edward.

From an early age Edward had visited Aunt Olivia and it has to be said he was the only member of the family who actually enjoyed the experience.

She found him a bright and interesting child, sharing her passion for politics, world affairs and the mysteries of the universe.

Edward, in turn, found Olivia fascinating to talk to and he was not a little intrigued by her self-indulgent lifestyle.

He could recognise in her some traits of his own character. She still found joy in life, but in a way which was too self-centred and eccentric to be admired by others with a Christian outlook.

Edward would visit his great-aunt at least once a week after school. He would do a little shopping for her and then they would sit down for an hour or so and "put the world to rights".

Olivia would regale Edward with her religious theories while Edward would expand on his latest philosophical ideas. They were both voracious readers with catholic tastes in literature. It was truly a meeting of minds.

It was not just Aunt Olivia's mind which fascinated Edward. It was her flat too.

The outside of the building was reached by a plain brown door squeezed in between a row of shops. When someone shut this door behind them a clanging echo was produced - a sound which was always imprinted on Edward's mind and which reminded him of the clanking-to of prison cell doors he had heard in television crime dramas.

Inside this door was a dark passage with a slate grey concrete floor. This led to two grim flights of stairs with iron railings which vibrated and made strange metallic noises as Edward ran up them.

The door to Olivia's flat was thick and heavy. Again, it would not have been out of place in a jailhouse.

This in turn led to another gloomy concrete passage through to the spartan kitchen and washroom.

But along another passage was the door to Olivia's living room and there the visitor found an astonishing contrast. Plush was the first word which sprung to people's minds in describing this part of her inner sanctum.

The orange and red textile wallcoverings and the thick-piled blue carpet gave an instant impression of opulence.

The three-piece suite was gargantuan and in a rich soft material, with deep blue and yellow stripes.

Edward loved this suite, with both sofa and chairs so comfortable and the textile so cool and pleasing to the touch.

Just being in the flat gave him a taste for a world of luxury and privilege.

But even more impressive to the boy were the ornaments which dominated the room, including the elephants, the largest of which was as big as Edward himself, and a dozen expensive looking urns and vases.

There was a distinct feeling of India and the Raj about this room.

Edward once asked Olivia how she had acquired her ornaments and she replied she had bought them at auctions. Family gossip, though, suggested the more likely source was a relationship she had once had with a maharajah.

For Edward it was a room steeped in mystery. In fact Olivia's whole lifestyle was shrouded in mystery. For example, although she had once told the family that she rented out 20 dwellings, no family member knew exactly where the properties were, and towards the end of her life she often pleaded poverty. Everyone assumed that she had gradually sold off the properties one by one so that she only had her own flat remaining.

When Olivia died of pneumonia after 40 years of widowhood, many in Sanderholme speculated that her luxurious lifestyle and her charitable giving to the church had left a large hole in her finances.

But those family members who knew her secret supposed that she had been salving her conscience by passing money to Joseph and his wife to spend on Gabriel.

Chapter Three

Unhealthy Obsession

During the late 1960s and early 1970s Sanderholme was a bright town to grow up in – a breezy seaside resort with a welcoming holiday atmosphere which rubbed off on the local people.

The town had a prosperous look about it, with freshly painted sea front hotels, a busy, clean beach, ideal for donkeys and sandcastle-making, and a couple of noisy, cheerful fairgrounds. It was a mecca for respectable working class families from the Midlands, Yorkshire and beyond.

Local children could play out in the streets and on the beaches without any fear of being molested. Women could take their dogs for walks along deserted sand dunes with no nagging thoughts that they might be mugged or raped.

There were some wonderful "characters" in the resort: hippy-style beach traders selling shellfish or candies from trays around their necks; street photographers with multi-coloured blazers and monkeys perched on their shoulders; Romany stall-holders offering gold jewellery and watches at incredibly low prices; camp showbiz entertainers who would mince a confident gait along the promenade or the pier; and stunning girl students from the length and breadth of the country who would come to Sanderholme during their vacations to earn some money working for the holiday businesses.

In their teenage years Edward and his contemporaries had had a field day in this zany, friendly atmosphere. Although he came from a wealthy family Edward was expected to work for his pocket money. He and his friends all had part-time jobs during the holiday season, such as serving in cafes, selling hot dogs or candy floss, or taking holidaymakers' luggage to and from the railway station in home-made barrows.

It gave them a few pounds to spend in the amusement arcades, coffee bars and fish and chip shops, and, when they got a little older (14 or more!), buying a few pints at the sea front pubs and discos.

The town did have its seedier side. Many of the people from inland cities who provided the seasonal work-force in the summer went "on the dole" in the winter.

Some of the less scrupulous of them would supplement their income in the winter by selling purple heart tablets to schoolchildren in the early Sixties and "pot" in the late Sixties. The less daring could earn a few extra pennies by "spinning" to cheat the slot machines in the arcades, a technique as useful as being able to pick a lock with a hairgrip.

The town had been a magnet for swaggering "teddy boys" with slicked back hair and sideburns, long jackets, drainpipe trousers, winklepicker shoes and a frightening range of flick knives.

By the late-Sixties these had been replaced by mods and rockers who would congregate in their thousands on the sea front at Bank Holidays and pick massed fights with each other. But their pitched battles were more of a spectator sport for the local people than any serious threat to anybody, save perhaps a few of the participants themselves.

This indeed was the time when the coastal holiday resort started to lose its sedate, cosy image and become a little more frenetic and exciting. But only a *little* more.

***

This seaside atmosphere permeated the cheerful office of Dunsill's Properties Ltd in 1974 – the year when Edward and Marilyn celebrated Christmas in grand style on the prickly office carpet.

When the office reopened after Christmas Edward's PA Shula was quick to detect a new atmosphere of sensuality. Her antennae told her that something had changed in the relationship between her boss and Marilyn, the receptionist.

She noticed smiles flashing between them which were warmer than those which politeness required between boss and employee. Marilyn had always been smartly dressed for work and attentive to her appearance. But now her skirts were noticeably shorter and her blouses were unbuttoned to show enticing amounts of cleavage. Edward was spending much more time in reception than he had previously.

When Shula went into reception she often had the distinct impression that Edward and Marilyn quickly changed the subject of their conversation. They had a shared interest in progressive rock music and often their talk would suddenly turn to that. They would be chatting about some album they had listened to – Emerson, Lake and Palmer, Pink Floyd, Yes, Jethro Tull – or about a concert one or the other had attended. But their sheepish expressions suggested that they were not nearly as interested in the music as in what they had been discussing – or doing! – before Shula arrived.

Once Shula happened to be walking past the office at 9pm when she spotted Marilyn leaving by the front door. She thought that perhaps the receptionist had left some personal item in the office and had gone to retrieve it. But then she noticed Edward standing inside blowing a kiss in Marilyn's direction.

Shula was angry. She was a very broad-minded and quite happy-go-lucky person but this behaviour riled her for some reason which she could not immediately understand. She kept her counsel but became even more alert to what she now realised was a romantic attachment between her work colleagues.

She found herself becoming increasingly irritated that she was in effect having to "play gooseberry" in her own working environment. There was more to her reaction than that, though. She was jealous.

It is an occupational hazard that relationships between bosses and their PAs often become so close that they develop emotional ties. Many spend more time together than they do with their respective spouses and partners.

Shula had not previously contemplated that she might have fallen slightly in love with her boss but now it suddenly dawned on her. She steeled herself against the notion, striving to convince herself that she was a one-man woman, totally committed to her fit and loving fiancé. But her actions and reactions contradicted this.

She too started to turn up to work in sexier clothes, her own short skirts revealing long shapely legs which would have reduced any red-blooded male to jelly. And she started to pick fault constantly with Marilyn's work, even where no obvious faults were apparent.

Working in close proximity to Edward, by whom she felt betrayed, she became moody and short-tempered.

Shula, though, had not reckoned with the guile of her opponent. Every time she found fault with the receptionist Marilyn would get into a huddle with Edward and complain about her treatment. At these times a good deal of mutual stroking and paddling of palms would occur.

This unsatisfactory situation went on for several months and then, one day, everything changed.

Shula noticed that, although Edward was spending even more time than ever in reception, the flashing smiles flashed no longer and the paddling palms paddled no more.

A couple of weeks later Marilyn knocked on the door of the office which Edward and Shula shared. Edward was out on business but Marilyn handed a letter to Shula.

"It's my letter of resignation," she said. "I am giving a week's notice from today."

"Oh, that's a surprise. I'm sorry to hear that," Shula lied.

"It's my boyfriend," said Marilyn. "He's going backpacking in Australia and New Zealand and he wants me to go with him."

Marilyn had a "reputation" in the area for having a variety of short-term boyfriends, "short-term" often meaning a one night stand in the back of a car. But, she told Shula: "Don't tell anyone, but I think I might have found someone really special this time."

Shula was quite taken aback, and almost touched, by this confidence from someone she had considered to be her enemy. She smiled and said: "I hope it works out for you, love."

"Thanks," said Marilyn. "I appreciate that. I realise I may have put your nose out of joint a little since I came here."

"I don't know what you mean," replied Shula, sharply.

"I think we both know what we mean," said Marilyn, smiling and then

38

quickly turning and going out of the room before Shula had the chance to argue.

***

When Shula passed Marilyn's letter of resignation to Edward later that day he calmly put it on one side and commented: "That's a pity. Can you draft a job advert for me to go into the newspaper and I'll look at it later?"

Shula was accustomed to Edward's inscrutability so that she was not at all surprised by his cool response.

In the weeks that followed her work skirts became longer.

One day she was searching through an office drawer for some sheets of carbon paper when she came across a letter inside an unsealed envelope addressed to Marilyn. It was from Edward:

"Dear Marilyn, I am utterly distraught to learn that you are leaving the office, and even more upset that you intend to leave the country. I accept that you have a boyfriend now and that you find him more to your taste than myself. However, please do not deny me one last chance to recommend myself to you.

"You are the most beautiful girl I have ever met in my life and I love you as much as it is possible for me to love anyone. We have had some good times, haven't we? I had hoped that you liked my company. I certainly like yours. I can't get enough of it.

"I think you will agree that I have the prospects to offer you a comfortable life. I have property and plenty of spare money. Backpacking may be fun for a while, but we could travel anywhere in the world and stay in the best hotels. I know that you are not mercenary but equally I know that you enjoy a good time. I will always be able to give you a good time.

"Please give me one more chance. Please give me a ring, either at home or at the office.

Whatever you decide, I will always love you. Even if you go to Australia, I will still be here for you when you return. I promise.

"All my love, Edward. XXXX."

As Shula put the letter back into the envelope there were tears in her eyes.

***

Outwardly Edward was easy-going with a mild temperament. Some thought him bland, and even shallow. "A wet fish" was how one friend had described him. But this belied what was going on inside his head. His mind was full of theories about life in general and about his particular place in it.

From his early teens he had been a romantic, falling in love easily and often with several girls at the same time. For that *is* possible. He was also an animal, capable of carnal lust without any thoughts of love.

When it came to Marilyn, though, the two elements of his manly thoughts - romantic love and sexual desire - combined in such a powerful way that his head was in a maelstrom.

The very thought of this raven-haired seductress both aroused him sexually and made him feel sick to the pit of his stomach. In truth his love, as love often does, had become a sickness, both physical and mental.

Thoughts of her were always at the front of his mind, exciting him, troubling him, especially in bed at night.

Troubles always seem worse at night. A lost five pound note or a missed appointment can assume tragic proportions in the wee small hours. Missed dates with the opposite sex can lead to thoughts so abject that they are far worse than the worst scary nightmare.

Wake up in the morning with the sun streaming through the bedroom windows, blackbirds singing, wood pigeons cooing from distant trees – and everything is put back in proportion.

He realised only too well that Marilyn was at the height of her sexual powers. Some had even referred to her as a nymphomaniac. He knew and accepted that when she left the office at night she was available to other men. She appeared to be capable of both romantic and erotic love, but the erotic was her prime driving force.

When he was with her Edward totally abandoned his usual moral scruples, always recalling the words of Ray Davies in the Kinks' song Days – "Days when you can't tell wrong from right".

Edward was one of the least jealous people on the planet, but even he felt tinges of the green menace when he heard tales of Marilyn's wild sexual behaviour.

The relationship between Edward and Marilyn was almost exclusively carried out in the office. In every nook and cranny of the office and on every piece of furniture. And on that accursed prickly carpet!

But there lay the problem for Edward. He still lived at home with his parents, Bertram and Margaret. Marilyn lived with her parents too - her father, Ted Stubbings, was a prosperous local butcher. Both sets of parents lived by traditional middle class values so there was little chance for hanky-panky to be carried on while they were at home.

On several occasions when Edward knew that his parents were out for the evening or away on holiday he had invited Marilyn to his home. But, on one pretext or another, she always turned down the invitation. Edward suspected, rightly, that she liked to compartmentalise her life. The reason for this was obvious – she had a number of lovers she wished to keep entirely separate from each other.

As the weeks passed Edward had felt a new coolness towards him from Marilyn. Now *she* rarely tried to seduce *him*. And she would sometimes reject his advances in quite an offhand way.

Marilyn had fallen in love - erotic and romantic love - with a hulk of a man, a bronzed Adonis called Mike. A man with no cerebral pretensions but with a breezy muscular charm. He had suggested backpacking in the Antipodes and Marilyn had readily agreed. Hence the letter of resignation.

When Shula passed the letter to Edward he displayed typical English phlegm – on the outside. On the inside he felt as if he had been hit by a large sledgehammer. He went into the office toilet and sobbed.

In the few weeks up until Marilyn's departure for Australia he showered her with begging letters and presents. He even offered to buy a luxury flat for her to live in. It was to no avail. Marilyn gave no concessions but was polite and understanding. She felt no animosity towards Edward but she pitied him his desperation.

After she embarked on her journey and the weeks turned into months Edward's hurt receded a little and he tried to be philosophical about his loss.

He took to heart a passage he had recently read in an Anthony Trollope novel referring to the hapless lover Johnny Eames: "He knew now - or thought he knew, that the continued indulgence of a hopeless passion was a folly opposed to the very instincts of men and women - a weakness showing want of fibre and muscle in the character."

And he read this from Ivan Turgenev: "Every kind of love, whether happy or unhappy, is a real calamity if you surrender to it wholly."

41

Edward therefore reluctantly accepted his lot and continued to live his life as normally as he could.

A whole year passed and then he was told by a friend that Marilyn was back in town. He decided to make one last throw of the dice. He hoped that a year abroad with her new man might have dampened their ardour.

Edward sent a new letter, accompanied by a huge bouquet of red roses, to welcome his love home. But there was a new body blow to come. He received a letter from Marilyn in the following terms: "Dear Edward, Thank you for your letter and for the lovely flowers. It was very kind of you to ask me out again, but I have to tell you that I have become engaged to Mike. Please do not send me any more letters or presents. Sorry about this, Marilyn."

Edward was defeated.

Chapter Four

The Holy Grail?

Our story moves forward again to 2016. Pleasure flights in small aircraft, mainly Austers, had been an overhead feature of Sanderholme for many years between the end of the Second World War and the early 1970s. But "Elf and Safety" rules had forced the operators out of existence.

However, if the flights had still been running, passengers looking down on the resort would have been struck by how little Sanderholme had changed physically in the years since the War.

The beach was still teeming with people in the summer, the end of the pier stood proud in the water, the sea front was bustling, the parks and gardens were blooming and the town centre was full of traffic and pedestrians.

But an old holidaymaker returning to the town and looking at it from ground level would have noticed some significant changes.

The majestic looking hotel buildings were still there, but half of them had been turned either into self-catering holiday flats or all-year-round bedsits and one-bedroomed flats, often occupied by workers from Eastern Europe.

The hotels and guest houses which remained intact catered mainly for short breaks and the previously vilified bed and breakfast "one nighters". Some hotels were offering the formerly unheard-of "room only" tariff. The week-long holiday had long since gone out of fashion.

The town centre had lost most of its smart "High Street multiple stores" and now there was a proliferation of charity shops, pound shops and outlets selling bankrupt stock.

The holidaymakers had changed too. One supercilious national newspaper columnist wrote: "The archetypal Sanderholme visitor is 'a chav' covered in tattoos, sporting rings in ears, nose and any other convenient orifice, with a huge beer belly, and wearing a tracksuit and dirty trainers. And that's just the women! Unattractive Nike no-necks of both sexes slope along, eating their crisps, smoking their fags and swearing at their children. There is a depressing poverty of aspiration here which contrasts sharply with the optimism of the post-war generations of visitors in the 1950s and 1960s."

Edward had been outraged when he read this. He was frustrated that the blinkered writer could not see that these modern-day visitors comprised, for the most part, solid working class families, thoroughly enjoying their trips to the seaside. Yes, there was still fun to be had at Sanderholme and the holiday trade continued to thrive.

***

Edward had been fascinated to hear Harry Greensmith's tale about his Great Aunt Olivia, her African Prince lover and her love-child.

When he told Harry about the fresh flowers he had found on Gabriel's grave the old man had been somewhat nonplussed. It was a complete surprise to learn that Gabriel had a son.

Edward was determined to find out more. He was particularly keen to trace the mystery son, Anthony. Could Anthony be his Holy Grail - the answer to his quest for an heir to the Dunsill bloodline? The "son" he had never had.

"I would be really pleased to find out more about Gabriel and Anthony," he told Harry. "I would love to actually meet Anthony, although the chances of finding him are probably a bit remote."

Harry, the keen amateur historian, saw an interesting challenge ahead.

"I'll do what I can to help you. It should be quite interesting," he said.

The old man went quiet for what seemed like several minutes. Then he became suddenly animated, as though he had had an Eureka moment.

"I know a man!" he declared. "A fount of all knowledge - at least about certain subjects, although not, I fear, about the birds and the bees."

"The birds and the bees?" said Edward with a quizzical expression.

"Yes, I'm afraid he is quite famous for his unusual misconceptions about human biology. If you will excuse me, I won't go into greater detail about that.

"His name's Peter Wattam. He's the churchwarden at Marshyard church and, as well as the birds and bees thing, he is also famous for keeping extensive and detailed records of everything that goes on in the parish.

"He's secretary for the parochial church council. The PCC chairman told me that no one can break wind at the meetings without Peter recording it in the minutes," chuckled Harry.

"He sounds just the sort of fellow we need," replied Edward. "Can we go and see him?"

Harry immediately telephoned the churchwarden and arranged a meeting for the following morning.

***

On a dull but fine morning Edward's car trundled along a narrow lane leading from the direction of the Marshyard village centre towards the sea. The marshland was table-flat and almost featureless, the desolation of miles of ploughed fields broken only by the occasional tiny copse and an odd scurrying pheasant.

An old red brick farmhouse, surrounded by tall trees to provide much-needed shelter, came into view. The car pulled into an untidy and very muddy farmyard, Edward taking care not to collide with any of the various pieces of lethal-looking metal which adorned it. He successfully picked out a path between scrapped tractors, rusty old ploughs, beat-up cars and vans and a dozen clucking free range hens.

When Edward saw two men approaching from the direction of the farmhouse he wound down his window ready to talk to them. But they were too agitated to even notice him.

The two men made an amusing contrast. One was bald-headed, crimson-faced, short and stocky with a short unkempt beard and wearing a muddy blue denim overall. But belying these unprepossessing features were an intelligent face and piercing blue eyes. The second man was in his early forties, tall, gangly and ungainly with a sagging bottom lip. Incongruously he was wearing a smart mid-brown suit and highly polished brown shoes.

"Where the hell do you think you're going?" the old man shouted angrily.

45

"We have the top field to plough this morning."

The younger man rounded on him and replied sulkily in a high whining voice: "But Daddy, I need to go into town to buy a new CD."

The old man reddened with fury and spat out: "You silly young fucker. You'll stay here and help me with the ploughing. Now come on."

He caught hold of the young man's arm and dragged him across the muddy yard.

"Daddy. Look what you've done. You've spattered my suit with mud. I've got to wear this for church on Sunday."

"Bugger church!" shouted his father. "We've got some fucking work to do."

As he said these words the old man caught sight of the car with Edward and Harry inside. His demeanour changed as he approached the vehicle.

"Good afternoon," he said, grinning wryly. "Can I help you, gentlemen? Oh, it's Mr Greensmith, isn't it? How can I help?"

Harry got out of the car, followed by Edward.

"It's young Peter we would like to talk to - about some church business," said Harry. "But I can see you're very busy. Perhaps we should come back at a more convenient time."

The father paused for thought and then answered: "Well, we do have some ploughing to do but I can spare Peter for a few minutes. Please come into the house."

The formerly irascible farmer turned into the perfect host as he ushered his guests into a large country kitchen. There they were greeted by an over-enthusiastic collie dog who proceeded to hump Edward's leg before being abruptly brought to heel by the farmer.

"Please don't mind the dog," said the old man. "He doesn't get to meet many people out here in the sticks."

"Don't worry," said Edward. "I'm well used to farm dogs. It's Mr Wattam, isn't it? We've met a few times before, I believe."

"Oh, yes. I remember. You're Bert Dunsill's son aren't you?"

Edward nodded and the two men shook hands.

"Your dad was a lovely man. I was so sorry to hear that he had passed away. We used to be on the drainage board together a few years ago. Lovely man."

"Thank you," said Edward. "I know he felt highly of you too."

The kitchen was warm and homely but poorly decorated with dirty brown paintwork, which probably started off 30 years previously as cream or magnolia, and a bare concrete floor. There were bills, newspapers and various ledgers scattered all over the kitchen table, on several chairs and on large areas of the floor. A crackly old radio perched on top of a black cooking range was giving out the shipping forecast.

Standing at a sink with her hands in a bowl of water was an elderly woman, the farmer's wife, a little stout lady with a florid complexion and rough hands resulting from years of clothes washing before the advent of the washing machine.

She had her back to the door and was so engrossed in her washing up that at first she did not acknowledge the visitors when they entered the room with her husband and son. When she turned round and saw them she quickly took up a tea towel and dried her hands.

In a broad Lincolnshire accent she declared: "I'm so sorry, Sirs, I were that busy with me weshing up I niver see you was there. Will you take some tea? I've got a pot on the boil. Please do."

Edward and Harry could sense that this was an offer it would be hard to refuse and agreed to partake of the brew. The woman cleared some wooden chairs around the kitchen table of the papers strewn on them and invited her guests to sit down.

The farmer, John Wattam, said he would have to attend to some work in the yard and left the kitchen, ordering the collie out with him. His wife, Mabel, served up the tea and then politely withdrew from the room, acknowledging that the visitors had some business with her son.

Peter Wattam was a unique young man, thought to be none too bright but, with a naive lack of self-awareness, strangely confident in his own abilities.

He had an encyclopaedic knowledge of current pop music, railways, cars, photography and the Church of England but otherwise was embarrassingly unworldly.

To help Edward to get the measure of the man Harry mischievously asked Peter: "Now then, young man. How are you getting on with your fiancée these days - young Ruby? You must have been engaged for ten years or so now, haven't you?"

"Twenty years!" replied Peter. "We're getting on just fine."

He drew up his chair closer to the guests and whispered conspiratorially: "Between you gentlemen and myself she let me get her cock out last night."

He put a finger up to his lips to appeal for this startling revelation to be kept strictly secret.

Harry cast a glance towards Edward who had his hands up to his face trying to conceal his laughter.

Harry quickly changed the mood by saying: "Now, gentlemen - to business!"

He explained to Peter that Edward was keen to know of any information he might have about Gabriel Dunsill and his son, Anthony.

"I know Gabriel's Dunsill's grave," said Peter. " 'Gabriel Dunsill, aged 41. Died March 1st, 1976. Beloved father of Anthony. Rest in Peace.' Nobody had been to it for years - until a couple of weeks ago. I was in the church, getting the records up to date, and a bloke came in. Said he was Gabriel Dunsill's son - Anthony - and asked me whereabouts his father's grave was. I showed him the grave, although at the time it was covered in nettles and dock leaves and you couldn't even see the headstone. He trod the nettles down and cleared it up a bit. Then he fetched some flowers and a pot from his car and put them on to the grave."

"Had you ever met Anthony before?" asked Edward.

"No. Never set eyes on him," replied Peter.

"What sort of chap was he?" asked Edward.

"Middle-aged. Quiet. Nice man. Didn't seem to want to chat much."

"Anything else you can remember about him?"

"He sounded English – probably a Southerner. He had a nice car – an Alfa Romeo. He had a big tattoo of a fire-breathing dragon on his arm."

Harry asked if there would be church records relating to Gabriel's death and funeral.

Peter said there definitely were records and he would find them.

"I can't go to the church today because I need to go into town to buy a CD - Katy Perry's latest. It's really good. But I can look tomorrow, after the Sunday service. If you could give me a telephone number I'll let you know what I find."

After both giving him their numbers, Harry and Edward thanked Peter and told him they would delay him no longer. They left by the front door of the farmhouse, followed by the trusty churchwarden. As they got into their car they saw Peter driving through the yard in an immaculate vintage Morris Minor, pursued on foot by his father who banged on the boot as it left him behind.

"Come here you lazy young bugger and get some work done," he screamed, but to no avail. The music shop was beckoning.

John Wattam took off his grey flat cap and hurled it to the floor in rage. Then, when he saw that Edward and Harry were still in the yard, he picked it up and, although it was bespattered with mud, put it back on his head. He gently nodded and raised the cap as a farewell gesture to his guests - and then gave a broad smile as brown muddy water trickled down his face.

The guests smiled back. They understood that Peter was, to say the least, an unusual son.

***

Early on Monday morning Harry received a telephone call from an excited Peter. He had found the details of Gabriel's death and his funeral on Friday, March 12th, 1976. The next of kin had, as might have been expected, been recorded as his son, Anthony Dunsill, who had an address in Islington, London. However, Peter said that during their recent meeting at the churchyard Anthony had passed him a piece of paper giving details of his new address in the event of any problems regarding the grave. This was Tora Cottage, Glenbernisdale, Skeabost Bridge, Portree, Isle of Skye. No telephone number or other information had been given.

"What's the gentleman going to do with the information?" asked Peter.

Harry said he believed that Edward was doing some family history and wanted to complete the family tree.

Peter continued: "If he wants to go to the Isle of Skye, he could go by train as far as Mallaig on the mainland. He could go on the Fort William to Mallaig Line. It's called the Jacobite line. It's meant to have the best scenery of any line in the world. Harry Potter travelled on it on the Hogwart's Express. Or he could go instead from Inverness to Kyle of Lochalsh - that's another beautiful line. I could find out all the connections for him if he would like, and all the timetables and prices. Please tell him that."

"I will be sure to tell Edward of your kind offer," said Harry. "And thank you so much for your time and trouble."

Peter, who had a rail timetable book in front of him as he spoke, went on to rattle off a number of other possible journeys which Edward might take. After ten minutes or so of this, Harry again expressed his fulsome gratitude but said he had an important appointment to keep and very regrettably must end the call.

Harry was a thoroughly decent man, not giving to lying. But on this occasion he was being "economical with the verite", as Alan Clark, the late Tory minister, diarist and serial womaniser, once famously admitted to. His appointment was not until the afternoon!

***

At 2pm Harry emerged from his flat, looking even more dapper than usual, sporting a large red carnation buttonhole. He walked briskly for about half a mile, passing the railway station and then walking along a busy road which had council houses on one side and the town's smart cricket ground on the other.

He turned off this road into a quiet tree-lined avenue with rows of neat semi-detached bungalows on either side.

Harry went down the gravel path of one of these bungalows and the front door was flung open before he had reached it.

"Come in, dear," said a polite and frail-sounding female voice.

Harry raised his cane and replied: "Hello, my dear. Lovely to be here again."

Standing in the doorway was an elegant, slender lady of some eighty-six years. She had immaculate silver hair in a bouffant style which contrasted with a deeply lined, heavily rouged face. She had not aged well facially but was valiantly attempting to conceal the fact. Her body, although somewhat scrawny now, still had an angularity which spoke of its past glories.

She was wearing a deeply plunging silver sparkly dress, more suitable for a night out at a posh restaurant or theatre than tea and scones on a summer's afternoon.

Harry kissed her on the lips, leaving a trace of bright red lipstick under his nose.

He was ushered into the tastefully furnished and comfortable living room where the refreshments were waiting for him. The best Doulton china tea set was prettily displayed on an engraved silver tray and there was a large selection of jam tarts, buttered scones and shortbreads.

"How are you, Sally?" he asked.

"Oh, bearing up, you know. I've not had much pain this week. I just keep taking the tablets and trying to keep my pecker up."

"How about you?"

"Oh, a touch of gout now and then. Otherwise tickety-boo."

"Do tuck in. I've made some gooseberry tarts specially for you. I think you'll like them."

"Gooseberry tarts! Ah. Now you're talking. I haven't had a gooseberry tart for years. It must have been when we used to have those nice teas at the tennis club after the matches. Do you remember?"

"I do. I used to make them, you know."

"Did you really? I had forgotten it was you. I say, these are just as good as I remember them."

"I got some Lady Grey tea for a change."

"Lady Grey. I haven't tasted that for years, either. I have Earl Grey at home – and Typhoo when the pennies are short."

"There was a special offer on at Tesco, so I thought. Ha! That'll do for Harry. He likes a nice cup of tea."

The conversation went on in this vein for some time, with prices at the various local supermarkets being compared and various brands of tea and coffee being evaluated.

"Do you know what I did in Morrisons the other day?" said Sally, pretending to hide her face in embarrassment.

"No. Go on. Surprise me."

"I saw this advert somewhere for Bogof washing powder."

Harry chuckled, already seeing the point of the embarrassment.

"I looked on all the shelves and I couldn't see it anywhere. So I called a young man over who worked there and he looked very puzzled to start with. 'Oh', he says, 'You mean Buy One Get One Free. There's an offer on for Persil.'

"Well I could have wished myself anywhere. How stupid was I? I felt like a right old dementia case."

"Well, if you didn't know, how could you be expected to guess what it meant? I sympathise," said Harry. "You know I went to the music section at

Tesco one day to look for a CD for my cleaner, Helen. When I visited her house once I had noticed a CD she had bought by a certain pop group. When I saw another one in Tesco by the same group I thought it would be just down her street. It was spelt I N X S. I thought it would be pronounced 'Inkses' – I was probably thinking of the Inkspots, you know – so that was what I asked for. The young girl who served me was very pleasant about it but she hadn't a clue what I was on about. So I spelt it out.

"She just doubled up with laughter: 'You mean 'In Excess',' she said.

"You see," Harry explained. "I N X S – In Excess. She was very nice about it but I bet everyone else in the store was told about this bumbling old duffer who had been in."

"We're just not safe to be let out on our own!" joked Sally. "Anyway have you had enough to eat and drink?"

"I certainly have, my dear. I don't know if we ought to be doing what we're going to do next on such full stomachs!"

"Don't be silly. We've done it plenty of times before," said Sally.

"Are you sure you are up to it today, Sally?"

"I've been looking forward to it all week," she replied. "Good God, we haven't done it for at least a fortnight! I'm getting serious withdrawal symptoms. I thought we would have some different music this week. Something romantic, to get us in the mood."

"Ah. What's that?" asked Harry.

"Tony Bennett. I do so love him."

"Yes, rather. He's a class act if ever there was one."

Sally went over to a CD player and put on the music.

Harry beckoned her over.

"Come on then, old girl. Let's see what we can do today."

Sally walked over and took Harry by the hand. He put his arm gently round her waist and took her other hand.

"Ready."

"Ready."

The couple danced, gracefully and with great precision.

They danced to the whole CD and then flopped down on to the sofa.

"You know I'm just about bushed," said Harry.

"I'll have a get a new partner if you can't stand the pace," teased Sally.

"It's just like the old days, at the Palais de Danse," said Harry. "Except then I could have kept going all night."

"And you did. I remember you. You had a string of ladies fighting over who would dance with you next."

They reminisced for another half hour or so and then Harry picked up his cane and prepared himself to leave.

"Same time next week?" he asked.

"Same time next week," said Sally. "I'll find some different music. Something a bit quicker. Some polkas, perhaps."

"You could give a chap a heart attack! Anyway, I will get myself fit walking along the prom and see you next week. Good-bye Sally."

He kissed her on the lips again and this time got lipstick on his chin.

***

When Harry returned home his first thought was to telephone Edward to give him the information he now had about Gabriel's son, Anthony. But he found that Edward had already been phoned by Peter, the assiduous churchwarden.

"What he had to tell me was really useful," said Edward. "But... he does go on a bit doesn't he?"

"Tell me about it," said Harry, laughing.

"I think I now know most of what there is to know about railway timetables, current pop music and the Bible," said Peter.

"He tried his best to turn me into a good Anglican. I got a bit serious with him at one point. I told him I believe that human nature stays largely the same whether in the microcosm of a small community or in the macrocosm of the wide world. I would like to have the comfort of a religion but I am resigned to living out my life – and death – in the uncomfortable position of being an agnostic.

"But that was not enough for Peter. He was concerned that I could not know the difference between right and wrong if I didn't believe in a God.

"I told him I did have a moral code, which was best summed up by Charles Kingsley's Mrs Doasyouwouldbedoneby in The Water-Babies."

"Peter came back at me in a flash and claimed that the idea of Mrs Doasyouwouldbedoneby must have come from the Sermon on the Mount, when Jesus said: 'All things whatsoever ye would that men should do to you, do you even so to them: for this is the law and the prophets.'"

"I was gobsmacked to tell you the truth. How can this, without wishing to be rude, yokel, who seems to know so little about the ways of the world, be so sharp and erudite?"

Harry laughed again: "He certainly seems to have made an impression on you. But don't be surprised. There are lots of homespun philosophers hidden out there in the Lincolnshire Fens and Marshes.

"Anyway, I can see you needed to get that experience off your chest. But will his information about Anthony Dunsill be useful?"

"I certainly hope it will," said Edward. "I shall be going on-line tonight to do an electoral register search for him and then take it from there."

That night Edward did go on-line and found that there indeed was an Anthony Dunsill living at the Isle of Skye address. He tried to find a telephone number through Directory Enquiries and social media, but to no avail.

Then, while he was sitting in his office, trying various searches on his PC, something rather extraordinary happened.

An email message arrived in his inbox. It said: "Marilyn Stubbings wishes to be a Friend on Facebook."

Edward was stunned. He quickly looked through her profile which confirmed to him that it was THE Marilyn — the great love of his life. His whole body shuddered with excitement. He immediately accepted her Friend request.

A few minutes later he received a Facebook message from Marilyn.

"Do you remember me from many moons ago?" she asked.

"Of course I do," Edward replied.

"How are you?" asked Marilyn.

Edward replied: "I'm very well, thanks. How are you? It's great to hear from you. It must be more than 40 years since I heard from you."

"It must be — at least that."

They messaged each other for at least an hour, reminiscing about times and people gone by. There was a respectful reserve in their conversation, neither of them venturing to mention their historic passions.

But Edward did make one totally astonishing discovery — Marilyn lived on the Isle of Skye!

She explained that she had met, married and divorced a Skye man and now lived with her only daughter, a 25-year-old.

Edward told her about his desire to trace and meet Anthony Dunsill. She had not come across anyone of that name, but, in another startling coincidence, revealed that she lived in a settlement called Tote, within comfortable walking distance of Glenbernisdale where Anthony lived.

Although reflective by nature Edward was never slow to make a decision. He decided he needed to go to Skye – as soon as possible.

"If I came to Skye could I possibly come and see you?" he asked.

Marilyn's response was beyond what he might have hoped for.

"Why don't you come over and stay with us while you look for Anthony?" she said.

Edward had had a long loving relationship with his wife, Elizabeth, and since her untimely death he had felt lonely and bereft. Now, for the first time since his bereavement, he felt a sense of excitement, sensing the possibility of a new chapter opening in his life. A trip to Skye might rekindle an old love affair and at the same time satisfy his longing for an heir to the Dunsill family name.

Chapter Five

Misty Isle

Five days later Edward's car was crossing the Skye bridge, after an eleven and a half hour trip from Sanderholme. Between crossing the border at Gretna and reaching Glasgow, Edward had felt weary from the long drive. But as soon as the route took him alongside Loch Lomond his spirits lifted and he drank in the many miles of beautiful majestic Highland scenery between there and the bridge crossing at Kyle of Lochalsh.

Edward had heard the Isle of Skye dubbed as The Misty Isle. But today it completely belied its reputation. The air was clear and the calm seas azure blue, reminiscent of the South Seas, with entirely uninterrupted views of the distant Outer Hebrides.

An hour after crossing the bridge the car trundled along a narrow single track lane to Tote, a hamlet which overlooked the sea loch Snizort Beag. It came to a line of bungalows and white-painted cottages straddling the top of a rich green meadow which swept right down to the edge of the loch. Edward was immediately struck by the tranquillity of the mid-afternoon scene. A herd of calm cattle chewed the grass of the meadow and a buzzard soared gracefully overhead.

The car stopped at one of the neat white cottages, appropriately named

Meadow Cottage, and pulled into the driveway. Edward knocked on the front door where he was greeted warmly by Marilyn herself, who was wearing a bright, multi-coloured summer dress. She hugged him and he kissed her on the cheek.

Marilyn was a well-preserved 60-year-old. Edward thought her figure just as alluring as it had been all those years ago. Her face was still pale and smooth, a few laughter lines seemingly the only obvious concession to age.

Marilyn noticed that Edward too had aged well. He remained slim with a well-groomed head of dark brown hair and the face of a forty-five-year-old.

She led him into her living room, a snug little room dominated by a large wood burning fire with black doors and surrounds. Edward's quick observations of the room's contents gave him some clues about Marilyn's current lifestyle.

The decor and furnishings were mainly in blacks, reds and purples. A small bookcase was dominated by books on herbs, homoeopathy, wacky religions and alternative lifestyles. Empty wine bottles were dotted around the room and there was a strong scent of pot pourri.

The sexy but largely conventional 17-year-old had clearly grown into an adult with a style very much of her own, with just a hint of hippydom.

However, there was clearly another influence in the room. There were CDs scattered on chairs, with artistes such as Green Day, Muse, Katy Perry, Rihanna and Jessie J prominent amongst them. Possibly the daughter's influence? thought Edward.

At Marilyn's invitation he sat down in a black leather armchair, which was comfortable but had a lump where a spring had broken and had clearly seen better days. After offering him a coffee, explaining that she only had decaffeinated, Marilyn disappeared briefly into the kitchen to prepare it.

Edward had expected to feel nervous at meeting his old girlfriend after so many years but she was warm and friendly and had put him at ease straightaway.

She returned with two coffees and perched herself on the arm of another chair so that she could converse with Edward more intimately.

"You're looking well," she said. "You haven't changed much at all."

"I can say the same thing about you. You look absolutely stunning," said Edward.

The old chemistry between them was still there – the keen eye contact and the unmistakable arousals of sensuality.

Their conversation began with commonplace subjects – Edward's journey up to Skye, the local weather forecasts and Marilyn's enquiries about various people from the past she had lost touch with.

Marilyn revealed that she worked as a receptionist and barmaid at a nearby hotel, a plush former hunting lodge with a reputation for fine dining and comfortable accommodation. Her daughter, Josephine, who had travelled the world as an air hostess, now ran her own business providing boat trips for tourists around Skye and other adjacent islands.

It was late afternoon on a Sunday, Marilyn's usual day off from work. She had planned a dinner of wild salmon for her guest, complemented by an excellent bottle of chardonnay.

After dinner another bottle of vino was opened and Edward and Marilyn sat down to do some more catching up.

It was around 7pm when Josephine arrived home. She bounded into the living room and went straight over to Edward to greet him with an enthusiastic handshake.

"Hi. I'm Josephine," she beamed. "And you must be Edward."

Edward replied: "Hello. So pleased to meet you."

He was more than pleased. He was entranced by this beautiful force of nature.

Josephine's looks had very little in common with her mother's. To start with she was a blonde, although not a natural one. She was tall and slim with a toned body, not so pale-skinned as her mother, and lightly tanned. She was wearing a white teeshirt over pert breasts and a pair of tight-fitting jeans with fashionable ripped holes in tantalising positions along her legs. Edward thought if she didn't do modelling, then she ought to do.

Where she did resemble her mother was in her flashing smile which could have lit up any room.

"You'll have to excuse me," she said. "I'm bushed. Just taken a party of German people on a seven hour trip to the Small Isles. It was a great day, though. We saw minke whales and a whole load of dolphins. They were a very happy party."

Edward thought that if this was what Josephine was like when she was "bushed" he would like to see her when she was feeling lively! "I would love to go on one of your boat trips before I go back home!" said Edward.

"Be my guest," said Josephine. "Complimentary, of course."

"Will you come?" Edward asked Marilyn.

"Oh, I don't know. My sea legs aren't very good. Walking's more in my line."

"Will you walk with me to Glenbernisdale then, to see if I can find Anthony Dunsill?" asked Edward.

"Yes, of course I will," said Marilyn. "I've got a day off tomorrow. We could go in the morning."

Edward was delighted by her positive response and readily agreed to the plan. Marilyn had already asked if he had contacted Anthony in any way prior to setting off for Skye. Even though he had no telephone number for him, he perhaps could have written, she suggested.

Edward explained that he was an impulsive sort of person and thought it would be more of an adventure to just set out and see what happened.

Marilyn had never thought of Edward as being particularly impulsive and she guessed what were his true motives. If Anthony had declared in advance that he did not wish to meet Edward then he would have had less reason to visit Skye and reacquaint himself with her. Now he had the perfect excuse for staying with this woman whom he considered the sexiest person he had ever met in his life.

And Marilyn did not mind that in the slightest. She had fond memories of Edward as a considerate man whom she knew had passionately and genuinely loved her. As a rampant 17-year-old she had enjoyed the physical side of their relationship but had never felt any deep attachment to Edward. Now, as a single 60-year-old it was beginning to dawn on her what she might have missed.

Now she had seen Edward in the flesh she was impressed at how well preserved he was. He was gym-fit and mentally as bright as a button.

As she plied him with several more glasses of wine she had one thought uppermost in her mind – seduction.

Josephine had made herself supper and gone to her bedroom, leaving Edward and Marilyn alone. It was midnight and Marilyn suggested it was time for bed. She led Edward to a spare single bedroom, really no bigger than a boxroom, pointing out a bunk bed which was to be his resting place for the night.

Edward set down his suitcase on the floor and said goodnight.

Marilyn put an arm around his shoulder and kissed him on the cheek. She did not let go. She pulled him closer to her and looked straight into his eyes, smiling widely. Edward said "Goodnight" again and kissed her on the lips. She clung on to him and they kissed deeply and passionately. Her hand strayed down to his bottom and he in turn clasped hers.

Marilyn pushed him away playfully.

"How did I ever let you go?" she asked, with a mock-sad face.

"You didn't have to. You don't have to," replied Edward.

"You don't *have* to sleep in *this* room," she said.

She took his hand and led him to her bedroom, a deep purple room with a comfortable double bed. Here they spent the night, rekindling the passions of 43 years previously.

***

The next morning Marilyn and Edward breakfasted together, Josephine having already left for work before they rose.

By 10am they set out on their walk to Glenbernisdale. Although it was a fine, sunny mid-August morning it had rained heavily overnight so they both donned wellingtons for their walk.

A muddy grass track interlaced with deep puddles took them from the side of Marilyn's cottage across to Skeabost, with the attractive tidal Loch Snizort Beag not far to their right and sometimes visible along their route.

The track continued past one of the most atmospheric locations in the whole of the United Kingdom, St Columba's Isle. Marilyn explained to Edward that this was the site of a fascinating burial ground which was still in use but which dated from medieval times. The tiny island had also once been home to the cathedral of the Bishop of the Isles.

She promised that on their return journey they would take a closer look at this historic spot.

After crossing a bridge over a frothing and roaring River Snizort, now in spate and a spectacular sight, the couple's path joined one of the driveways past the hotel where Marilyn worked.

A tree-lined drive, with a golf course on one side and the fast-flowing salmon river on the other, led them past the magnificent white structure which was now the hotel. Marilyn promised to take Edward for a meal there before his return to England. The scene was so idyllic and the company so exhilarating that he thought he would never wish to go home.

Past the hotel was another tree-lined walk near the lochside, a few bungalows and their gardens slightly interrupting the view of the water at certain points.

A walk of about ten minutes led to the main Portree to Dunvegan road. After they had crossed this a roadside path of about 50 yards took Edward and Marilyn across a bridge over the narrow but noisy River Tora and then to the junction with the lane leading to Glenbernisdale.

At the junction Marilyn pointed out three cottages which were joined together, two in a line along the lane and the other, with its frontage along the main road, forming an L-shape with the other two. She said the main road cottage had been the home of the famed Gaelic poet and songwriter

Mairi Mhor nan Oran, popularly known as Big Mary of the Songs. Mairi had been an outspoken champion of the crofting movement in the 19th century and had become one of Marilyn's heroines.

Edward was struck by her enthusiasm for this literary crusader. Marilyn had obviously come a long way both culturally and intellectually since her days as receptionist at Dunsill's Properties Ltd.

The Glenbernisdale lane was a pleasant one. On the left hand side of the road were several grass fields, the home to a couple of horses, a pony and a pig. Just beyond the fields the torrents of the River Tora could be heard but not seen as they flowed in deep cuts through dense woodland.

The solitary, but friendly pony came across to meet Edward and Marilyn, probably in the hope of receiving some titbit, but also apparently happy to make do with nuzzling up to both of them.

Marilyn told Edward to look out for deer at the edge of the wood but none made themselves available on this particular day.

"You're more likely to see them at dawn or dusk," she pointed out.

The right hand side of the lane began with a patch of untamed, scrubby woodland which gave way to a series of fields and tracks rising to a line of bungalows and houses which formed the main part of the settlement. After about half a mile Edward caught sight of a gatepost with a black mailbox fastened to it. Under the box was a roughly hand-painted sign saying "Tora Cottage".

"Here it is!" said Edward, getting excited.

His euphoria became somewhat dampened as he surveyed the scene in front of him.

Most of the properties he had seen along the lane had been immaculately painted in white. Although rough tracks amid fields of long grass led up to all of them, the track up to Tora Cottage was rougher and more rutted than the others and the grass was longer and more clogged with thistles and other weeds, including the yellow ragwort plant so dreaded by horse owners. Bits of rusty scrap metal poked out from the undergrowth and the remains of a touring caravan completed the insalubrious picture.

The cottage itself was a substantial building, much bigger than the other properties on the lane and with extensive grounds. But its exterior was offputting with its dingy grey brickwork and ill-painted doors and window frames. There were plants growing out of the gutters running along the eaves and out of the chimney pots.

Edward and Marilyn picked their way through the muddy potholes until they reached the front door. There was no sign of a bell, a door knocker or even a door handle! So Edward hammered on it with his knuckles.

A mixed race man of about 40 years with long dreadlocks and a slim torso opened the door. He was naked from the waist up and wearing dirty skin-tight jeans and no shoes.

"Hi there. What can I do for you guys?" he asked in a none-too-friendly manner.

"I'm looking for a Mr Anthony Dunsill," said Edward. "Have I got the right house?"

"Sure," said the man. "I'll get him."

He disappeared inside and a few seconds later another man came to the door.

In most respects he was a middling sort of man – middle-aged, medium height and neither fat nor thin, with greying hair receding at the forehead. His dress was unexceptional - grey flannel trousers and a dark blue teeshirt. But what stood him out from the crowd was his doleful brown eyes which gave him a sleepy, solemn demeanour.

"What can I do for you?" he asked in a non-committal manner.

Edward, polite to the point of being apologetic, replied: "I am so sorry to bother you. But I have been tracing my family tree and I believe we may be related to some degree. My name is Edward Dunsill and I believe that your grandmother and my grandfather were brother and sister, which makes us, I think, second cousins."

Anthony, for it was he, looked bemused and a little suspicious. After a few seconds' thought he held out his hand and said: "Pleased to meet you, cousin. Will you come inside?"

Marilyn, who was standing quietly by Edward's side, was introduced as "an old friend".

They were shown into the living room, which had all the hallmarks of a disorganised and slightly seedy, bachelor pad.

There were half-eaten plates of food, full ashtrays and a proliferation of empty beer bottles and cans. Waste paper bins were overflowing with takeaway packaging and there was little sign of a duster or vacuum cleaner having been used in many months. A sweet smell permeated the room.

The mixed race man, who was lounging unceremoniously on a ripped leather settee, was introduced as Jordan.

He said a peremptory "hi" to Anthony but was much warmer in his welcome for Marilyn, insisting that she took his seat and then posting himself close to her on the settee.

After again apologising for taking up the men's time, Edward produced a piece of paper from his pocket upon which was printed the family tree. He explained the relationship between himself and Anthony and then gingerly brought up the subject of Great-aunt Olivia.

"I've heard something about my grandmother," said Anthony, without elaborating on this statement.

Then Jordan chipped in: "Yeah. She was a racy old bird, I'm told. Played the field a bit with the gents as it were."

Edward grinned: "Well, I suppose you're right. I wasn't going to put it that way myself."

Anthony, who spoke gruffly with a London accent, said: "Don't worry about that. I reckon we all have bloody skeletons in the family cupboard."

Edward asked: "Did your father talk much about his mother to you?"

"Not a lot," replied Anthony.

Edward was keen to know more about Gabriel and Anthony and their past lives.

At first Anthony gave few details, except to reveal that Gabriel had travelled the world as a cigarette salesman, while his wife and only child remained in London. Edward gradually coaxed more information out of him. Gabriel had been a chain smoker which had probably led to his untimely death from cancer at the age of 41. Anthony had been only ten at the time and had been left an orphan. The year before he died Gabriel had split up from Anthony's mother, leaving her in a state of poverty to bring up her son. She had become an alcoholic and had died after falling in front of a bus while in a drunken stupor. Anthony had left his home in Kentish Town to live in Islington with his maternal grandparents.

Like his father Anthony had been a restless young man. He too had travelled extensively, mainly in the Far-East, taking jobs in bars and restaurants and eventually settling in Vietnam, training to be a chef and marrying a local girl in Hanoi. The relationship, which had produced a daughter and a son, had broken down after 15 years and he had returned to the UK, not knowing what to do next with his life and feeling depressed.

While working at a restaurant in Hanoi he had met and befriended a bar manager – Jordan – and they had always kept in touch. Jordan was working for a chain of hotels which owned three premises on the Isle of Skye. When he learnt that his latest job would be on Skye he urged Anthony to join him. He convinced Anthony that he would be able to find work in the island's busy and growing tourist industry. So far he had only managed to get work washing pots at a Portree café, but he hoped that with his experience he would find something better in the catering trade before too long.

Anthony's way of talking was somewhat uncouth and untutored but at the same time he showed a reticence which bordered on shyness which Edward found quite disarming.

By contrast, far from shy and reticent was Jordan, who constantly butted into the conversation to remind Anthony of details, while simultaneously flirting with Marilyn in a very up-front way. Marilyn was lapping up the attention, so much so that even Edward, the least jealous of men, found himself becoming a little irritated.

When Marilyn invited the two men to join Edward and herself for dinner at her cottage the following evening, Edward had some mixed feelings. He desperately wished to get to know Anthony better with the ultimate aim of installing him as the "Dunsill heir". He had been particularly heartened to learn that Anthony had a son, who provided a further extension to the family line. On the other hand he wished that Marilyn had not extended her invitation to Jordan, to whom he had taken an instant dislike.

Jordan offered the couple a lift back home in his old Audi estate car which was parked in the yard at the back of the cottage. Edward and Marilyn declined, saying they would enjoy the walk.

"What do you think?" said Edward as they strolled along the Glenbernisdale lane.

"Well – you got what you wanted didn't you?"

"Yes, I did," replied Edward.

And he had got what he had come for. He had established contact with a true scion of the Dunsill line, with the bonus of at least one more generation to follow. Although they might not openly admit it most people who carry out genealogical research would love to find that they are descended from, or currently related to, someone famous, preferably a member of the aristocracy. Many lose interest in their family trees when that proves not to be the case.

Edward was not immune to an element of what might be called genealogical snobbery. He would rather have discovered that Anthony Dunsill was a prominent astrophysicist, actor or potential peer of the realm, than that he was a pot washer at a café and the son of a poverty-stricken drunken mother. But beggars couldn't be choosers and he began to feel it was his duty to raise up Anthony and his son to greater heights – and wealth. That was to be his new mission.

Having crossed the Skeabost bridge over the River Snizort Edward and Marilyn turned for the last leg of their journey back to Tote. But they had one interesting detour still to make. They branched a few yards left to walk over a small footbridge to St Columba's Isle. Just in front of the bridge was an information sign which informed them that the island contained the burial chapel for 28 Nicolson clan chiefs.

After crossing the neat wooden bridge they set foot on the "island", which, although steeped in history and interest, is only just deserving of the description "island". True, on two sides it is bordered by the River Snizort but all that separates the rest of the "island" from dry land are two very small rivulets, easily crossed by one stride.

The central feature of the burial ground is the ancient chapel, veiled, eerily, in overgrown surroundings, and having lost its roof many years ago. Four of the tombs inside date back to the Crusades. Among the carved slabs, a 16th century stone effigy of a knight still reclines. The prone image of the knight, with his high conical helmet and a sword, which he is holding point down in front of his legs, was a totally unexpected and mysterious sight which set Edward back on his heels.

The island, dedicated to St Columba - although it is not known for certain whether the saint ever visited it - cannot be described as a totally quiet place. The incessant flow of the River Snizort, together with many tweeting birds and the sounds from cattle in an adjacent field, means there is always a background noise. But it does have an atmosphere of an intense, almost prehistoric, peace.

Among the many fascinating gravestones which Edward inspected was one so sinister that he felt as if he had been hit in the face by it. Its headstone was inscribed with a crudely hewn skull and crossbones. Such symbols are not uncommon in ancient burial grounds. No one truly knows why such a seemingly unsympathetic symbol should have been put on a grave. There is no evidence that it has anything to do with pirates. The most likely theory is that it is to remind everyone of their mortality – a far cry from the cuddly toys, football scarves and other sentimental effects which are left on modern graves. But it made Edward feel distinctly uncomfortable and he indicated to Marilyn that it was time to go.

As he stood contemplating the implications of this particular grave Marilyn came up behind and threw her arms around. He turned round to face her and she pulled him towards her and started to kiss him. But he gently pushed her away.

"What's the matter?" she said. "Do you know what I was thinking? I was thinking that it would be rather sexy if we were to go into that chapel and make love on top of that knight. A threesome!"

Edward winced.

"It wouldn't feel right. And anyway it's broad daylight. Someone might come along. You live here. What would that do for your reputation?"

"Spoilsport," declared Marilyn. "It would be a kind of religious act reconnecting us with the spirits of our ancestors."

"I don't' see that," said Edward, becoming a little annoyed and finding himself quite shocked by her suggestion. "Don't you think it would be – well – a little undignified for two old-aged pensioners to be having it off in a graveyard?"

"I thought you were more of a free spirit than that," mocked Marilyn. "But I can see that you're scared that we might get caught in the act. What if we were to return after midnight? In fact that would add to the mystical experience."

"You're crackers," retorted Edward. "Come on. Let's go. I'll have a think about it."

He took Marilyn by the hand and bustled her away.

"I'm disappointed in you, Edward," was Marilyn's last word on the subject for the time being.

After dinner that night the wine was flowing again in copious quantities and the couple were feeling mellow and thoughtful as they cuddled up on the sofa. Josephine was "out on the town", or at least as much as you can get "out on the town" in the village of Portree.

"I think you were a little bit scared by St Columba's Isle," ventured Marilyn mischievously.

Edward would normally have vehemently denied any such suggestion. However, after a moment's pause for thought, he replied: "There was something about that place that I found unsettling. I can't put my finger on it. I suppose it was almost a feeling that we shouldn't have been there – that it was a place for the dead not the living.

"Yet rationally I cannot believe I have just said what I have just said."

"It is a spiritual place," said Marilyn.

Edward replied: "You may think that. But you see I don't believe in the spirit, or at least not in any accepted, conventional sense. You will probably think less of me when I say this... but I don't think there is such a thing as a soul, just as I don't think the heart is anything but a mechanism for pumping blood around the body. We just have a mortal brain and although science has gone a long way to helping us understand how that brain works there is still a long way to go.

"So you see I don't think there's anything spiritual about that graveyard — just a lot of old bones and headstones. And yet there's something different about the place, something very ancient and very hard to comprehend. I can't begin to explain it and really I think I may be talking a load of old rubbish."

"No," Marilyn interjected. "I think you are beginning to see the light. Of course we have souls, the immortal part of us that lives on when the body has given up."

"I can't believe that," said Edward. "Wait here a minute."

Edward got up from the settee and went into Marilyn's bedroom where he had left his suitcase. A few seconds later he returned, thumbing through a small dog-eared notebook.

"Ah, I've found it. A quote from Thomas Edison about the soul. Listen: 'Our intelligence is the aggregate intelligence of the cells which make us up. There is no soul, distinct from mind, and what we speak of as the mind is just the aggregate intelligence of cells. It is fallacious to declare that we have souls apart from animal intelligence, apart from brains. It is the brain that keeps us going. There is nothing beyond that.' That's precisely what I believe."

"So why were you frightened in the graveyard?" asked Marilyn.

"I wasn't frightened!" protested Edward. "I just felt a sense of, I don't know — unease. That somehow this was a place for the dead and not for us."

Marilyn joked: "You're a crazy mixed-up kid, aren't you? Why can't you accept there are some things that really aren't rational? I believe we can communicate with our ancestors — with the dead as well as the living - if we become attuned to the wavelengths of the spirit world."

Edward suddenly felt a wave of sadness drowning him. All his beliefs, honed over decades by his delving into philosophy and great works of literature and by his observation of everyday life, had now been called into question. Not called into question by Marilyn, whom he suspected of being into all kinds of "weird things", but by his own doubts after gazing at the knight and the skull and crossbones on the headstone.

"Shall we go to the cemetery again at midnight?" asked Marilyn after a while.

"No, not tonight," said Edward. "I would rather commune with the living — in your cosy warm bed."

"Okay," said Marilyn, smiling one of her most winsome smiles.

Chapter Six

Changing Tack

Harry Greensmith had picked up his walking cane and donned a natty straw trilby and was just about to leave for his morning "constitutional" when his doorbell rang. His visitor was Peter Wattam, the illustrious churchwarden of Marshyard.

"Good morning, Mr Greensmith. I wonder if I might take a few minutes of your time?"

Harry showed him into the sitting room.

Peter said he had been busy cataloguing his thousands of photo albums and had come across something which might interest Harry and his friend Mr Dunsill. He produced a photograph of a man standing at the side of a vintage Alfa Romeo car.

"This is that fellow Mr Dunsill was asking about – Anthony Dunsill," said Peter.

"Oh, I see," said Harry. "How did you get hold of that?"

"I took it myself – at the cemetery."

"Do you usually take pictures of people who visit your cemetery?" asked Harry.

"Oh, no. Only when they have interesting cars or something like that. He

69

had a classic Alfa Romeo Spider S4, 1991 model, 2000c cc with injection. Lovely car. The man said I could take a picture of it."

Harry thanked Peter for his thoughtfulness and asked if he could keep the photograph to show to Edward on his return from Skye. Peter said Edward could keep the photo as he had made a copy.

"I'm going into town now. There's a new James Blunt CD I want to buy," said Peter. "And then I'm going to get my hair cut. Mummy and Daddy say it's looking a bit straggly."

Harry bid him good-day and went out on his walk.

***

Marilyn was working at the hotel the next day and she sent Edward into Portree to buy provisions for the evening meal with Anthony and Jordan.

After making most of his purchases at the Co-op Supermarket he took a stroll by the harbour. There, standing on a cabin cruiser moored at the busy harbour-side was Josephine, who was preparing to take a party of Japanese tourists on a wildlife watching tour. Sea eagles, cormorants and shags and seals were among the cast of creatures expected to provide the entertainment , but there was always the chance of a celebrity appearance by a porpoise or two, a pod of dolphins or even a whale.

It was a warm sunny day and skipper Josephine was dressed for the occasion with a flimsy white teeshirt and brief blue tight-fitting shorts. She waved to Edward as she saw him approaching and he stepped to the edge of the quay to talk to her.

"Are you coming with us for a trip?" she asked.

Edward explained that he had to get back to Tote with the food shopping so that Marilyn could prepare the meal when she got home.

"Perhaps tomorrow then?" she said." You must come out before you go back to England."

Edward said he would love to go on a trip.

"Tomorrow morning then? I'm taking a party of people on a 'Cast Ashore' day to the isle of Isay. It will take most of the day, but Mum will be working so it will be something for you to do. We'll take a bottle of wine and some lunch."

Edward readily agreed to this plan. The idea of a day on a boat with the lovely Josephine was very appealing.

After a little more sightseeing around Portree, Edward returned to Tote where Marilyn was already waiting for him. They worked together preparing dinner, the main feature being a whole fresh salmon.

At 7pm a car drew up outside Meadow Cottage, with Jordan at the wheel. He and Anthony alighted to be greeted at the door by Edward and Marilyn. The visitors handed over two bottles of wine to their hosts and were shown inside the living room.

There followed an hour of pre-dinner drinks and chitchat, with Jordan doing most of the talking. He was very well travelled and had stories of adventures in many countries, but predominantly ones in the Far-East where he had worked in numerous bars and restaurants. But he revealed that before becoming involved in the catering trade he had had a spell in the British Army and then as a mercenary helping various African Governments to fight off revolutionary forces.

Marilyn was lapping it all up and tossing in occasional observations such as "wow" or "that's incredible".

In fact Edward's misgivings soon changed from his concern for Marilyn's finer feelings to a belief that she must think his own life as small-town property owner boringly humdrum in comparison to that of their new acquaintance.

By contrast, Anthony, who, after all, should have been the "star" guest of the evening, was almost dumbstruck, whether through a sense of his own inadequacy in the realm of adventure, or because he couldn't get a word in.

Dinner came and went successfully, with both guests and hosts drinking large quantities of wine. When they settled down again for more conversation, Jordan became increasingly garrulous, talking quietly but very quickly and peppering every sentence with profanities.

Edward was becoming frustrated because he wished to use the occasion to find out more about Anthony and assess his suitability as the bearer of the Dunsill bloodline.

Then the evening took a twist which Edward found utterly deplorable. Jordan started to relate various enjoyable experiences he had had with drugs. Edward tried to change the subject by starting to engage Anthony in a discussion on family history. But Marilyn shocked him when she butted in and suggested they all try a cannabis joint.

"I've got some super stuff I've been saving for a special occasion," she declared.

Jordan was enthusiastic, Anthony nodded in agreement and an angry Edward said they should "count him out". He did not wish to cause a scene or be thought of as a killjoy so, with as much diplomacy as he could muster, he made the excuse that he had had far too much to drink and had to turn in for the night. His companions did not seem at all put out by this and continued happily rolling out their cigarettes.

Edward did not sleep well that night, although he did feign a deep sleep when Marilyn eventually flopped into bed at around 5am. He was worried that everything was starting to go wrong. His hopes of drawing Anthony into the family circle had been dealt a severe blow. Also he had begun to doubt Marilyn's moral fibre. Did he really want as a companion a 60-year-old druggie whose idea of a good time was to drink to excess, smoke joints and have sex on top of a graveyard slab?

***

Around 8.30am the next day Edward, lying naked in bed, was awoken by a knock on the bedroom door. Marilyn was still sound asleep and snoring loudly, so he jumped out of bed, quickly put on his boxers, and went to the door. It was Josephine.

"Have you remembered our boat trip this morning?" she said.

"Oh, yes. Of course," replied Edward.

"Well, we will need to be off soon. I'm meeting our party at the boat at 10 o'clock."

"Oh, okay. Fine," said Edward, who in his concern about the previous night's encounter had temporarily forgotten about the trip he had been so looking forward to.

"I'll get washed and dressed and have a bowl of cereal and then I'll be ready for the off."

Josephine smiled sweetly, but cocked her head to one side, in a gesture intended to express some doubt as to whether he would achieve that.

But Edward, who had drunk a little less than the others at the dinner party, was true to his word and by 9am joined Josephine in her lime-green Land Rover Sport, heading for Portree.

Josephine told Edward that she had arrived home at 1am to find her mother and two men talking drunken gibberish. She had made her excuses and gone straight to bed. Edward wondered if she knew they had been smoking cannabis, but thought it best not to mention the subject.

He had also noticed that Jordan's car was no longer outside the cottage. That meant that one of the drug and alcohol-fuelled men must have driven home in the early hours. He again found himself shocked and disappointed. Even though both Tote and Bernisdale were quiet settlements with little traffic, the fast and quite busy Portree to Dunvegan road lay between them. Edward himself was no saint but he found himself recoiling at such irresponsible behaviour.

When they reached Portree Harbour they climbed aboard Josephine's smart 10ft long motor vessel, which was large enough to carry 12 passengers and two crew members. Josephine and Edward were to be the captain and crew that day, although Edward was told his role would mainly be to dispense cups of tea to the customers.

After the necessary preparations had been made for the voyage Edward and Josephine sat on deck awaiting the arrival of their guests. Soon a gaggle of Japanese tourists arrived, each armed with the inevitable camera and already snapping away ferociously, capturing everything that moved and everything that didn't.

The happy party was welcomed aboard and there were enthusiastic handshakes all round. It soon became obvious that most of the Japanese had very limited English so Josephine had to use a variety of visual aids and physical demonstrations to explain the day's arrangements, the safety requirements and what wildlife they should look out for.

The weather was warm and sunny and the sea quite calm as the vessel cast off for the day's adventure. The Japanese were delighted with the opportunities afforded for photographing a variety of accommodating wildlife. Between shots one or two of the party even had the chance to look at birds and seals without the intervention of a camera, a tablet or mobile phone.

The boat made good progress to the now uninhabited island of Isay, once owned by pop legend Donovan. The main purpose of the "castaway" trip was to leave the party on shore for seven hours so they could explore the island and let their imaginations roam over its history and its long lost populations. Partial shelter, if the weather required it, could only be provided by the roofless ruins of old houses.

The boat pulled up at the remains of an old jetty where the customers were put ashore.

"What do we do now?" asked Edward.

"We could go back to Skye – to Stein. That's not far away and there's a nice old inn there – the oldest inn on Skye," said Josephine.

"That sounds all right," said Edward. "But it's so lovely here. Could we look around this island ourselves?"

"Sure we could," said Josephine. "We could eat our picnic and drink our bottle of wine. And then just sunbathe. It would be really relaxing."

"Sounds like a plan," said Edward.

"But we'll have to move the boat from here," said Josephine. "The whole point of this trip is that the punters think they have been cast away – abandoned to the elements. I like them to think that the boat has gone away and they're stuck on their own desert island – at least for seven hours.

"We'll move to the other side of the island. It's quite a big island as islands go, so there's not much chance they'll find us."

She put the boat out to sea and rounded the island, mooring at an isolated inlet as far away as possible from where they had left the tourists.

They scrambled ashore, Josephine leading the way and Edward carrying a well-stocked picnic hamper. They sat down on an exposed grassy bank and contemplated the magnificent sky blue seascape with uninterrupted views of the Outer Hebrides.

They tucked into their picnic and slurped their bottle of red wine.

They chatted away happily, telling each other about their lives, their successes and failures and their hopes for the future.

Josephine was a very positive person. On the surface she had had a difficult childhood. Her mother had gone from partner to partner, marrying a couple of them in the process, and had moved numerous times to various parts of the United Kingdom. Josephine's father, an occasional actor, had abandoned them for an elderly male thespian.

It seemed that Josephine herself had never let her mother's dysfunctional lifestyle drag her down. She had done well at school at Winchester and had studied Modern Languages at Southampton University. While there she had become a keen yachtswoman, spending many hours sailing on the Solent and gaining a coastal skipper qualification.

It was there she met her first serious boyfriend, a bronzed Eton-educated muscleman, who shared her passion for boats and the sea. Their relationship grew closer, even though they spent a great deal of time apart, Josephine working as an air hostess and her lover, Royston, becoming a hedge fund manager in the City.

After two years in their respective jobs the drawing power of the sea proved too strong for them. At that time Marilyn had taken up with her latest beau, an oil rig worker who lived in his old family home at Tote on the Isle of Skye – Meadow Cottage.

After spending some holidays together on Skye Josephine and Royston hit upon a business venture which appeared to fulfil all their dreams. They would run motor boat trips for tourists and also buy some small yachts so they could teach sailing skills.

And that's precisely what they did, Royston's well-to-do parents financing the scheme.

For the first year everything went swimmingly, but then it all went seriously awry. Josephine did not reveal everything to Edward that day on Isay, skating over the problems which had led to the couple's break-up.

But the fact was that Josephine was an attractive, sexy and friendly young lady – a free spirit who was not yet ready to be tied down to one partner. Royston, on the other hand, was possessive, jealous and something of a control freak. Despite their superficial compatibility, zest for life and shared interest in the sea they were on a collision course. And collide they did.

After Royston spotted Josephine canoodling in a bar one night with a handsome American tourist, he punched the unfortunate man, slapped Josephine across the face and stormed out of the bar and the relationship.

He took the yachts away and relocated to the south coast of England, leaving Josephine with the cabin cruiser to run the boat trips. She gladly took up the challenge and was now in her second successful season.

While Josephine was telling her story, in a breezy and confident manner, Edward was entranced by her. She was glowing with health and youthful vitality and he rated her even sexier than her broodingly sensual mother.

"Time for some sunbathing, I think," said Josephine. "Don't mind if I strip off, do you?"

"Be my guest," said Edward, bashfully but with a strong feeling of anticipation.

She removed her teeshirt and then struggled out of her jeans, leaving her in an attractive blue bra and brief blue knickers. Her flat stomach and very long legs impressed Edward greatly. He decided it would be polite to follow suit and stripped down himself to his boxer shorts.

Josephine produced two yellow plastic bottles from the picnic hamper.

"Here," she said. "You'll need these – suntan lotion and insect repellent. Midges love Isay."

Edward applied the creams liberally and then passed the bottles back to Josephine.

"I'm already covered head to toe in the stuff," laughed Josephine. "But I wondered if you would mind rubbing some suntan lotion into my back. It's difficult to reach it yourself."

"A pleasure," said Edward.

Josephine rolled over on to her stomach and Edward gently applied the sun cream,"

"You can rub it in a bit harder than that," she joked. "I won't break."

Edward laughed and rubbed more robustly.

"Wow. You've missed your vocation," she said. "You should have been a masseur. Just unclip my bra will you? You could do wonders with the itchy spot I have just there."

Edward, becoming excited, was pleased to oblige and continued his massage."

"Ooh. That's absolutely gorgeous," said Josephine. "I'm enjoying this a lot. You certainly have missed your vocation."

"You're not the first person to tell me that," said Edward. "But it's quite easy really, especially when the client is as absolutely gorgeous as you are."

"Well. You're not too bad yourself, for an old 'un," she replied.

"I'll make you pay for that," was Edward's rejoindure, as he pummelled her back vigorously.

Josephine quickly reared up and turned towards him, her bra hanging loosely. She playfully punched his chest, shouting: "I'm going to get you back now!"

Edward grabbed her by the wrists and then looked into her eyes.

"Absolutely gorgeous," he said.

He let go of her wrists and pushed her arms around her back. She moved closer to him and French-kissed him. Then she pushed him away and flung her bra aside.

"You can massage these now, if you like," she said, smiling.

Edward cupped her pert breasts in his hands and gently massaged them.

She put her hand down his boxers and grabbed his erect penis.

"Come on," she said. "Show me what an old 'un can do."

She unzipped a backpack which lay on the ground beside her and pulled out a packet of condoms.

"Here," she said, passing the packet to Edward.

He was surprised that she was so well prepared. He guessed from the fact the packet was not full that he was dealing with "a lady of experience".

Josephine took off her knickers and Edward removed his boxers. She lay back on to the warm grass and pulled him on top of her.

***

"What are you going to say to my mother?" said Josephine as she cuddled up to Edward, gently pulling at his chest hairs.

"Say to your mother?" asked Edward. "Do you want me to say anything to your mother?"

"No, of course not. I was joking," said Josephine. "But I'm not going to share you."

Edward looked fondly into her eyes and replied: "Do you think I would want to share you with anyone?

"To be quite honest I've begun to have some reservations about your mother. Somehow she doesn't seem to have grown up since I knew her as a young girl. I know that must sound a bit rich coming from me, after what we've just done. Hardly the action of a mature old-aged pensioner, was it?"

"No," said Josephine, wagging her finger like a school ma'am. "You're a naughty boy. But I like you!"

Edward laughed: "I know. I know. But about your mother... from what I've seen myself and from what you've told me she doesn't really seem the type to make much of a commitment. And then there was the cannabis last night. Sorry, I hadn't mentioned that. It's really a little, well, Sixtiesish, isn't it? You're not into the wacky baccy yourself are you?"

"No. I only go in for healthy pursuits," she winked. "You're right about my mother. She's a hopeless case. She's always been man mad and not too particular about what sort of man she gets tangled up with. You must think I take after her and perhaps I do. But I know exactly what I want out of life. She never has. I've got ambitions."

"What are your ambitions exactly?" asked Edward, typically wondering if he could do anything to help her to further them.

"I want to expand my boat trips business so that I have a presence on every decent sized island in Scotland. And when the business is strong enough for me to employ managers then I want to sail a yacht around the world – hopefully take part in the Clipper Round the World yacht race or something similar.

"And I want a baby, or maybe babies, and a husband who will look after the babies while I'm away yachting."

Edward told her he was impressed by her enthusiasm and hoped she would achieve all her goals. He tweaked one of her nipples and declared: "I can see you're a winner."

Josephine looked at her watch. "Two hours left," she said.

"Shall we do it again?"

Chapter Seven

Horny Dilemma

When Edward returned to Meadow Cottage that night he realised he was facing a dilemma. On their journey home Josephine had reiterated that she was not prepared to share him with her mother. She did agree, though, when Edward insisted that Marilyn should be told nothing of what had taken place that day.

Edward was a little taken aback by all this. He had thought that they had just enjoyed a spontaneous, never-to-be-repeated, day of passion. Why should this beautiful, confident young woman wish to, as it seemed she did wish to, prolong the relationship?

He was not so vain as to believe for a moment that this was anything to do with his sexual prowess. He could not get out of his mind the fact that he was an old-aged pensioner and that she was a vital twenty-something.

Could it be that she was emotionally needy in some way, perhaps even looking for a father figure? Or, perish the thought, was she looking for a sugar daddy, perhaps to replace her former partner's rich parents in financing her business?

Whatever the true reason for Josephine's attitude, Edward could not help being flattered, and, truthfully, excited.

While Marilyn and Josephine busied themselves preparing an evening meal, he wracked his brain as to how he could extricate himself from Marilyn's bed that night. He needed time to think, so he decided on a course of action that would at least put the dilemma on hold for 24 hours.

He used his mobile phone to contact Anthony. He suggested that he might drive over to see his new relative after dinner that evening, to do a little in-depth family history research and Anthony, having consulted Jordan, said that would be a very good idea. Edward knew that Marilyn was working at the hotel that evening so there was no chance of her suggesting that she might accompany him.

His plan was to say later that he had had too many drinks with Anthony and could not possibly drive home. He was relying on Anthony to be hospitable and offer him a bed for the night, or at least a place on a sofa.

This is exactly what happened, except that very little family history research was done and a great deal of drinking was. Edward found that every time he sat next to Anthony in earnest, pen and notebook at the ready to jot down facts and reminiscences, Jordan would chip in with the offer of another drink. He also offered drugs, but Edward was sufficiently disapproving of the suggestion to ensure that they were not offered a second time.

This did not stop Jordan and Anthony, though, the latter becoming increasingly incoherent as the night progressed.

At one point Jordan, now slurring his words, turned the conversation to Marilyn, describing her as "a very fit old bird".

"I must say, Edward my son, that I fancy the pants off her," he declared. "A pity she's gone on you."

Edward shrugged his shoulders: "I don't know about that. We certainly got on well years ago, but I couldn't keep her then and I suspect I wouldn't be able to keep her now if something better came along. She's a genuinely friendly, loving person, but she's a something of a butterfly, I think, when it comes to the opposite sex."

"You mean she puts it about a bit," said Jordan.

"Well, she certainly used to," replied Edward.

He found Jordan's tone and manner quite offensive, but he was a quick and decisive thinker and a new thought came to him now which he determined to put into immediate effect.

Jordan was to be his "Get out of jail free" card. It had been obvious when they met at Meadow Cottage that Marilyn had been attracted to Jordan. Now Jordan had admitted that he was attracted to her. Job done! Edward would do all he could to encourage the relationship, thereby allowing him to continue his tryst with Josephine.

He straightaway put his plan into action.

"How would you two like to come over to Meadow Cottage again – tomorrow night, say? If Marilyn's not working, that is?"

Jordan looked over to Anthony, who by this time was starting to nod off.

"Anthony," he shouted. "We've been invited to go over to Marilyn's place again. Would you like that?"

"Oh, yeah," said Anthony, stirring himself.

"But we can't do tomorrow night, because we're both working," said Jordan. "That's a fucking shame. I think we're working every fucking night for the rest of this week."

"What time do you finish?" asked Edward.

"About 11ish," said Jordan.

"I think Marilyn finishes around time that too," said Edward. "Could we make it a late night tete a tete? Could you bring us a takeaway from Portree?"

"Good plan, guvn'r," said Jordan.

"Yeah. Suits me," grunted Anthony.

Edward rang Marilyn on her mobile and she happily agreed to the idea.

The rest of the night was mainly dominated by Jordan, telling a series of long-winded stories about his life. The picture he painted was of someone who had lived a selfish existence, leaving jobs and women at the drop of a hat and living on the edge of the law, carrying out various scams. The more he spoke, the more Edward disliked him.

He even started to feel guilty about his scheme to pair Jordan off with Marilyn. After all, what had Marilyn done to deserve this? She had shown Edward great hospitality and kindness, as well as taking him to her bed. On the other hand, she was a 60-year-old woman, well able to make her own decisions. That was how Edward argued with himself in an effort to square his conscience.

Blasted conscience!

Edward had always struggled with the concept of conscience, questioning

81

whether it was innate to human nature or just, like religion might be, an artificial concept invented by society in order to place restraints on behaviour.

As a young man visiting the theatre he had nodded agreement with a Murderer in Shakespeare's Richard III, who says of conscience: "I'll not meddle with it; it makes a man a coward; a man cannot steal but it accuseth him; a man cannot swear but it checks him; a man cannot lie with his neighbour's wife, but it detects him; 't is a blushing shamefaced spirit that mutinies in a man's bosom; it fills a man full of obstacles...".

But as he got older and more mature Edward began to believe that people might, after all, have an innate sense of morality – not one codified by religion, the law, or even the customs and traditions of society by which he set great store.

He took the first tentative steps along the road to believing that the phenomenon of people being revolted by their own sins was of the very essence of their humanity. He did not need any external sources to tell him what was right and wrong. This basic morality was programmed into his genes.

At various times of his life Edward, like the Murderer, would have liked not to meddle with Conscience but he always found that deity at his elbow.

As he sat listening to Jordan's profanities his conscience troubled him. How could he think of throwing Marilyn to this wolf, just so that he could carry on a questionable affair with Josephine, a woman young enough to be his granddaughter?

Then suddenly a radical thought struck him so hard that he felt dizzy: Josephine had said that she wanted a baby, or babies.

"Eureka! This could be the solution I've been looking for," he said to himself.

Edward had slowly and reluctantly come to the conclusion that Anthony was not the "heir" he had been seeking. He wanted someone he could cultivate as a worthy successor to the Dunsill line; someone he could build up, give money to, possibly even set up in business. But Anthony, the almost monosyllabic pot washer with dubious habits and an even more dubious housemate, did not present very fertile ground for cultivation.

Now Edward began to give serious consideration to the notion that he might father a male child by Josephine, offering pleasure in both the undertaking and the result.

Then the conscience problem reared its head again. What would his daughter Julia think about his producing a baby with a woman ten years her junior? She was broad-minded but even her liberality had its limits.

However, whatever reservations he had about Julia's reactions were subsumed by his overwhelming sense that it was his duty to propagate Dunsills.

He had convinced himself that duty was the guiding principle of his life, choosing to ignore a quotation from George Bernard Shaw which he had once read: "When a stupid man is doing something he is ashamed of, he always declares that it is his duty."

So it was his *duty* to have a child by Josephine and he was determined to get on with the task as soon as possible.

Not wishing to fall foul of Scotland's draconian drink driving laws Edward did not leave the Glenbernisdale cottage until noon the following day. Even then he did not see or hear anything of his two companions who were still "sleeping off" the previous night's excesses.

He had phoned Marilyn who told him that she was already at work but that she had left plenty of food for him at Meadow Cottage if he wished to have his lunch there.

Edward had other plans, though. He had already telephoned Josephine and arranged to meet her for lunch in Portree. They met at a recently refurbished hotel on the village's main street.

Decisive as usual, Edward intended to confront Josephine straightaway with his "radical idea" of fathering her child, or children if that's what it took to produce a male Dunsill. He realised he was taking a big risk. She might dismiss him angrily as a very dirty old man, or even just laugh in his face.

After ordering their meal in the well appointed dining room, they had time for a chat. Josephine, as confident and relaxed as she had been the day before, was not at all embarrassed about what had happened between them. In fact she was the first to refer to the matter.

"I really enjoyed your company yesterday," she said.

She added, with a wink, "You are an extremely fit man – for your age."

"Cheeky," replied Edward. "Does my age matter very much to you?"

"No, not a bit. I hate ageism."

"You don't feel just a little embarrassed in the company of someone as old as me? You don't feel it cramps your style?"

"No."

She patted his hand as a gesture of reassurance.

"Then I have something to say to you. You might find it a little shocking. If you don't like it then I apologise in advance and then please forget I ever said it. I hope it won't in any way spoil our new friendship."

Josephine laughed: "You're not going to tell me you're a mass murderer are you?"

"No. Not quite as shocking as that."

"Then go ahead. I'm really intrigued now to know what it is," she smiled.

"Okay then. You promise you won't be cross with me?"

"No. I won't be cross with you. Now get on with it!"

"Well. I thought we gelled pretty well yesterday, didn't you?"

"Yes. We got on great."

"I listened very carefully to what you said about being ambitious in business."

"Yes I am."

"Well, I think I could help you there – with some investment."

"I'm all ears."

"I also heard you say very clearly that you would like a family."

"Yes – that's another strong ambition of mine."

"Well – and please don't take offence – I was wondering if I might help out there too."

Edward slapped his hand in front of his mouth, as if to stop himself saying anything even more provocative.

"Do you mean what I think you mean?" asked Josephine calmly. "Are you actually suggesting that you might give me children?"

"I know it's ridiculous. But I did just wonder if you might consider it. I know we only met a couple of days ago and I know I'm a silly old fool. But I did just wonder."

Josephine gently took his hand: "I am flattered that you would think of such a thing. And I'm sure we would have a lot of fun making babies. You'll guess though that this is a bit of a bombshell. Can I ask why – why would you wish to saddle yourself with me and a new family at your age? Sorry to keep on about your age. It's very naughty of me. But I'm thinking of you. You

84

already have a daughter and grandkids. What would they think? And what would they think about you spending their inheritance on my business and then having a new set of kids to support?"

"I know. I know. You are being far more sensible than me," said Edward, blushing a little.

"You haven't answered my question. Why?"

"Two reasons, and I have to admit they are both very selfish ones. You see I have a duty to fulfil – a duty to the Dunsill family. I fear my family name, which has been a name to be reckoned with in our part of the country for generations, will die out unless I do something about it. I need to bring a male Dunsill into the world."

"Wow," said Josephine. "That's quirky. But don't you also have a duty to your daughter and your grandchildren? Can't one of the grandchildren pass on the family name, if that's so important?"

"They're both girls."

"But these days a lot of women keep their maiden names as part of their new surnames when they get married - have a double-barrelled name including their husband's name as well."

"I've thought of that. But it's not the same. And anyway it's too late. My daughter and my grandchildren already have their surname. It's Jones."

He uttered that name with a cringe of distaste.

"Dunsill-Jones would be all right, wouldn't it?"

"No. It's too late, and anyway it would look pretentious to suddenly add a name and make it double-barrelled."

"It might look pretentious, but surely not so drastic as starting a whole new family."

"I'm an old-fashioned old git, I know. But I have a strong belief that a healthy society needs to have traditions and continuity and one of the best ways of achieving that is for inherited genes to run through old families."

"I think you're pretty mad, actually," said Josephine. "I don't begin to understand why a name is so important. A rose by any other name and all that. If that's what you think, though, then I respect your right to believe that. But there was a second reason for wanting to have a family through me?"

"Ah, yes. That second reason is that you're the most beautiful girl I have ever seen in my life. You're vibrant, brimful with the vital spark of young life.

I love your unaffected manner and your go-getting approach to living. Silly old bugger that I am, it was love at first sight."

Josephine laughed.

"You are a silly old bugger. But I can see that you could charm the birds from the trees. My mother said you were charming but that you were too reserved and quiet when you were young. You're not reserved and quiet now, are you?"

"I am usually. And people think I'm cautious too – a bit of a stick in the mud. They don't really know me. They don't know what exciting thoughts race through my head every day of my existence. It's just that I don't usually share them with anyone else. Not until today. That's how I feel about you."

Josephine went quiet for a few moments, a new seriousness coming over her. Then she said: "If we were to have children and they were to have your name, then we would need to be married, wouldn't we?"

"Yes."

"I don't know if I'm ready for marriage. I'm still a bit of a wild child, I think."

Edward replied: "Don't worry. I would want you to stay just as you are. I'm not a jealous person, I hope. I wouldn't expect you to be faithful to me, sexually I mean. You are far too young for me to expect that of you. I am pretty sure you would make a lovely mother for my children. I could either be there all the time, or keep my distance, whatever you would like."

"Are you sure you could do that – not that I'm saying I would be putting it around all the time?"

"I'm sure."

Josephine paused for thought once more and then continued: "As I said, I'm flattered. I do trust you to be kind and understanding. And I do fancy you. I just need a little time to think. Come with me on another castaway day tomorrow, then we can talk some more. And, who knows, maybe even make a baby."

Edward was flabbergasted by her last remark, which he had not for a moment expected to hear.

He stretched across the table and kissed her on the lips and then said: "So another trip to Isay then. Isay Dunsill. Could Isay be a boy's name, do you think?"

In response to this Josephine feigned a reproachful look.

***

Julia Jones was dusting the spacious hallway of the old Sanderholme farmhouse which she and her family had moved into just a few months previously following the deaths in quick succession of her paternal grandparents.

The move had been her father's idea, of course, keen as he was to keep the fine old house, now a listed building, in the family. He thought it a great pity that people with the name of Jones were living there, but it was better than nothing!

Julia was a well-preserved 35-year-old, a tall slim brunette with a pleasant homely face and a page-boy hairstyle. Her complexion was mainly pallid, but she had slightly rosy cheeks which, to the discerning eye, might have marked her out as a farmer's wife not averse to taking her turn in the fields.

Her husband, Clive Jones, had taken over the farming side of the Dunsill family business. He was a burly man, with much rosier cheeks than his wife's and a cheerful rustic disposition. Their two daughters Eve, 10, and Samantha, 8, were happy and boisterous girls, who owned a pony each and spent much of their spare time riding them and caring for them.

The marriage was recognised throughout the Sanderholme area as a successful one, bonded by love and financial good sense. Like Julia, Clive came from a farming family. The couple had met at a Young Farmers' social and their union had resulted in a fruitful merger of the two families' farming interests.

Edward had always been more interested in the property side of the business than in farming, so bringing Clive on board had been a godsend.

The premature death of Julia's mother, Elizabeth, who had been the perfect doting grandmother, had been a nasty shock for the whole family. But the natural healing properties of Time had done their work and, for the most part, this well-balanced group of people had come to terms with their loss.

Julia did worry a little, though, about her father and how he was coping. He had always been a loving and dutiful parent and had remained strong throughout the trauma of Elizabeth's passing. But he was prone to developing obsessions, or, as his wife had called them, crazes.

His first adult obsession had been Marilyn. Other obsessions throughout the years had been the study of philosophy; reading great literature, with the unlikely target of reading at least five books a week; marathon and half-marathon running; and endurance horse riding. The latest was the study of family history.

Julia had begun to be concerned that this latest craze might be turning into an unhealthy one. It had gone beyond his usual academic enthusiasms. He had confided in her that he had become desperate to ensure that the family's male line and name was continued. In spite of his promises that this would make no difference to the expectations of herself and her family, Julia was unsettled. She thought he was being foolish and told him that he should be content with the loving family he already had. Edward had hugged her and assured her that he was indeed content and that what he was searching was merely "the icing on the cake" on his otherwise satisfactory life.

Knowing her father as well as she did, Julia was not entirely convinced. His behaviour had recently changed and he was spending a good deal of time away from his business, making mysterious trips to far flung parts of the country to "trace the family tree".

He told Julia that he was visiting archives offices, cemeteries and long lost cousins who might be able to provide him with useful snippets of information. But one day he had accidentally left his diary on the sofa in her sitting room and, with totally natural curiosity, she had examined it.

Yes, it did contain details of some appointments at archives offices but she could not help but notice that the "long lost cousins" detailed in the diary were all female. And she recognised one or two names of women who had been mentioned over the years as former girlfriends of her father before his marriage.

His latest visit to Skye was the farthest he had been to date and the most unexplained. He had merely left a message on Julia's mobile phone to say that he was going to the Scottish Highlands in search of family history clues and that he hoped to be back home in a week or so.

Julia had tried to contact him on his mobile but he had not responded. Like many of the older generation Edward was notorious for leaving his mobile phone at home, describing it himself as "the most immobile mobile phone in the world". She tried emailing him several times too, but he had not replied.

Julia was not entirely surprised by his lack of contact. He seemed to be in a world of his own these days.

And at this particular time she had other more pressing reasons for concern.

Her husband, Clive, was a creature of habits. His routine on five days a week was to rise at 5.30am, wash, shave and breakfast while listening to Radio 4, go out to work on the farm, return home for lunch at noon, go back to work at 1pm and return home for dinner at 6pm. On Sunday he went to church in the morning, followed by the pub, and returned home in time for the Sunday roast lunch. He took part in various family activities at weekends, usually involving the daughters and their ponies. As a result he was a familiar figure at gymkhanas and equestrian events organised by the local hunt.

However, in recent weeks something had changed: Clive would often miss his mealtimes. This might appear to be a trivial matter, but Julia knew that this was almost unthinkable behaviour for her husband whose hearty appetite was legendary. He normally slept like a log for seven or eight hours a night, but now he was restless on several nights of the week, tossing and turning and breaking into sweats.

Other routines were also falling by the wayside. Even during his normal working hours he had become more willing to take his daughters to the local stables where they kept their ponies and had their riding instruction. And he would often stay with them until they had finished whatever tasks they had to perform there.

Then one day, out of the blue, youngest daughter Samantha said to Julia: "I think Daddy loves Rachel."

Rachel, a short but well-proportioned and pretty 30-year-old blonde, was the girls' riding teacher.

"What do you mean?" asked Julia.

"Well he's always kissing her."

"Kissing her? When?"

"Every time they meet – and every time they say goodbye."

"Do you mean just a peck on the cheek?"

"Yes. But sometimes on the lips," giggled Samantha.

"Oh, I expect they're just being friendly," said Julia, who quickly changed the subject.

But Julia began to think. Could this be an explanation for Clive's unusual behaviour of late? Could it also explain why he always seemed to smell strongly of aftershave these days?

A maggot of doubt burrowed into her.

She said nothing for days but just quietly observed Clive's comings and goings and his changes of mood. She went with him and the girls to the stables and watched closely for any signs of chemistry between the vivacious Rachel and her husband. She detected nothing beyond the normal intercourse between two naturally friendly people. She noticed, though, that there were no kisses between them, either on meeting or departure and she wondered if they were being deliberately coy in her presence.

Then something else happened which heightened her suspicions. One Sunday afternoon when her girls returned from the stables she was in the kitchen preparing a meal and they were in the adjacent lounge. She overheard a conversation which was whispered, but whispered so loudly as to be audible.

"They were kissing again today," said Samantha.

"I didn't see them," said Eve.

"They were – they were kissing in the tack room. I went in to hang my bridle up and they stopped when they saw me."

"Don't tell Mummy," said Eve. "She'll be cross."

"I won't," said Samantha, rather unconvincingly as she was known to be the chief gossip-monger of the family.

Julia was gutted, but she said nothing when Clive entered the kitchen a few moments later having put his Land Rover in the garage.

She worried all night about what she had heard and her anxiety remained with her the next morning as she breakfasted with Clive and then woke up the girls, fed them and took them to school.

She spent the morning furiously cleaning and dusting, trying to take her mind off what she had heard. But it didn't work and she decided to tackle Clive on the subject when he returned home for lunch.

He arrived on time and in a good mood but soon sensed that all was not well.

"I need to talk to you," said Julia, as soon as he had taken off his farmer's cap and hung it up in its usual place on a peg in the spacious hallway.

"What's the problem, love?" asked Clive.

"Are you…" she stopped to search for the right words. "Are you carrying on with Rachel?"

"Carrying on?"

"Yes. I've overheard the girls saying you and Rachel keep kissing each other."

"Kissing?"

"Yes, kissing. It's not the first time it's been mentioned, and you have been spending an awful lot of time at the stables recently."

Clive was quick to respond: "You know Rachel. She's quite tactile and affectionate, isn't she? She often gives people a kiss — just to say 'hello' or 'goodbye'. That's all it is. Of course we're not 'carrying on'."

"You're sure that's all it is?"

"I'm absolutely sure, love. And, as for me spending a lot of time at the stables, well we both want to encourage Eve and Samantha in their riding, don't we? You've often said that yourself and I know that up until recently I've rather let work take over everything. I thought I ought to spend more time with the girls and give them some support. Please don't say you don't trust me."

"I do trust you," said Julia. "But just be a little more careful. Our daughters have probably misinterpreted things."

"Yes. Don't you worry, love. I'd never be interested in anyone but you."

Julia told Clive she was reassured. But this was a lie. Although she recognised Rachel as being a lively, confident and quite friendly person she had never noticed that she was especially tactile or affectionate. She remained suspicious.

Chapter Eight

The Boat Builder

Edward was well satisfied with the outcome of his lunch with Josephine and quite taken aback that she had not dismissed out of hand his suggestion that they might produce a baby. He felt positively rejuvenated.

Josephine had gone back to work for the afternoon, taking a couple of wildlife tours around Portree harbour and Edward had gone along for the ride and to help serve teas and coffees. Then they took another party out on an evening "sunset cruise", Skye being noted for its magnificent and much photographed sunsets.

They returned to Meadow Cottage in separate cars at around 10.30pm. Edward had told Josephine of the plans for later that night when Anthony and Jordan would be joining them, bringing with them a takeaway from Portree.

He had briefly told Josephine of his scheme to pair off Jordan and Marilyn and she had been enthusiastic in her approval. He had already deduced that the daughter had little respect for her mother, whom she had described as "regrettably, a little bit of a tart". Edward had a strong English sense of irony and the phrase "like mother, like daughter" had occurred to him.

At a few minutes past 11pm Marilyn arrived home. Josephine said that she would like to join the "takeaway party", so the three of them chose their dishes from a Chinese restaurant menu which Edward had picked up on his way back to the cottage. Then he phoned Jordan with their order.

Half an hour later Jordan and Anthony arrived by car and the food was quickly dispensed. Bottles of beer and wine were opened and modern jazz CDs put on as background music.

Jordan was as loquacious and cocky as ever and Anthony as taciturn and non-committal. Edward and Josephine were sociable and giving not the slightest hint that they had any relationship other than as very recent acquaintances. And Marilyn was as usual the perfect hostess, friendly to everyone and freely handing out drinks and other goodies.

There was a short period when Edward began to fear that his plan was going very much awry. Jordan appeared to be paying far more attention to the beautiful Josephine than to her mother and Josephine appeared to be quite willing to accept his attentions.

However, when Jordan turned away for a few seconds Josephine looked at Edward and curled her lip to show her disapproval of the younger man. Then she moved her chair away from Jordan's and tried to engage Anthony in conversation. She persevered for a long time, even though he spoke about little else than how boring he found his pot washing job.

The result, though, was that Jordan, a little put out by Josephine's defection, turned his full attention to Marilyn. She had been sitting alone on the living room's sofa but Jordan moved over to join her and the two soon became engrossed in each other's company. There was lots of flirtatious eye contact and touchy-feelyness. Edward noticed that Marilyn had placed her hand on Jordan's leg, dangerously close to his crotch.

Then, as Edward had feared was inevitable, Jordan suggested that they all smoked a joint. Anthony showed his first enthusiasm of the night, declaring "Yeah, great idea" and Marilyn was her usual compliant self. Josephine looked at Edward and raised her eyes heavenwards.

Edward shook his head disapprovingly. His upbringing had given him a deep respect for the rule of law and he could not stomach this blatant flouting of it.

"Shall we get some fresh air?" he said to Josephine.

"C'mon, Eddie. Let your fucking hair down and join us for a smoke," said Jordan.

93

"No, thanks," said a po-faced Edward. "I'll be back soon."

Josephine got up to join him and they walked out of the front door.

The weather still being remarkably good for Skye, it was a balmy, clear evening.

"Just look at all those stars," said Edward, as they stood in the lane outside the cottage. "There's thousands of them and they look so close. The sky seems like a black flat blanket draped over us."

"I know. It's absolutely wonderful. I sometimes feel as if I could just put my hands up and touch some of the nearest stars – and it's like this so often. Did you know that nine parts of Skye are designated as Dark Skies Discovery Areas because there's so little artificial light pollution? It's amazing how many tourists come to the island for that reason alone. I'm seriously thinking of extending my sunset cruises to take in the Dark Skies. I'd have to install some extra lighting on the boat for the sake of the passengers, and then, of course, I would turn them off when we reached the relevant points for looking up at the sky. In fact I'll get on to this straightaway – in the morning."

Edward continued to be impressed by Josephine's ambitions for her business and this strengthened his resolve to be part of her future.

The couple sauntered hand in hand down the lane. The way ahead was lit by a small torch which Josephine had produced from the back pocket of her jeans. There were very few sounds to be heard on such a still night. The good people who lived in the cottages along the Tote lane were tucked up in their beds with their curtains drawn and their lights turned out. Marilyn's raucous laughter was coming from Meadow Cottage, as the mellowing effects of the cannabis had plainly not yet come into play. Some cows, mooing and lowing contentedly, could be seen moving around in the bright moonlight.

"There's an ancient Pictish stone here, at the side of the road – just here," Josephine pointed out, shining her torch on to a large grey standing stone. I'll show it to you in the daylight tomorrow. It dates from the 7th century. It's been here for over a century but before that it was built into the door frame of a house near here."

"That's interesting," said Edward. "We'll take a closer look at that in the morning."

They carried on along the lane, talking about possibilities for the future, including the business, the baby and marriage.

Josephine clasped Edward's hand tightly, stopping him in his tracks and pulling his face close to hers.

"I will," she whispered.

"Will what?" he whispered back.

"Marry you."

She kissed him on the lips.

"That's wonderful," said Edward. "I promise you won't regret it. I'll look after you."

"I know you will."

Edward could hardly believe that Josephine had so quickly agreed to his ideas. He felt elated.

They walked for about half an hour backwards and forwards on the lane, neither being at all anxious to return to Meadow Cottage. When they did get back they were in for a surprise as only Anthony was in the living room. He was slumped face downwards on the floor, snoring loudly and with a pile of vomit on the carpet by the side of his mouth.

There were empty bottles and stubbed out cigarettes on the floor and on chairs.

"That's disgusting," exclaimed Josephine.

"Mum, where are you?" she shouted.

There was no reply so she looked in the kitchen, the bathroom and the toilet and, finally, knocked loudly on her mother's bedroom door. There was still no response so she sneaked inside the bedroom, worried about what she might find. But no one was there.

Meanwhile Edward had unsuccessfully tried to rouse Anthony.

"Just leave him there," said Josephine. "He'll probably just sleep it off. I'll get a bowl of water and an old towel or something and I'll clean up this mess. It's making me feel sick just looking at it."

She smiled and added: "Nice relatives you have, Edward."

"Nice mother you have!" joked Edward.

"Ok. Touche," said Josephine.

"That rhymes. You're a poet and you don't know it," quipped Edward.

Josephine playfully slapped him on the head.

"Come on, help me clear up this mess," she jousted. "Don't just stand there making silly jokes."

They set to work clearing up the room and as they completed the job the front door was flung open.

Marilyn and Jordan, holding each other up, almost fell into the room.

"Oh, dears, you're back," slurred Marilyn.

"Oh dear more like," said Josephine. "Don't worry. We've cleaned up the sick."

"Sick?" asked Marilyn.

"Yes, look at Anthony. We found him like this, laying on the floor with his face in a pile of sick."

Marilyn giggled and went over to look at Anthony's prone form.

"He's in a bit of a state, isn't he?" she said.

"He's fucking pissed and off his head," was Jordan's perspicacious comment.

Josephine looked closely at her mother and saw that her pretty floral dress was spattered with mud and bore a number of grass stains. Then she looked at Jordan and noticed that his tight fitting white jeans were similarly soiled.

"Where have you two been?" she asked.

"Just for a little walk, dear," said Marilyn. "It's such a lovely night."

Josephine merely replied: "Um."

Edward was appalled by the state the couple had got themselves into, but at the same time quietly pleased that his plan seemed to be working very well.

Jordan and Marilyn staggered over to the sofa and slumped down on it, clinging on to each other as if scared to let go in case they fell on to the floor. Within a few seconds they were both asleep.

"Leave them there," said Josephine to Edward. "It's bedtime now. Coming to join me?"

She took Edward by the hand and led him to her room.

***

The next morning Edward and Josephine were up bright and early, making coffee and eating a breakfast of cereals, toast and marmalade. Marilyn and Jordan were still asleep on the sofa, arms wrapped around each other. Anthony had somehow managed to wake up and fall face down into an easy chair.

Hoping not to wake anyone, Edward and Josephine crept quietly around the cottage preparing themselves for the day ahead when they would be going on their second castaway cruise.

But the Skye weather had changed unexpectedly and dramatically overnight. A strong blustery west wind had swept in from the Atlantic and it was raining heavily. As soon as Josephine poked her nose out of the front door she decided that that day's cruise had to be cancelled. She picked up her mobile phone and gave the bad news to her clients.

"So. I've got a day off," she said. "What shall we do?"

"Did we ought to see what the others want to do – when they finally wake up?" asked Edward.

"No! I'm not staying in here with these three saddos," said Josephine. "They'll probably not get going until lunchtime anyway."

"Yeah, you're right. What shall we do? What *do* you do on Skye on a wet, windy day?"

"What I should do is go and sit by my boat at Portree harbour and tout for trade. But I fancy a day off and I don't think the weather's going to change any time today. So how about we take a drive around the island? It can be really atmospheric on a wet day, especially in the Cuillin mountains. You won't be able to see for long distances, but what you can see might be quite spectacular – elemental. I'll drive."

Edward loved her spirit. Someone who liked driving around in the pouring rain was just the sort of person he admired.

"We could stop for some lunch somewhere," she said.

"Sounds like a plan," said Edward.

From Tote they drove to Dunvegan, one of the largest villages on the island, noted for its castle perched on the edge of a beautiful sea loch, the ancient seat of the Chiefs of the Macleod clan. They drove past the castle and parked in one of the wider passing places overlooking the loch.

"Take my binoculars," she said, "and point them towards those islands."

Edward did as he was told, looking through the closed car window. The rain was still pelting down but the visibility had improved enough to allow a good view of several small islands in the loch.

"Seals," he said. "Lots of them."

He had spotted several groups of seals, both adults and babies, basking on the sandy edges of the islands.

"There's nearly always seals to be seen just here," said Josephine. "The Dunvegan estate makes loads of money taking visitors on boat trips to look at them. Edward, just look down there, in front of us."

Edward put down the binoculars and saw that just a few yards away from them in the water was a single seal, its black face, grey whiskers and big, soft, black eyes clearly visible above the waterline. The animal stared at them, then disappeared under the water, eventually resurfacing just a few yards away and examining them again.

"We have seals at Sanderholme but we seldom see them as close as this, except at the local seal hospital," said Edward.

"People love seals," said Josephine. "They like eagles and whales and porpoises, which we often see on my boat trips. But although the seals are very common around here there's something cute about them that attracts people. And they're reliable too. One of the boats round here offers people their money back if they don't see any seals on their trip. I bet they don't have to pay up very often. I don't think I'll risk it though.

"How much money do you think you will be able to invest into my business?"

The directness of this question took Edward by surprise.

"I've not thought about actual figures yet," he said.

"If I'm going to expand the business I need to buy a second boat and employ a couple of extra staff," she said. "£100,000 should do for starters."

Edward needed all his reserves of decisiveness to respond quickly to this bold statement. Inwardly he was becoming nervous, worried that he had dived in too deep. Eating into his consciousness was a gnawing feeling that by becoming too involved with Josephine, both emotionally and financially, he would be failing to do his duty to his close family. He might be risking their inheritance and even forfeiting their respect. And all for a silly notion about a family name – "a rose by any other name" and all that. After all, the Dunsill family genes had already been passed safely to the next generation in the persons of his two granddaughters. But, however irrational it might be, he still had this overarching desire to perpetuate the Dunsill family tradition.

He had to give Josephine a positive answer, otherwise his whole project would be in tatters.

"That shouldn't be a problem. We'll work out a business plan."

Josephine kissed him on the cheek.

"Thanks."

"Shall we have lunch?" asked Edward. "Is there anywhere around here you can recommend?"

"Let me take you to the oldest inn on Skye," she replied.

They motored a few miles away to the Waternish peninsular, renowned for its spectacular sunsets, and just around the corner from the isle of Isay, where Edward and Josephine had consummated their new relationship.

They arrived at the popular 18th century inn which overlooks the picture postcard Loch Bay and was once Donovan's "local". Normally at lunchtimes there would be drinkers seated at lochside tables at the front of the inn but on this particularly rainy day they were packed inside among the numerous diners. There were no spare tables so Edward and Josephine decided to wait until one became available.

They bought two glasses of wine and then perched on window seats in the bar area. Most of the people in the bar were dressed casually, some of them in shorts and teeshirts and others in walking gear. It was clear that this was a tourist hotspot, highlighted by the number of foreign languages and accents which could be heard. But sitting at a table were two elderly men both smartly dressed in tweeds and speaking with the soft and slightly clipped tones of the Highlands. They were talking quietly but were close enough for Edward and Josephine to pick up their every word. It seemed that they had both lived on Skye for many years.

Edward pricked up his ears when he heard one of the men talking about Glenbernisdale and the bus service between there and Portree. It was obvious that he was a long-standing inhabitant of the settlement.

He caught the eye of one of the men, who smiled at him and said:

"Are you on your holidays?"

Edward replied that he was and a conversation started about the weather.

"You live at Glenbernisdale then?" asked Edward as soon as he was able to change the subject.

"Aye", said the man. "I've been there all my life and my parents before me. My brother here was born there too but he moved to Orbost for his work."

More pleasantries were exchanged between the four of them, when it emerged that the slightly older of the two men, who was aged 75 and a widower, was called Fergus and was known locally as Fergus the Boat Builder. His brother was Douglas, a bachelor who lived with two wealthy spinster sisters and worked as their gardener, chauffeur and general factotum.

Josephine enjoyed an in depth talk with Fergus about the qualities of various types of boat, about which they were clearly both experts.

Then Edward asked Fergus, the brother who still lived at Glenbernisdale, if he knew of the two men who lived at Tora Cottage.

Fergus looked at his brother and laughed: "Aye. I ken them. They live just a couple of houses away from me."

"Do you know them well?" continued Edward.

"Nae too well," said Fergus. He laughed again and this time his brother joined in.

Edward smiled and asked: "Is there something funny about them?"

"It's just that we were talking about them as you came in. Are they friends of yours?"

"Not exactly friends," said Edward. "Acquaintances. One of them is a very distant relative."

"Aye," said Fergus, nodding.

"They like their drink," said Douglas. "Fergus is a little disapproving of them, as he does not drink himself."

"Oh, I see," said Edward. "I understand."

"You mean they're piss artists," Josephine helpfully interjected.

"I didna' say a word," said Fergus, his shoulders heaving as he tried to suppress further laughter.

Douglas nodded to Josephine in agreement, furtively so that his brother would not see him.

Edward was keen to learn more and, to keep the men's attention, offered to buy them both a drink.

"That's very kind of you," said Douglas. "I'll have half a pint of the 80 shillings. Fergus here doesn't drink, but he will have a sherry – a schooner of sherry is his usual."

Edward smirked and cast a knowing look toward Josephine, who was desperately trying to hide her laughter behind a strategically placed hand. He went to the bar where the barman was already pouring out the sherry into a huge vessel which had a large label stuck to it bearing the name of Fergus. Edward soon returned with the half pint for Douglas and the teetotal Fergus' favourite tipple, and they expressed fulsome thanks.

"As my brother said, I don't take a drink – but I do like a little sherry. But those friends of yours, from Glenbernisdale, they are heavy drinkers well enough. Not like the other gentleman who came to Tora Cottage. He was a respectable man – a very nice man."

"Aye. He was a friendly chap," affirmed Douglas. "He wasn't there long but my brother missed him when he left. They spent hours talking to each other."

"Aye. We had some really good crack," said Fergus. "He was an interesting man. I can't understand how he got involved with that black man. He seemed a different sort altogether."

"Did he live there with the mixed race guy who lives there now?" asked Edward.

"Aye. The black fella came first and then the white man joined him later. I haven't seen the white man – the one I liked – for a few weeks. I hope he's not left for good. I was disappointed because he never came to say goodbye. That surprised me. I would have thought he would have done. Then this other chap came – the miserable looking one."

"Fergus!" interrupted Douglas. "Be careful what you say. That man is probably this gentleman's relative."

"Yes. I'm afraid it must be," said Edward, smiling.

"I'm sorry," said Fergus. "I had better keep quiet."

"No need," said Edward. "He's only a distant relative. And I must admit he does look a little miserable sometimes."

The conversation flowed for the next hour or so, allowing time for the sober boat builder to indulge in a second schooner of sherry. His face became increasingly florid and he took a great shine to Josephine, taking her hand and whispering some special stories into her ear. They had found a particular bond, he the master boat builder and she the boat trip entrepreneur.

Douglas, who was the self-acclaimed drinker of the two brothers, in the meantime had sipped quietly at his half pint. He decided that it was time to get his brother home "to have a sleep before teatime". There was much shaking of hands and an invitation to take a dram at the teetotaller's Glenbernisdale cottage before Edward returned home to England. The ancient boat builder also took the opportunity of giving Josephine a smacker on the lips.

Edward returned the schooner to the bar, joking to the barman that Fergus was a "great character".

"Ah, Fergus the boat builder," the barman replied. "I've lived here for 50 years and no one can ever remember him building a boat."

Chapter Nine

Doubts

At the Sanderholme farmhouse Julia was feeling uneasy. As she tried unsuccessfully to preoccupy herself by methodically cleaning every room in the house the thought suddenly struck her that everyone was leaving her.

Clive spent less and less time at home and when he was there he was often distant and uncommunicative. She sensed that his mind was on Rachel. Even her daughters were spending progressively more time at the stables in the company of their father and his alleged lover.

She had lost her grandparents and her mother, and now her father, who had been her rock within recent years, was behaving erratically and seemingly keeping her out of the loop. Even when her beloved and highly dependable mother had been alive Edward had always been the patient, listening parent, full of sensible advice when she had had boyfriend problems or other crises in her life.

She longed to have his advice now. She needed someone to confide in about her perceived marital problems and Edward was the only person she could rely on to inject sound commonsense into her situation.

But where the hell was he? In Scotland – but where in Scotland?

He had told her that he had met recently with cousin Harry to talk about the family tree. So, clutching at straws, she determined to visit Harry to see if he might know her father's whereabouts.

She laid aside her mop and bucket, took a shower and dressed to drive into town.

She was greeted warmly by Harry, who had not seen her for several years, and he ushered her into his sitting room. He courteously begged her to be seated.

After exchanging some pleasantries, Julia explained that she needed to talk to her father but had received no response to her phone messages and emails. She wondered if Harry might know where his current researches might have taken him.

Harry said that Edward had, in fact, telephoned him a couple of days previously – from the Isle of Skye, to tell him that he had located his relative Anthony. Julia was very put out by the fact that her father had thought it more important to contact Harry than to reply to her many messages. But she kept her composure, not wishing to make Harry feel in any way uncomfortable.

"Apparently he's staying with an old friend who he met by coincidence," said Harry. "I wrote down the telephone number of the house. He said his mobile signal was in and out so he was using the landline."

Harry went over to a desk and copied a telephone number on to a piece of notepaper, which he then passed to Julia.

Julia expressed her gratitude.

"I'll ring him as soon as I get home – the monkey," she said.

Harry laughed and then put a finger in the air indicating that he had remembered something.

"I have a photograph here that you might be interested to see."

He went back to his desk and returned with the photo of Anthony which Peter Wattam had left with him.

"This is Anthony Dunsill – the relative that your father has traced on Skye."

Julia looked at the photograph carefully.

"I don't think I have ever seen him before," she said. "How does he fit into the family?"

Harry gave a full explanation, relating the history of Great-aunt Olivia and the family scandal surrounding her, a story of which Julia was totally unaware.

She normally had little patience with her father's family researches, but even she found this story quite riveting.

As she was about to leave, Harry took her hand and said: "Just one more thing."

"Yes", said Julia.

"You are into computers and emails and all that sort of thing aren't you?"

"Well, yes, up to a point."

"I think your father would be very interested to see this photograph. Could you possibly email it to him while he is on Skye? He might want to show it to Anthony."

He explained fully how he had come to have the photograph.

"Of course I will," said Julia, adding pointedly. "If, of course, he can be bothered to look at an email from me."

***

As soon as she arrived back home Julia rang the telephone number Harry had given her. Marilyn answered the call.

Julia asked if Edward Dunsill was there.

"Oh, yes. Who is it speaking?"

"It's his daughter, Julia."

Marilyn gave a friendly reply and said she would fetch him.

Edward came to the phone and gave a cheery and effusive welcome to his daughter.

But Julia was not to be easily charmed out of the resentment she felt from having been ignored.

"Where the hell have you been?" she raged. "I've been trying to get hold of you for days. I've phoned, left messages on your mobile, sent umpteen emails."

"I'm sorry dear. I've been rather busy. You're right to chastise me."

His apology proved not to be as disarming as he had hoped.

Julia continued to rant and rave at him for his neglect and selfish lack of concern for her. She was particularly critical of the fact that he had found time to contact Harry Greensmith – 'your bloody cousin umpteen times removed'."

"Anyway, Dad, where are you staying? Harry said it was with an old friend."

Edward explained truthfully that an old employee of his, Marilyn, had established contact with him on Facebook. By an uncanny coincidence Marilyn was living on Skye, the very place he needed to visit in his search for Anthony. Diplomatically, he omitted to mention that Marilyn was a former girlfriend, that he had shared a bed with her, and that he planned to marry and impregnate her twenty-something daughter.

Not knowing who might be listening in to their conversation, Julia was unwilling to discuss with her father there and then her suspicions about Clive. Instead she asked him to ring her back as soon as he was on his own. Edward, feeling thoroughly ashamed of his neglect of his much-loved daughter, readily agreed to phone her at an agreed time of seven o'clock that evening.

Julia, who could never be angry with her father for long, came down from her high horse and began to speak to him in her usual friendly manner.

"By the way," she said. "Harry Greensmith gave me a photograph of Anthony Dunsill that he asked me to scan and email to you."

"A photograph? How did he come by that?"

"The churchwarden at Marshyard took it when Anthony visited the graveyard there."

"Oh. How exciting. I'll be able to show it to Anthony. Please do send it on to me."

***

Julia's phone call was made in late afternoon after Edward and Josephine had returned from their extended pub lunch and a car tour to see the imposing, almost sinister, Black Cuillin mountains. They had found Marilyn surprisingly bright and breezy after her drink and drugs binge of the previous night. Jordan and Anthony had finally awoken and gone away.

On the drive home Edward and Josephine had made a crucial decision: they would tell Marilyn that they had become "an item". Not for the first time Edward was surprised at Josephine's "full frontal" approach to situations. He was riven with guilt and worry about how to break the news to Marilyn, whereas Josephine's stance was: "Just tell her. She's a grown woman. She's given blokes enough shit in her time."

Edward could not believe his luck, then, when Marilyn, having waited for Josephine to leave them alone together, beckoned him to sit down and made the following declaration: "Edward, you're a love and it's been great getting together with you again. But I'm afraid I've got to move on. You see I think

106

I've found someone who's more on my wavelength – as daft as I am, I suppose. Me and Jordan have been getting on really well, as you might have noticed. He's a cool guy and of course he lives on the island which is good."

Edward's sense of relief was at odds with a tinge of regret that Marilyn was taking a disastrous step in opting for such an obvious low-life as Jordan. But it was "job half-done" with only the news about his plans with Josephine left to impart.

"I understand," said Edward. "I'll move my things out of your room straightaway and I'll make myself scarce from the cottage in the next day or two – unless you want me to move out immediately."

"No, of course not," said Marilyn. "Stay as long as you need. There's no hard feelings, eh?"

"No hard feelings," replied Edward.

"Listen. I have something to tell you – something which may come as a bit of a bombshell. It's about Josephine and me."

"Josephine?"

"Over the last few days we've got to know each other very well and we really get on. Without beating about the bush, we've decided to get married."

"Christ almighty," said the shocked mother.

"I know there's a huge age difference, but I keep myself pretty fit and Josephine has assured me that it isn't a problem."

"The cow. She's done it to me again. It's not the first time by a long chalk that she's pinched one of my lovers."

Her statement took Edward by surprise but he regained his composure quickly and asked: "Have any of these lovers wanted to marry her?"

"No. Marrying's not been their aim at all. You know you're old enough to be her grandfather?"

"Of course I know that. You're not going to go all puritanical on me are you? Hardly your forte I would think."

"Far from it," replied Marilyn. "Free love and free will have always been my way. In fact, love, you would have been the puritanical one had you seen me last night."

"I saw you. Drugged and pissed up to the eyeballs and curled up with our friend Jordan."

"He had the balls to do what you didn't anyway," said Marilyn, becoming slightly annoyed.

"What do you mean?"

"Last night we took a walk to St Columba's Isle and consecrated our relationship in company with the knight."

"The night. I don't understand."

"The knight in the ruined chapel – on his slab. You know, the cosy threesome I suggested."

Edward was stunned to silence, a feeling of abhorrence flooding into his mind. Although not a religious man, he considered what had taken place to be an act of desecration, an abominable and sinister way of behaving.

"Yeah. I really got turned on. The feeling of that cold stone…. A feeling of communing with the soul of a dead…"

"Stop!" said Edward. "I don't want to hear any more. You've gone beyond the pale."

"And you haven't gone beyond the pale wanting to marry my 25-year-old daughter?"

"It may be culturally questionable. But it pales into nothing when compared to your perverted behaviour."

"You've got no imagination. That's your problem. And that's why Jordan is much more to my taste. Josephine's a scheming bitch, but she's got imagination too. She'll soon get fed up with you," said Marilyn, storming out of the room and slamming the kitchen door behind her.

Edward was left for a few minutes to cogitate on what had occurred. But then Marilyn reappeared and sat on the arm of his chair. She stroked his arm and said: "I'm sorry. I didn't mean to have a go at you like that. You've always been good to me. I know that. I wouldn't choose you as a husband for my daughter. Let me put that differently. I wouldn't choose my daughter to be your wife. I know you would be kind to her and fair to her. I would just give you one word of advice. Watch your bank balance!"

***

A vision of Marilyn and Jordan having sex with, or at least alongside, the prone stone knight preyed upon Edward's mind. During the days since he had visited the ancient graveyard with its strange oppressive atmosphere he had wished to find out more about it.

That evening Marilyn went out to work. Josephine had deliberately made herself absent so that Edward would have the opportunity of privately breaking the news of their engagement to her mother. She had said she would visit friends and not be back home until late.

So this gave Edward the opportunity to do some historical research, his very favourite pursuit. He found a couple of posts on Google which suggested that the knight in the ruined chapel was merely an effigy which had been created as a memorial to a Nicholson clan chief. The old boy was probably not buried underneath the stone image at all. So Marilyn's twisted idea that she had been in some way having a threesome with Jordan and the soul of a medieval knight was far-fetched as well as disgusting.

Carrying out research on the internet can often lead one to stray from one related topic to another and Edward found himself looking at posts concerning other graveyards on the island.

He came across the bizarre and desperately sad story of Lady Grange, who is buried at Trumpan churchyard on Skye's Waternish peninsular.

Lady Grange (1679–1745), maiden name Rachel Chiesley, was the wife of Lord Grange, a highly successful Scottish lawyer.

She was described as "a wild beauty" and Lord Grange fell in love with her and made her pregnant. But at first he refused to marry her because her father had murdered the Lord President of the Scottish Court of Session and Lord Grange feared that marrying the daughter might jeopardise his legal career. However, he changed his mind when Rachel threatened him at pistol point.

Before separating acrimoniously they enjoyed 25 years of married life "in great love and peace" and produced nine children. They had divided their time between an Edinburgh town house and a country estate where Lady Grange filled the role of factor.

But Lady Grange was no quiet housewife and mother. She is known to have had a violent temper and to have been a heavy drinker. She took the unnatural step of disinheriting all of her children when they were infants.

In the run-up to the separation from her husband she had discovered he had been having an affair with an Edinburgh coffee house owner. She was also stripped of the job as factor for her extravagant spending.

In April, 1730, Lady Grange threatened to commit suicide and to run naked through the streets of Edinburgh. It is said she had kept a razor under her pillow and intimidated her husband by reminding him she was a murderer's daughter. She also barracked him with obscenities in the street and in church and swore at his relatives.

Lady Grange was a supporter of the Hanoverian monarchy, but her husband had sympathies with the Jacobites, who wished to restore the Stuart dynasty to the thrones of England and Scotland. She produced letters which she claimed were evidence that her husband was involved in a treasonable Jacobite plot against the Hanoverian government. So to keep her out of the way he had her kidnapped.

She was abducted by two highland noblemen and several of their men. There was a bloody struggle, during which she was tied up and gagged. She was taken to Weseter Polmaise, near Falkirk, where she was held in an uninhabited tower.

She was eventually transported to the remote Monach Isles, off North Uist in the Outer Hebrides. Housed with a farmer and his wife, she lived in isolation for two years, not even being told the name of the island on which she was living.

From there she was taken to the remote Atlantic island of Hirta, part of the St Kilda archipelago, one of the remotest and wildest parts of Britain.

There she lived alone and miserable in a tiny and uncomfortable stone storage hut, said to resemble a giant Christmas pudding and measuring only 20ft by 10ft. It had an earthen floor, rain ran down the walls and in winter handfuls of snow had to be scooped up from behind her bed.

No one on the island spoke English and Lady Grange had little or no Gaelic when she arrived there.

She spent her days asleep, drank as much whisky as was available and wandered the shore at night bemoaning her fate.

Eventually a letter from Lady Grange found its way to her solicitor. Appalled by her condition he paid for a sloop with 20 armed men on board to go to St Kilda. But by the time it arrived the lady had been removed from the island.

Now aged 61, she was transported to various locations, possibly including Assynt in the far north west of the mainland and also Harris and Uist in the Outer Hebrides.

She arrived in Skye in 1742. It is thought she may have been kept for 18 months in a cave before being housed with Rory MacNeil at Trumpan in

Waternish. She died there on May 12th, 1745, and McNeil had her "decently interred" in the local churchyard. Intriguingly a second funeral was held at nearby Duirinish some time later, where a large crowd gathered to watch the burial of a coffin filled with turf and stones. It is rumoured that this was her third funeral, Lord Grange having conducted one in Edinburgh shortly after her kidnapping.

Edward was excited by this extraordinary tale. On the surface it appeared to be a litany of incredible cruelty imposed by an unfaithful husband on a wife who had borne him nine children. Lady Grange could possibly be an icon for our age, a proto-feminist brutally abused by a bunch of reactionary Scottish aristocrats. Shades of Lord Lucan perhaps?

But Edward mused that life is never as simply black and white as that. Looked at from a different angle Lady Grange was a violent and uncontrollable woman, a threat to her whole family and clinically insane at least in the latter part of her life. Why did none of her nine children seek to rescue her?

Edward spent hours Googling to discover more about this extraordinary woman. He felt an obsession coming on! This was a definitive part of his character. Where others would have interests, pastimes and enthusiasms, he could all too quickly develop obsessions. His obsession with preserving the family name of Dunsill had not been one which had gradually evolved in his mind. It had come upon him in a flash and there had been no going back since then. Now he had a nascent new obsession – Lady Grange. Did he have the capacity to maintain two obsessions at a time? Only time would tell. Meanwhile he determined to visit the Trumpan churchyard to try to locate Lady Grange's grave.

***

Edward was still Googling at midnight when Josephine arrived home.

"Is Mum in?" she asked.

"No. Still at work I should think."

"She's usually in by now. Well – did you tell her?"

"I've told her."

"And?"

"She took it quite well – in the end."

"Quite well. That's good. But 'in the end'?"

"She doesn't like the age difference."

"Oh, well. Never mind. She'll get used to it."

"There's some more news."

"Oh?"

"She and Jordan are now an item."

"Oh my god. She never learns. I saw it coming. Still. Let them get on with it. It's her funeral."

Edward was struck again by Josephine's devil-may-care attitude.

"I've had to move into the spare room."

Josephine put her arms around him.

"Bollocks to that. We're almost engaged, aren't we? You're very welcome to come to my room. She took his hand and led him to her bedroom once more.

Marilyn did not return home that night. She spent the night with Jordan at Glenbernisdale.

***

The next morning Josephine and Edward were up early. Josephine had a short boat trip booked and Edward decided he would drive over to Trumpan to see if he could trace Lady Grange's grave.

He approached the graveyard via a narrow, potholed lane which had spectacular views over the Little Minch. It was a bright, fine day again, the water was calm and azure blue and the grey outlines of the Outer Hebrides could be seen clearly in the long distance.

He parked in the car park opposite the gates to the churchyard. A corncrake was calling in the adjacent meadow – a bird rarely heard in the United Kingdom and even more seldom seen.

He entered the well-kept cemetery with the ruined church in the centre and a mixture of new, old and ancient graves around it.

Edward searched among the oldest gravestones but was beginning to think his journey had been in vain. Then, immediately in front of the church ruins, he saw a light grey rectangular stone on which he could just make out the words "Lord Grange" and then, even more faintly, the words "Wife of" and the date "1745". This was it!

Edward felt a tinge of excitement. But there was another cause for surprise. Placed carefully under the headstone was a cluster of white lilies. The flowers had faded somewhat but they had clearly been put there within recent weeks.

Edward pondered on the question of who would have put flowers on the grave of a woman who died in 1745. Perhaps it might have been someone with a family connection. Maybe someone like himself with a passion for history. Or could it be that Lady Grange had indeed become a feminist icon as he had surmised she might?

He stood at the graveside in reverence for several minutes, his mind blown away by the strange tale of the ill-fated lady.

He was overcome with a deep sympathy and a mesmerising fascination for this woman who was simultaneously a frightening termagant, a pathetic abused woman and an extraordinary life-force. He decided he would return to the graveside on another occasion and pay his own tribute to her.

As he drove away from Trumpan he was contemplating his future with Josephine and the enormity of what he was planning. His thoughts turned to how his daughter would react to the news of his intended nuptials.

It was then that he remembered that he had promised to phone Julia the previous evening. Immersed in his study of Lady Grange, he had forgotten all about it. He was only too aware that he had let down his daughter frequently in recent months and he had a keen sense of his selfishness.

He pulled over into a passing place on the single track road and phoned Julia on his mobile.

He started by profusely apologising for failing to ring her previously. There was a sharpness in Julia's tone which was even more pronounced than in their previous conversation. But he knew he deserved it.

"I have something important to tell you," she said. "Although perhaps you won't be interested."

"Don't be silly. Of course I will be interested."

"I am sure that Clive is having an affair – and that it's been going on for quite a long time now."

"What?" said Edward, incredulously. "Who with?"

"Rachel, from the stables."

"Rachel? Are you sure about this?"

"I'm pretty sure there's something going on. Clive denies it. But he's changed. He's spending more time at the stables than he does at work. And you know that's not like him. And both the girls have seen them kissing. Clive says it's just her being her typical affectionate self. But I think there's more to it than that."

Edward tried to reassure her. He had always liked Clive and was willing to give him the benefit of the doubt. Being only too well aware of his own weakness for the opposite sex he could well believe that Rachel might have led Clive astray.

His advice to Julia was to keep her own counsel until she had some definite proof for her fears. She should be watchful but not do anything which would precipitate the end of what had been a very happy union.

Julia was a reasonable woman and was ready to accept her father's advice. The last thing she wished for was the breakdown of her marriage. But at this time, more than at any time in her life, she craved her father's support and attention.

She asked him pointedly when he was planning to return home. She did not wish to antagonise him by saying so, but she felt his mission to Skye was a silly waste of time.

Edward went quiet. His daughter was his closest confidante and he felt that he needed to tell her as soon as possible about his relationship with Josephine. However, he realised that she was in a fragile emotional state and was loth to cause her even more upset.

The result was that he dodged her question.

"I won't be here for much longer – a day or two perhaps. I'll let you know tomorrow."

"Don't be long, Dad. I miss you."

"And I miss you. Of course I do."

Julia, now in a much better frame of mind towards her father than at the start of their conversation, was about to close her call in an affectionate way. Then she remembered something.

"By the way I've emailed that photo to you, the one of your relative that Harry Greensmith gave me."

"Oh, yes. I must look at that and print it out. I'll give a copy to Anthony....though." He paused.

"Though what?" said Julia.

"Though I'm not sure he'll be all that interested. I get the impression he isn't really bothered about this family stuff at all. In fact not much seems to interest him."

114

"Oh, dear," Julia laughed. "Is he not quite what you are hoping for?"

Edward laughed too.

"I hate to say this. But I fear our Anthony is a little bit of a moron."

Chapter Ten

Suspicions

It was mid-morning and Jordan's car pulled up outside Meadow Cottage. Marilyn alighted from the vehicle looking unusually dishevelled. It appeared that she had dressed hurriedly and not had time for brushing her hair or putting on her makeup.

She entered the cottage first, followed by Jordan. Edward greeted them in a friendly manner and Marilyn responded with her usual casual amiability. Jordan, though, seemed a little offhand and Edward had a distinct feeling that he was now "in the way". A lot had changed in the last 24 hours.

He decided it was time for him to move out of Meadow Cottage and push ahead with his whirlwind marriage plans as quickly as possible. There was an unusual dichotomy in Edward's character. His default position in everyday life was cautious conservatism but he often took radical decisions at breakneck speed on the important issues.

He phoned Josephine who was just returning from her morning boat trip and arranged to meet her for lunch at a Portree hotel.

Edward arrived first but very shortly afterwards Josephine breezed into the restaurant. Her lovely long hair looked unusually straggly, strong maritime winds, acting like a pair of curling tongs, having swept it out of its normal immaculate straightness. From the waist up she was every inch a mermaid.

Having exchanged a tender kiss on the lips, the couple bought some drinks and ordered their meals. Then they got down to the serious business of planning the future.

"I think we need to move out of Meadow Cottage," said Edward. "Staying there with your mother might prove tricky. And anyway I got the distinct impression this morning that she, and even more so Jordan, would like to see the back of me now."

"Are you saying we should move in together somewhere?"

"Exactly that," Edward replied. "I suggest we get along to the local estate agents as soon as possible."

"Can you afford to buy somewhere or would we rent?" asked Josephine.

"I think buy. Don't you?"

"Yes. The only thing is …. oh no. It doesn't matter."

"What?"

"Well I did wonder whether you would be able to afford to buy somewhere and still invest in my business."

Edward smiled and took her hand: "No need to worry about that. I'm not short of a bob or two."

Josephine smiled back and said: "It's just that I've seen an advert for a boat for sale which would just fit our bill."

"Great."

"But it's a little but more expensive than we were talking about yesterday."

"How much?"

"About £200,000."

"Wow. Okay. I'm sure I can manage it. I have property I can sell."

Josephine stroked his arm and said: "I am worth that much to you?"

"I believe in you and your business. And I love you and want to give you a baby."

Josephine smiled again and nodded.

"Okay. After lunch we could go to the estate agents. There's two offices in town," she said.

Their house hunting got off to a promising start. The couple agreed that their ideal property would be a traditional white Highlands cottage, with at least three bedrooms to accommodate themselves, their putative child and any visitors. For Josephine, the seagoer, a sea or loch view was essential. Fortunately both local estate agents had several properties on their books which met those requirements and so some viewings were arranged for the next couple of days.

The pair returned to Meadow Cottage around teatime to find both Jordan and Anthony sprawled on the sofa, drinking from cans of beer and watching a horror movie on Marilyn's DVD player. Marilyn had gone to work.

Anthony was polite in his usual gruff kind of way and offered Edward and Josephine some "tinnies", which they in turn politely refused. Jordan was uncommunicative and Edward again had the feeling that his presence was no longer desired.

Josephine said she would have a shower and a lie down before they decided what to do about dinner. Edward set up his laptop on the kitchen table to check his emails.

One of the emails was from Julia and attached to it was the photo of Anthony which she had obtained from Harry Greensmith. Edward opened it and saw the image of the man standing behind the Alfa Romeo, with Marshyard church in the background.

Edward stared at this picture for some time, cocking his head from one side to the other to study it from various angles. He put his hand to his mouth in contemplation. For from whatever perspective he viewed the photograph his conclusion was the same. This was not Anthony.

The man in the photo was tall and willowy with an impressive mane of well-groomed brown hair. He was wearing tweeds and a collar and tie and looked every inch an English gentleman.

By contrast Anthony, the couch potato swilling beer in the next room, was of medium build with receding grey hair and with no discernible dress sense.

What conceivable life event could have changed him so dramatically?

Edward went into the sitting room and said to Anthony: "I'm sorry to disturb you. I know you're watching your film, but could you possibly pause it for a moment and come and look at something?"

"Sure," said Antony.

He turned to Jordan who nodded grumpily and used the remote control to stop the film.

Edward took Anthony to the kitchen table and sat him down in front of

118

the laptop.

"A friend of mine from Sanderholme has sent me this photo, which he says is of you. But, unless you've changed quite a bit, it doesn't really look like you."

Anthony peered at the screen.

"That's because it's not me. Your friend must have made a mistake. "

"The local churchwarden took it and passed it to a friend of mine."

Anthony replied: "Yeah. Well he must have made a mistake. That bloke ain't as good looking as me. Where's this photo meant to have been taken anyway?"

"At Marshyard churchyard. You will remember I told you about seeing your father's grave there."

"Yeah. Well I have been to the grave a few times. But obviously that's not me."

Edward said: "You must be right, because it obviously isn't you. The churchwarden's a bit of an oddball. He must have got mixed up.

"Yeah," said Anthony. "I'd better get back to the film."

Dealing with Julia's email and the photograph reminded Edward that he had promised to let Harry know how he was getting on with his family research. He decided to phone his cousin there and then.

Edward explained his success in meeting up with his relative. But knowing that Anthony was in the next room he gave no hint of his disappointment about the man's character.

He did, though, raise the matter of the photograph, giving his opinion that Peter Wattam must have got mixed up. Harry expressed some surprise.

"I know he's a sandwich short of a full picnic, but he has the reputation of being extremely well organised and good on detail, almost to the point of being annoying," chuckled Harry.

"In fact I know of a number a family historians who have contacted him and been amazed by the depth and accuracy of all his church records.

"I'm quite intrigued by this," he continued. "I think I'll get in touch with Peter and ask him to check his files again. He'll be devastated if he thinks he messed up."

Edward thanked Harry, saying if the real photo turned up he would be delighted to see it.

Harry, who loved a little light detective work, phoned Peter straightaway and told him about the discrepancy.

As anticipated, Peter received the news with total disbelief. In fact he became so animated that he stammered and spluttered himself into quite a state, the pitch of his voice becoming even higher than usual.

"No, no. I'm quite sure that the bloke in my photo was Anthony Dunsill. It's quite clear in my files, the caption and everything. I keep everything to do with the church three times – once in my computer, once on a disk and once in the church archive. I'm sure I couldn't have made a mistake. Blimey, even the Bishop has praised my files. It's a rum do," Peter concluded.

These assurances were repeated four or five times, each time with greater emphasis, and Harry accepted them each time too. So a conversation which could have taken a minute lasted for at least twenty.

Harry phoned Edward back and repeated that he had absolute confidence in Peter's accuracy.

The two men discussed a number of possibilities, including the outside chance that there might be two Anthony Dunsills.

When the telephone conversation was over Edward decided to put that latter possibility to Anthony.

When he returned to the living room he found Jordan and Anthony engaged in what seemed to be deep conversation. But they quickly turned their attention back to their film when they saw him.

Edward asked Anthony if he thought there could possibly by two Anthony Dunsills, both of whom had visited the cemetery.

"I've never heard of another person of that name. I haven't heard of anyone in our family with the same name. But you never know, do you? You didn't know I existed until a few days ago, did you?"

Edward was intrigued by this answer. It was certainly not beyond the realms of possibility that there might be two relatives with the same name. But then Edward recalled that Peter had specifically referred to *his* man as being Gabriel's son.

He went back into the kitchen and mulled over the matter further. Josephine joined him and he told her of the puzzle regarding the photograph.

She said she was sure there must be some mistake. After all, Anthony must know himself who he was. Edward could do no more than agree.

Clive Jones had been late for dinner that evening, which these days came as no surprise to Julia and would normally have passed without comment. But this particular evening was different. Her daughters had been to the stables and returned home with the news that "Daddy is at the stables talking to Rachel. He says he'll be home soon."

When Clive did finally arrive at 8pm Julia was at the kitchen sink taking out her frustrations on an unfortunate saucepan which had been careless enough to get covered in cooking fat.

"You've been with her again, haven't you?" was her welcome to her husband.

Clive looked serious as he sat down at the kitchen table.

"Come here, love, and sit down a minute. I need to talk to you."

"I haven't got time to sit down. I've got to finish the washing up. Your dinner's in the oven."

"Please. Leave the washing up, love, and sit down."

The luckless saucepan found itself being hurled into the sink with a death-rattling clatter and then suffered the indignity of having a pan scourer thrown on top of it.

"What is it?" she asked.

"I have something to tell you. I'm not very good at words as you know, so you'll have to forgive me if I'm blunt."

"Go on then."

"I've fallen in love with Rachel and I'm going to move in with her. I'm so sorry. You don't deserve this and you can do anything you like to me. Kill me if you want."

Julia put her head into her hands and trembled before bursting into tears. She ran out of the kitchen, shutting the door behind her. She knew it was the end of her marriage.

Clive stayed at the table, with a feeling of numbness which for the time being was keeping the pain he was suffering at bay. He felt a shame too deep to put words to. The numbness was soon to be followed by a feeling of utter desolation. What had he done?

The way of farmers when confronted by dire situations is to go to the shotgun cupboard and put an end to it all. Several farmer friends he knew had ended their lives like that. He looked towards the cupboard, which was fixed to one of the kitchen walls. But he was not brave enough even to take that easy way out.

After an hour or so of sitting and staring into space a strange calm came over him. He had faced telling Julia his terrible news and she had reacted in just the way he had expected. He knew she was not a violent person – not even an angry person. He knew her well enough to know that she would not strike him or go into wild hysterics and she had behaved true to her character. In other words, the worst was over. His guilt would remain with him forever. But he would survive.

Meanwhile, Julia's tears were uncontrollable. She dreaded meeting her daughters in this state, but fortunately they were in their bedrooms, perhaps doing their homework but more likely watching the latest films on Netflix or messaging their friends.

She had a feeling that they were shrewd enough to know what was going on between their father and their riding instructress. They loved their father, though, and telling them he might be leaving her – and perhaps them too - would be an unpleasant ordeal. She decided it was something best left until the next day – when her eyes were not so red.

***

The next morning Edward found himself at a loose end. Josephine had risen early to take a party of Chinese people over to the nearby island of Rona, uninhabited for many years except for a caretaker and visitors to three holiday cottages on the shoreline.

On a whim he decided to visit Fergus the boat builder at Bernisdale. He took the usual walking route past St Columba's Isle and through the hotel grounds. It had been a rainy night and the River Tora, always noisy but otherwise usually insignificant, was a raging torrent of foaming white water.

As Edward approached Fergus' cottage he could see it was set high on a hillside, with excellent views of the Cuillin mountains in one direction and the famous Storr hill in another, and with a pleasant coniferous forest in the foreground. The gushing Tora was slightly further away from the roadside at this point, but could still be heard cascading into a deep ravine before flattening out harmlessly to join up with the remote and rarely visited Loch Niarsco.

The cottage needed a lick of paint and some work doing to its garden, a sign of the advancing years of its occupant.

When Edward knocked on the front door Fergus pushed aside his net curtain and beckoned him to step inside.

He was a scrawny looking old man, with sunken cheeks and eye sockets, but when he extended a bony hand to Edward there was a friendly twinkle in his eye and a quaint toothy grin.

"Aye. It's bonny to see you," he exclaimed. "Will you take some tea, or perhaps something a little stronger. An itsy-bitsy wee dram perhaps?"

Edward noticed a bottle of Skye's classy Talisker whisky on a sideboard of the old-fashioned living room. He had never tried it before but had heard that it had a unique peaty flavour.

"I'll try a little whisky then," he said.

"Neat, or with a little water?" asked Fergus.

"A little water, please."

With an unsteady hand Fergus proceeded to pour out a very large whisky. By the time the water had been added it almost reached the top of the glass.

"You'll excuse me if I don't join you," said Fergus. "I'm not a drinking man. I'll just take a small sherry."

With that he poured himself a schooner of the harmless ruby red liquid.

The two men enjoyed a long conversation, ranging from life on the Isle of Skye, to boats, and to Edward's farming ancestors. Talking was thirsty work and necessitated several healthy top-ups of the whisky and the sherry.

Discussion about Edward's ancestors naturally led on to the subject of Edward's successful quest to find Anthony.

The effusively garrulous Fergus became unusually quiet when the subject turned in that direction. Edward was already aware that the boat builder had little time for his relative and his exotic companion.

Eventually the old man did venture a somewhat guarded opinion on his neighbours.

"They're a strange pair, that's for sure."

"In what way?" asked Edward.

"Well, they're meant to be working but it takes them all their time to get up in the morning. When they do appear they look as if they've tumbled out of bed. And there's always piles of beer cans outside their front door. They don't even bother to put them in the recycling.

"Aye. And then there's that smell which lingers all around their cottage."

"Smell?" said Edward.

"Aye. Wacky baccy, I think. Other folk have noticed it too. Now, I don't mind all that. I'm broad-minded even though I don't drink myself and was brought up strictly in the church. But there's something a bit odd about it. I shouldn't say those things, though. He's your flesh and blood and you must be delighted to have found him."

"Hardly flesh and blood," said Edward, "but certainly part of our wider family."

Edward was interested to find out a little more about the third man whom Fergus had said lived at the cottage with Jordan before Anthony's arrival.

"Aye. He was a very nice man – gentleman-like. He had travelled the world and had all kinds of good stories to tell. He had lived in Vietnam for many years – ever since the war ended."

"Probably that's the connection with Anthony and Jordan. They have both lived in Vietnam."

"Aye. Anthony. That was his name."

"No, I meant he must have known Anthony who lives here now."

"Oh, another Anthony?" said Fergus.

"What do you mean?" asked Edward, thinking that Fergus was showing the confusion of old age.

"Well the nice man who used to talk to me. He was called Anthony."

Are you sure about that?" asked Edward.

"Aye. I'm sure. I didn't know the chap there now was called Anthony too."

Edward smiled and nodded. He was still not sure whether the sherry may have been playing tricks with the boat builder's memory.

"Come to think of it he said he originally came from Lincolnshire. It's where you come from isn't it?"

"Yes, from a holiday resort called Sanderholme."

"Oh, aye. Funny that. He mentioned Sanderholme. I don't think he came from there. But he had some connection. Knew it well, I think."

"Another connection with your current neighbour Anthony," said Edward. "Gabriel, this Anthony's father, came from the same area too. There must be some connection there somewhere. I must ask Anthony about it."

"Very strange. Very strange," said Fergus. "It's a small world. A small world."

Fergus looked closely at Edward and could see he was perplexed and confused. He decided to change the subject and the mood.

He went over to a chest of drawers and produced some large rolled up sheets of paper. He unfurled them in front of Edward and revealed several drawings of a boat, shown from different angles and in various cross-sections.

"This is the boat I am planning to build next. My masterpiece," he said.

He went on to explain in great detail the processes he would have to go through to build the boat, which he said would be ideal for carrying tourists on day cruises around the Hebridean isles. The plans certainly looked professional enough and Edward pretended to be very impressed and interested in all this. But at the back of his mind throughout the long exposition was that the barman at the old inn had said no one could ever remember Fergus building a boat. He began to think that he was wasting his time listening to the ramblings of a fantasist – and a fantasist who had consumed far too much sherry.

Eventually Edward managed to prise himself away from his congenial host, but not without giving a promise to make a return visit before he left Skye.

Before returning to Tote he could not resist visiting Tora Cottage to see if Anthony was at home and to interrogate him about the other Anthony.

He found that Anthony was indeed at home. Edward was relieved to find that his relative was alone in the cottage, with Jordan out at work. Not only did he find that it was difficult to get into a proper conversation with Anthony without Jordan butting in but the latter's body language had hinted at a new hostility towards him.

It was not long before Edward recounted his conversation with Fergus about "the other Anthony" who had lived at Tora Cottage.

Anthony replied bluntly that before he moved in himself another man called Anthony had lived there with Jordan. He was another of Jordan's friends from Vietnam and the facts that he bore the same Christian name and had spent time in Lincolnshire were pure coincidences. The man had since returned to the Far East.

Edward asked what the man's surname was. Although Sanderholme was a busy holiday resort for much of the year the resident population of the town

125

and its surrounding villages was quite close-knit and there was a chance he might recognise the name.

Anthony said he didn't know the surname and then asked Edward if he would like a beer.

Having already quaffed a fair amount of Talisker, Edward declined the offer, but continued to ask about the surname. He said he was sure Jordan would know the man's surname and he would ask him the next time he saw him.

Anthony made no comment about this and Edward sensed he was uncomfortable with the whole subject of "the other Anthony".

After further exchanges of mundane conversation Edward left and headed back to Meadow Cottage.

As he walked along he ran through in his head the new information he had received since the previous evening. What was emerging was at least a conundrum and at worst something rather worrying.

He recalled the various discussions he had had with Anthony since their first meeting. From the outset he had been frustrated by a certain vagueness about his cousin's answers to his questions. At first he had put this down to a lack of interest in family history on the other man's part. This was nothing unusual as Edward had found this attitude to be fairly common when he quizzed people about their family trees. He understood that many people considered family history research to be at best a waste of time and at worst an unwanted intrusion into their lives. For some the whole subject was boring, for others there were skeletons in the cupboard they would rather not see revealed.

He had dismissed Anthony's reticence as resulting from a lack of interest from a person who appeared to have a limited intellect. But now other factors had come into play.

As well as the photograph which did not match there were the coincidences regarding the name Anthony and the Vietnam and Sanderholme connections.

Then there was the nature of Jordan, whom Edward considered to be an unsavoury person, undoubtedly an illegal drug taker and, from his own accounts of his past experiences, someone who had always lived at least on the edge of criminality.

Edward's default position in life was to think the best of people. Usually his non-judgemental attitude had proved to be an advantage as it had helped him to go through life without making enemies and without too much personal trauma. However, occasionally a touch of naivety made him vulnerable to those of a less wholesome character.

He was beginning to suspect that this was a time when he needed to be a little more cynical about the motives of others.

He decided he needed to share his concerns with someone else. But who? Marilyn was now completely under the influence of Jordan. Julia would have no patience with him and just tell him to come home to his real family. There was only one person he could turn to – Josephine. After all, she was to become his wife.

He wanted to see his fiancee as soon as possible and his first thought was to drive over to Portree to meet her off the boat late that afternoon. But he had been drinking and so driving there would be out of the question. The rain had abated for the time being so he decided to spend the afternoon strolling around the local countryside until Josephine's return in the early evening.

***

When Josephine did appear she listened to him sympathetically and began to have suspicions of her own. She did not really approve of Anthony and Jordan anyway. She thought her mother was being led astray by Jordan – or rather further astray than she had always been - and that Anthony was just a drink-sodden nonentity. It had also occurred to her that Anthony, the much sought-after long lost relative, might be a competitor for Edward's wealth.

She agreed with Edward that something was not right. She suggested that they should both visit Fergus again to try to find out any more details they could about the mysterious "other Anthony". She added: "And let's take that photograph with us."

It was early evening as Josephine's Land Rover Sport arrived at Fergus's cottage.

They both went to the door and waited for a response to Edward's knock. When Fergus opened it Edward was immediately struck by a change in his appearance. The old man was deathly white. The effect of too many schooners, Edward conjectured.

Also they were surprised when they did not receive the warm welcome they had been expecting.

"Oh, good evening," said Fergus brusquely. "What can I do for you?"

"I wondered if we could have another little talk to you about your neighbours. We have a photograph here we would like to show you," said Edward.

"Aye," said Fergus, who seemed agitated. "There is nothing I would like better than to talk to you, but I am just waiting for my brother to come for me. We have to go out this evening."

"Oh," said Edward. "We quite understand. Could you just take a quick look at the photograph?"

"Sorry," said Fergus. "I have to go inside and get ready. Please excuse me. Goodbye."

With that the old man closed the door and could be heard drawing the bolt across, a strange act for someone about to go out.

"That was weird," said Josephine. "He really didn't want to see us, did he?"

"No, you're right," replied Edward. "Earlier on I couldn't stop him talking. Although … he did seem to try to change the subject once when I was asking him about Anthony."

Chapter Eleven

Identity Crisis

The next day Harry Greensmith was getting ready to go on his daily afternoon walk on Sanderholme sea front.

As he was carefully placing a carnation in the buttonhole of his cream suit there was a knock on the door. It was Peter Wattam.

He told Harry that he had some information about Anthony Dunsill, which he was sure would be of interest to Harry and his friend.

His curiosity aroused, Harry invited Peter inside and asked him to sit down. Peter produced some paperwork from his sports jacket pocket.

"I was at church yesterday and I was talking to Mr and Mrs Odling, from Marshyard Tofts. Do you know them?"

"It's quite a common name in Lincolnshire. Do you know their Christian names?"

Peter looked at his paperwork and read the names "Edith and George".

"I don't believe I know them," said Harry. "But I might do if I had a few more details."

"Well," said Peter. "Mr and Mrs Odling were next door neighbours of Mr and Mrs Dunsill."

He looked down at his papers – "Joseph and Myrtle, parents of Gabriel

Dunsill and grandparents of Anthony Dunsill."

"Yes."

"We got talking about Anthony Dunsill."

"Yes."

"They know him."

"Yes."

"He stayed with them a few weeks ago, around the time when I met him at the churchyard."

"I see," said Harry, somewhat underwhelmed by the news. If he had been told this before Edward went to Skye it would have been very useful information. But now Edward had actually met Anthony it didn't seem to matter very much.

"They're a bit cross with him," continued Peter.

"Why?"

"Well they haven't heard anything from him since he left their house. He promised them he would get in touch as soon as he reached Skye. But he didn't and they are a little bit worried and a bit cross with him. It's a bit of a bugger if you ask me. After they put him up. You would have thought he would have rung them, after a long journey like that up to Skye."

Peter spoke on this theme of Anthony's ungratefulness for another ten minutes or so, before Harry intervened.

"I'll tell you what. I'll contact Edward's daughter. I'll get her to email Edward and ask him to tell Anthony to get in touch with the Odlings."

Peter was ecstatic.

"What a good idea," he said. "They are quite worried, and a bit cross. You see they have known Anthony all his life."

"All his life?"

"They said so. They even went to Vietnam and stayed with him and his family."

"Really? He has a family in Vietnam then?"

"Yes," said Peter, consulting his notepad. "He has a wife and two children, a boy and a girl."

Harry was puzzled.

"What was he doing in England and how come he has an address on the Isle of Skye?"

"I don't know," said Peter. "It's a bit of a bugger, isn't it?"

"You're right," said Harry, smiling and adding, quite out of his usual way of speaking: "It's a bit of a bugger."

"Have you heard the latest Little Mix album, Glory Days?" asked Peter.

"No. I can't say I have."

"It's a very good album. I'm just going into town to buy it. They're lovely gels those Little Mixes. Cor, not half!"

"I can't say I know them," replied Harry. "Are they English?"

Peter proceeded to give him a rundown on the names and antecedents of each member of Little Mix. He started to outline their full discography but was eventually interrupted by Harry, who said he must have his "constitutional" before teatime.

***

On his return Harry duly telephoned Julia with the message about the Odlings. She politely agreed to send her father an email although, being currently obsessed with her marital problems, she had to feign some interest in the matter.

When Edward received the email that same night it only added to his concerns about Anthony. He felt it was strange that his new-found relative had never thought it interesting enough to mention that he had recently been staying with the neighbours of his late parents, people so close that they had even stayed with him in Vietnam.

Edward decided it was another matter which needed to be probed. It was fortuitous then that Jordan and Anthony should have called at Meadow Cottage that same night, bent on another drinking and drug-taking session with Marilyn.

On their arrival Anthony was his usual non-committal self while Jordan was an uncharacteristically quiet and brooding presence. Edward again felt he had outstayed his welcome, at least as far as Jordan was concerned.

Edward emerged from the kitchen with Josephine, with whom he had been sharing the details of the latest email.

"I have had a message from your friends, the Odlings," he told Anthony.

Anthony replied: "Oh?"

"Yes. They are a little worried that they have not heard from you since your visit to Marshyard."

"Oh, I see," said Anthony. "I'll have to get in touch with them."

"I didn't realise you had stayed with them at Marshyard," said Edward.

"Oh, yes," said Anthony. "Didn't I mention it?"

"No. They're obviously very good friends."

"Yes, very good friends."

At this point Jordan interrupted to ask where Marilyn was. Josephine said she was washing her hair and would join them shortly.

"I'll tell you what," said Jordan. "We'll go and have a drink at the hotel and come back later on."

"There's no need for that," said Josephine. "I'm sure Mum will only be a few minutes and we've got plenty of drink in here."

"No. I fancy a pint of their strong beer," said Jordan, insistently. "Come on, Anthony."

"So you'll get in touch with the Odlings?" asked Edward.

"Yeah," said Anthony. "I will."

When the two men had departed Josephine looked at Edward and declared: "There's something I don't trust about those two. I don't think they want to get involved in this whole family history business. I don't know. There's something fishy."

Edward replied: "You might say there's something fishy. But I smell a big ugly rat. I hesitate to be so definitive about it, but I don't think our Anthony here is *our* Anthony Dunsill at all. I think for some reason he's pretending to be Anthony Dunsill and that the person who was at Tora Cottage previously was the real Anthony Dunsill."

"I had been thinking exactly the same thing, ever since I saw that photograph," said Josephine. "There's some sort of scam going on here."

Edward nodded.

"If we could get in touch with these Odlings then we would be able to resolve the identity question. If they were on email we could send them a picture of the Anthony who visited the churchyard. It's a pity we don't have a photo of our Anthony here."

Josephine took her smartphone from her jeans pocket and fiddled with it.

"Here," she said.

Edward looked at the phone.

"You've got one! How did you get that?"

"I took one the other night when you got the emailed photo. He didn't realise I had taken it. He was half asleep sat in front of a film on TV."

"But why did you take it?"

"I was beginning to have my suspicions. I didn't want to labour the point at the time because I didn't want to disillusion you about Anthony. I've thought from the start there was something shifty about that pair."

"I've got one of Jordan too," she said, showing him another image in the phone.

"You're a genius," said Edward, kissing her on the cheek and patting her bottom.

Edward telephoned Harry, who was able to find the Odlings' telephone number in the phone book.

Then Edward put through a call to the elderly couple at Marshyard Tofts. George Odling answered.

"I believe you wished to know something about Anthony Dunsill. I'm a relative of his, Edward Dunsill."

"Oh, yes. I've heard of you. You're connected to Dunsill's Properties, aren't you?"

"The very same."

"Yes, we were a little worried about Anthony because he hasn't been in touch since he stayed with us a few weeks ago – and that's not like him. But how did you know that?"

"Well, a relation of mine, Harry Greensmith, was talking to Peter Wattam and he said that you were concerned about Anthony."

"Oh, yes, Peter. I see. Yes, I did mention it to him."

Edward continued: "Well, the thing is - this might sound a little strange - I am doing some family history research and I am trying to find out something about Anthony Dunsill, who I believe is a relative of mine."

"He will be," said George.

"My problem is that I've found two Anthony Dunsills through my research and I'm not sure which is which."

"Two, you say. I only know of one. But then it's a big world isn't it?"

"I was wondering if I might send you photos of both Anthony Dunsills so that you could tell me which is the one who was brought up by your neighbours, Joseph and Myrtle."

133

"Yes. I could do that. That shouldn't be a problem."

"Do you have an email address?"

"Yes, I do. I don't use it very often. I'm getting a bit old in the tooth for that sort of thing. But if you want to send me the photos by email I could certainly have a look at them for you."

He gave Edward his email address.

"Great," said Edward. "I'll send the photos over now, if you don't mind."

"Sure. I will try to reply to you straightaway. If you manage to get in touch with either of these Anthony Dunsills, would you ask the one that stayed with us to please contact us. I've got a mobile telephone number for him, but it keeps saying the 'person is unable to take your call'. I know he is living on the Isle of Skye. He has bought a cottage which he is sharing with a friend and he's intending to settle down there. I don't have the address, though. He was going to give us his address to use, but I think he forgot."

"I'm on the Isle of Skye now," said Edward. "That's where my search for Anthony Dunsill brought me."

"Do you have an address for him there?"

"No, not yet," Edward lied.

"If you get one we would be pleased to have it, for future reference," said George. "We don't want to lose touch. I was best friends at school with his father, Gabriel. We have known Anthony all his life, since he was a young boy. He has grown up to be a really charming man."

Edward was excited to learn that George had known the elusive Gabriel and went on to ask more about him. George said that Gabriel had been a good friend to him at school but had always been rather spoilt by his doting "parents", Joseph and Myrtle. He had never settled to anything in life, always looking for something better than what he had. He had, though, thought the world of Joseph and Myrtle and had visited them as often as he could, often bringing his wife and son Anthony back to Marshyard for short stays. When Gabriel's wife had fallen under the bus and then Gabriel had died of cancer, Anthony had sometimes stayed with his grandparents at Marshyard for extended holidays. He had always liked to pop round to the Odlings for a chat and a cup of tea and had stayed friendly with them after his grandparents' death.

"Sometimes he treated us like a substitute mother and father, I think," said

George.

Edward was now quite convinced that the Anthony he had met was an imposter.

He decided now was his golden opportunity to find out more about the real Anthony.

"Anthony has a family in Vietnam, you said?"

"Yes, a wife and two children. We had the pleasure of staying with them for several weeks a few years ago when my wife and I and our son and daughter went on a Far-Eastern tour. A lovely family. Such a pity there was a break-up."

"Yes. What went wrong?"

"I'm afraid Anthony strayed. I don't know all the details – you don't like to ask – but I think there was another woman involved. The affair didn't last, though, and Anthony finished up on his own. He is still in contact with his wife and children. I think he has hopes of patching things up with his wife eventually. They were never divorced and had become quite friendly again."

"So why did he go to live on Skye? It seems a world away from Vietnam."

"A friend of his had already moved there and had persuaded him they could open a restaurant together. Apparently Skye's quite an up and coming place for foreign tourists. I rather gather Anthony thinks he will be more or less a sitting partner – that he will leave his friend to run the place from day to day while he still spends half of his time in Vietnam. I hope it succeeds for him."

"It will be a bit expensive, sharing his time between Skye and Vietnam," suggested Edward.

"I don't think that will worry Anthony. He's not short of a bob or two. I wish I was a few pounds behind him."

"Oh, I see. That sounds all right then."

"As a matter of fact we were going to write to his wife to ask her if she had heard anything from him," continued George.

"You have contact details for the family, then?"

"Yes. An address in Hanoi. We exchange Christmas cards with them every year."

"Do the Vietnamese celebrate Christmas?"

"Some of them seem to. Anthony's wife is a Catholic. I believe there are a lot of them in Vietnam – a throwback to the French colonial days."

"Do you have an email address for them, or a telephone number?"

"No. I'm afraid not."

"I wondered," said Edward, "if you would be prepared to let me have the address of Anthony's family. If I wrote to them it could be a great help for me in filling in details of my family tree."

"I can't see there would be any harm in it. After all, I know that you are a respectable local man. When you send me the photos I will send you the address with my reply. How about that?"

"That would be absolutely great. You have been most helpful. Hopefully I will be able to help you by putting you in touch with Anthony. I'm like a dog with a bone, so I shall be pursuing this straightaway."

Edward sent the two photos and, true to his word, George replied immediately. He confirmed that the photo supplied by Peter Wattam was the Anthony Dunsill that he knew. He had never seen the man in Josephine's picture. He also provided Edward with the Hanoi address he had requested.

Josephine and Edward spent some time discussing the latest revelations.

"So what do we do next?" asked Josephine. "Get the police involved?"

"No," said Edward. "I'm going to Vietnam on the next available plane."

Chapter Twelve

Fool's Odyssey?

Mabel Wattam shut the front door of the Marshyard farmhouse behind her and bustled out of the yard with the air of someone with a mission.

The roly-poly, florid-skinned farmer's wife strode out as fast as her stocky legs would carry her.

It was 9 o'clock on a late August morning. She had dutifully prepared breakfast for husband John and son Peter and they had already been out in the fields working for a couple of hours.

The sun was out but its rays were as yet weakly breaking through a patchy early morning mist. This mainly consisted of a shimmering haze but there were also denser patches which hung oddly over the water in the dykes which run parallel to each side of the narrow lane.

The day promised to be fine and hot, but the canny elderly woman knew better than to trust the English weather and she wore a dark grey mackintosh and a red beret, complemented by sturdy brown shoes. Over her arm she carried a sensible straw basket the contents of which were covered by a white tea towel.

The lane was a public road merely serving the Wattams' farm and a pair of semi-detached red-brick cottages before reaching a dead end on the land side of the sea bank. The road was so little used that grass grew down the middle. The land farmed by the Wattams had been reclaimed from the sea in the 19th century, protected from the tides by the high sea bank and drained by a network of dykes, rivers and pumping stations. It is part of a large area of flat fertile Marsh and Fenland on the east coast, stretching from Lincolnshire southwards as far as Suffolk, famed for its rich soil and as the country's chief vegetable growing area.

The landscape along Mabel's route could be described as featureless. Apart from the odd copse, kept intact for the benefit of game birds and the shooting fraternity, the only trees were around the scattered farmhouses and farm cottages which could be glimpsed in the far distance. The cottages had once been home to an army of highly skilled but poorly paid agricultural labourers, their homes being "tied" to the farms they worked on. But mechanisation means that full-time work in the farming industry has greatly declined. The cottages now provide relatively cheap housing for the general populace, many of whom commute into nearby towns for work.

As Mabel strode out she disturbed a cock pheasant which had been sheltering in the long grass on the side of a dyke. There was a great flapping of wings which momentarily startled her. Further along the dyke-side she could hear the scurrying of a rodent which had similarly been alerted to her presence. Apart from these sounds and the odd twittering bird her journey was a silent one.

After about half a mile she crossed another lane and passed by two deserted wheelie bins and a semi-derelict wooden post box, the features mentioned at the beginning of our tale.

She continued along the rough track alongside a straight drain for a further half mile at which point a cluster of sycamore trees came into view. Mabel followed a muddy path between the trees for about 50 yards before entering a clearing beyond which was a dilapidated looking red brick farm cottage. At the side of the detached building was an equally neglected brick barn with grass growing out of its roof. The house itself was poorly decorated with rotting wooden window frames and a number of tiles missing from the roof. What had once been a vegetable garden was choked with weeds and strewn with odd pieces of rusty metal and the splintered remains of a wooden fence.

Hanging limply at an odd angle on the unwelcoming front door was a sign bearing the prosaic house name, Far End Cottage.

There must be many such properties hidden away in the depths of the countryside. One particular feature, though, set this aside from all the others: the bottle garden.

In a large patch of land at the side of the cottage was a vast array of bottles, planted carefully upside down in the soil with the bottoms poking out of the ground like a crazy mosaic of maladjusted flowers. The glass bottles were of all shapes, sizes and colours. There were milk bottles, wine bottles, beer bottles and jars. There was something bizarrely attractive about the display, if mildly disturbing.

As Mabel approached the front door it was scraped open and a buxom and rather dishevelled looking woman appeared from inside the house. She had lank and unkempt platinum blonde hair and was wearing a short-sleeved black top and black tracksuit bottoms. Her chubby arms were decorated with fearsome tattoos. At first glance her appearance was unprepossessing but beneath her heavily caked make-up was a bonny smiling face and her figure was full but voluptuous.

This was Kathleen Wattam, daughter of Mabel and John and sister of Peter.

Kath, who was in her mid-forties, was well known in the Marshyard area, having had a chequered history with the opposite sex. Her nickname, acquired for reasons largely lost in the mists of time and the marshes, was "Ten-Bob Kath".

She was an embarrassment to her family, who generally kept her at armslength but who looked out for her every time she found herself in trouble.

"Hello, Mum," she said. "How are you doing?"

"All right, duck. I've brought you some dinner."

"Oh, great. I'm bloody starving."

"When did you last eat?"

"Oh. I can't remember. Yesterday, I think."

"You think?"

"Yeah. I think I had some soup."

"You're not looking after yourself, duck"

"I've been busy."

"Doing what?"

139

"Looking after my garden. I managed to get some more bottles from the Co-op."

"From the Co-op? You didn't just take them, did you?"

"Of course not. They gave them to me."

"I don't know, duck. I can't understand why you do it."

"Do what, Mum?"

"Waste your time with those bottles."

"It's lovely. It's my hobby."

"It's a rum 'un."

"It's art – that's what it is."

"Art? It's a good job you live out here. If people saw what you were doing they would think you were crackers."

"Oh, bugger people. I do as I like."

"That's your trouble, duck. Still niver mind. I'm not here to fall out with you."

"I'm pleased to hear it. Are you coming in for a cuppa?"

"Yes, duck. I'll have a cuppa. I just wanted to see you were all right."

"Yes. I'm ok."

They went into the cramped living room, stepping over scores of bottles waiting their turn to be planted in the garden.

Kath moved a pile of clothing from a chair so that her mother had somewhere to sit.

Mabel noticed that they were men's clothes.

"Oh. You haven't got another man here?" she asked with a sigh.

"No. Course I haven't."

"I don't know anything about 'course you haven't'. I thought that Sid of yours had gone away a few weeks ago."

"He did. You know he did. I just haven't got round to getting rid of his clothes yet."

"I believe you. Thousands wouldn't."

"It's true."

"Has he gone for good then?"

"Yeah. I wouldn't have him back. He was all right. But just disappearing like that – he wasn't fair to me. He's still never been in touch. Anyway I've had it up to here with men."

"I should hope you have, Kath. You knew nothing about him. He might have been a wrong 'un for all you knew. When will you ever learn not to go taking up with every Tom, Dick and Harry?"

"I've learnt my lesson this time, Mum. I'll stick to my bottles in future. I don't get any trouble from them."

"Oh, those bottles. Why don't you get yourself a proper hobby? You could help me make some kneelers for the church. It'll look a treat when I've finished them."

"The church has never done ote for me. Snobby lot of folk that goes there."

"Well, we're not snobby as you call it. It's just respectable God-fearing people that goes."

"Hypocrites, the lot of 'em. I tried it once, you remember. It's not my scene."

"You spoilt it for yourself, duck. Throwing yourself at the vicar's son like you did. You couldn't expect people to welcome you to the church after that."

"Why not? He was a bit of all right he was. It was only his snobby parents who put him off me."

"Oh, well. I'm not saying any more about it. And messing about with that young choirboy like you did. How did you expect decent people to welcome you to church? But it was a long time ago. Most folk won't remember much about it now. I'm sure if you wanted to go back to church that no one would mind."

"No. You stick to your church. I'll stick to me bottles. Anyhow it's fun emptying them ready for the garden."

"You're not still drinking too much are you, duck?"

"Na. Don't worry about me, Mum. I knows when to stop."

"I hope you do. I hope you do. I never met him but I'm told that your Sid spent all his time drinking at the Queen's Head. He might as well have lived there. At least he won't be egging you on with your drinking now."

"No. Good riddance to him," said Kath, making a two-fingered gesture.

***

Rationally, Edward knew that he was about to embark on a fool's errand by travelling to Vietnam. But his obsession with family history was stronger than his desire to bang Anthony and Jordan to rights for whatever misdeeds they

141

were perpetrating.

There is no doubt some egocentric value to be derived from seeing one's family name survive after one's death, especially if one is obsessed with and steeped in history, tradition and custom. History, tradition and custom are not to be mocked: they help us to understand who we are and they help to bind together society as a living organism – one with a past, a present and a future.

History, tradition and custom are an important part of our *humanity*. But they are not the overriding wellspring of our *animal* existence.

Of course animals do have history, traditions and customs associated with them. But they have no awareness of those things. Their raison d'etre is to survive, to reproduce and to provide the conditions necessary for their offspring to do the same. In that respect humans are no different. Our superior intelligence leads us to find trillions of other activities and thoughts to fill in the time between our birth and our death. These are mere ephemera, though, relative to the vital biological task of propagating the species.

We humans have become so arrogant that we pretend we have a higher purpose than our animal cousins. We kid ourselves that we are made in the image of God. But we know nothing of God or even if there is a God or Gods. We have spent thousands of years trying to fathom out the meaning of life, of time and of space. But we are no nearer to finding an answer to all of this than we were when we started. When we can't explain we use the ultimate cop-out - that "God moves in mysterious ways".

Religious study and practice can be an interesting way of filling in that time between birth and death. Religious intolerance often leads to wars and massacres which may help in culling the population when it threatens to outstrip the planet's resources. But too often religion is used to deny the only observable truth, that our essential work is to preserve and reproduce our species. What more useless existence can there be than that of a chaste contemplative monk or nun?

Look at the way we behave. We dress, manicure and tone our bodies to please the opposite sex. We acquire material possessions to lure them. Some men play the caveman to attract a mate; others use charm, wit and intelligence to the same end. Likewise some women deploy subtle methods of seduction; others play the strumpet. The end game is the same – to reproduce the species. Our whole culture points in that same direction. In modern times the methods

142

may be more sophisticated and more varied than in the age of the caveman and cavewoman, but the objective is unchanging.

Having reproduced, we make our nests – a cave, a semi-detached in suburbia or a luxury apartment in Dubai. It doesn't matter which. We raise our children in the best way we know how and we go to our graves having done our duty.

Those children of ours do not *belong* to us, their parents. They are part of our *society*. Like ants and bees we operate as an organic whole. Yes, we are individuals. Yes, we have families. Yes, we are citizens of our country, defending our territory against external aggression and not above invading others' space if we believe we need additional resources in order to rear our children successfully.

We are all part of society – a society dedicated to preserving our species and propagating it. Edward's obsession with the family name was a mere trifle compared with that all-encompassing goal. He knew it, but, like the rest of us, he was kidding himself.

***

He had never travelled to the Far East before so he began his Vietnamese odyssey in a spirit of adventure.

The first leg of his journey was arduous enough – a long drive from the Isle of Skye to Gatwick, so that an overnight stay at the airport's Hilton Hotel was for a restorative break.

His flight to Hanoi had one stop-off at Istanbul airport. The first leg of the flight passed without incident, two meals having been consumed and enjoyed even if the food had a tendency to be congealed. The highlight was the excellent rolls and butter.

At Istanbul he could not leave the terminal building but the atmosphere of the airport was everything he had been expecting. Istanbul is the archetypal melting pot of different races, languages and cultures, providing the gateway to the east for westerners and the gateway to Europe for oriental people.

The terminal lounge was choc a bloc that day, with standing room only. But Edward was soon offered a seat by a group of friendly joshing group of young Algerian men. They told Edward they were moving on anyway but in fact theirs was an act of pure kindness.

As he sat in contemplative mood, Edward's attention was drawn to a dusky eight-year-old Asian boy who had placed his mobile phone on the charging facility provided by the airport. He was pacing up and down impatiently, occasionally taking the phone out of the charging base to see if it was ready, and then putting it back with a sigh.

"It's taking a long time," he said to Edward in broken English.

"You are English? I learn English," he added proudly.

Edward nodded, smiled and said: "Well done. You have very good English."

"Thank you. My name is Mohammed."

This did not surprise Edward in the slightest and he was beginning to warm to the child's innocent self-confidence and friendly, if bemused, smile.

"I live in Stockholm. My father is from Bangladesh and my mother from Russia."

He was the epitome of the sort of person – a racial and religious anomaly – that one would expect to encounter in Istanbul.

Although Edward was temperamentally and culturally a staid Englishman, there was something about the mixing of races and cultures which excited him. And nothing had done more to open his mind on the subject than the prospect of finding a Vietnamese heir to the Dunsill name.

As he chatted to Mohammed, a Bedouin Arab walked by in full traditional costume, a dead ringer for Omar Sharif in his role of Lawrence of Arabia's ally Faisal.

A procession of Muslim women and girls passed by, following the lead of their husbands and sons. Edward noted with some pleasure that none of them was wearing the burka.

Mohammed's phone eventually got charged and he waved goodbye. A competent little rich boy who would go far in the world, thought Edward.

As Edward found himself alone for a few minutes he decided to tackle the cryptic crossword in his Daily Telegraph. He was useless at cryptic puzzles and his mind started to wander. He had almost nodded off when he felt a light tap on his shoulder.

"Excuse me. Are you English?" said the man standing in front of him.

His interlocutor was a tall erect man in his seventies, wearing a cream straw hat and a beige linen suit. He had the bearing and tones of a patrician, though age had taken its toll on him and his hand was shaking with the onset of

144

Parkinson's.

"Yes," said Edward.

The man explained that he was travelling to Saigon but could not find his flight listed on any of the departures boards. Edward fancied he could provide an immediate answer to the man's problem.

"Perhaps it's listed as Ho Chi Minh City rather than Saigon," he said.

"Oh, really" said the man, the period of history following the demise of colonialism having passed him by.

He was the kind of Englishman who has chosen never to forget the atlases and globes he saw as a child – the ones with a preponderance of pink or red denoting the British Empire.

"I'll have a look," said Edward.

There, on the nearest board, as he had guessed, was the answer to the old man's quandary. Consecutive entries read "Hanoi" and "Ho Chi Minh City". The flight numbers and the times of departure were the same. Edward explained this to the man, who expressed his gratitude, but who still looked confused.

"But why does the flight go to Hanoi first? I was told it was a direct flight from Istanbul to Saigon.

"Probably the same aircraft will stop at Hanoi and then carry on to Ho Chi Minh City," ventured Edward confidently.

"Oh, I see," said the man unconvincingly.

"I'll stay here then," he said.

When he alighted from the plane at Hanoi and entered the transfer lounge Edward could hear the patrician voice again. The man was arguing with a member of the airport staff, who was trying to explain to him that he should not have left the aircraft as he was continuing to Ho Chi Minh City.

"The crew told us to leave the aircraft," he said.

"That instruction was for the passengers for Hanoi," the airport man replied.

The old man looked bewildered and was becoming angry.

Edward stepped in to help.

"I think you need to get back on to the plane," he said," and that will take you to Ho Chi Minh City."

"But I want to go to Saigon," said the man.

At that point the airport public address system announced: "Passengers for Flight TK1997 for Saigon should go to the departure lounge immediately."

"Saigon?!" thought Edward.

He felt defeated and moved away. As he looked back he saw the old man, arms flailing with exasperation, continuing his argument with the hapless airport official.

Chapter Thirteen

Our Man in Hanoi

Edward took a taxi from the airport to his hotel situated in a busy area of Hanoi about a mile from the city centre. The journey gave him the opportunity to view the imposing Red River and to gain his first impressions of this country of some 93 million people.

Men and women in typical oriental conical hats were hard at work in the fields and in the prolific roadside houses and businesses. Every few hundred yards along the dusty roadside little groups of Vietnamese people were sitting on plastic stools and enjoying food and drink provided by street sellers.

Incongruously there came into view a portentous illuminated archway. Edward speculated that it was some local equivalent of the Brandenburg Gate or the Arc De Triomphe. But he was told later it was nothing more than the entrance to a complex of rich people's accommodation. Vive la Revolution!

The journey showed Edward a side to the city which he at first found difficult to countenance – the traffic. Hanoi traffic comprises a seething, apparently anarchic, mass of motor-cycles and pedal cycles, interspersed with the odd car, bus and lorry trying to push its way through the maelstrom by force of its motor horn. It did not take Edward long to realise that the multitude of horns were not sounded in anger as on British roads, but were more of a kindly warning of "I'm coming" or "Please let me through. I don't mean to be rude but I'm bigger and faster than you.".

When unable to make progress along the road the motor-cycles simply mounted the pavement and continued their journeys there. As a result pedestrians had to keep their wits about them at all times.

As for crossing the road themselves, the pedestrians just ventured out in front of the moving traffic, relying on the goodwill and driving skills of those coming towards them. "Like water moving around a stone" was how Edward later heard this described. Pedestrian crossings appeared to be totally redundant and red traffic lights habitually ignored.

The motor-cycles and their passengers were a sight to behold. Three, four, or very occasionally five passengers hung on to some of them. Parents wearing crash helmets rode with infants wearing no protective headgear at all.

Fashionable and sexy business ladies with short skirts, nylons and high heels tried to maintain some degree of dignity by perching sidesaddle on the motor-cycles. A dozen large cardboard boxes trundled past Edward's taxi, concealing the pedal cyclist who was propelling them. A passenger of one motor-cycle held a full length ladder vertically.

Women in conical hats pedalled past with huge displays of beautiful flowers balanced on their handlebars. Several motor-cyclists were carrying large ornamental trees.

The saddest sight was a farmer's motor-cycle with a tightly packed crate of hens tied to the back. The heads of three hens were lolling out between the bars of the crate as if they were fighting for air. It was unlikely all the birds would reach their destination alive. Fowls are surely the most abused creatures in the world.

Such were the sights and sounds of Hanoi as our traveller was transported to his three-star hotel, chosen because it was a walkable distance from the address he had been given for Anthony's family.

By the time Edward had checked in, unpacked his best clothes and had a shower it was early evening. He decided to take a stroll out with the aim of acquainting himself with his surroundings and finding something to eat.

He walked along a narrow street with tiny shops at either side. There were all manner of food shops, with fruit, vegetables and meats set out on the pavements and the vendors crouched down behind them. There were repair shops for motor-cycles, hairdressers' salons, and pet shops with caged birds and tropical fish.

Many of the shops doubled up as dwellings for their owners or tenants. Edward smiled to himself when he noticed a woman asleep in bed in the window of a perfume store.

He constantly found himself jumping out of the way of motor-cycles which even traversed what was little more than an alleyway.

As he walked from one street to another very similar one he became aware he was being watched and sometimes pointed at by grinning Vietnamese people. Many would say "Hello, hello" to him as he passed, especially young men and children. On this first evening he judged their grins to be a form of mockery. He thought they were poking fun at his Western appearance. He later came to realise that foreigners were not seen too often in this particular part of the city. The smiles were part-friendly, part-quizzical and there was no malicious intent whatsoever.

He sat down at a table outside a crowded beer house and wondered how he was going to order his drink. He need not have worried as a Hanoi beer was immediately placed in front of him by a pretty smiling teenaged waitress.

"Hello," she said.

She paused and added: "How old are you?"

Edward was surprised by this question but in the days to come it was one he would be asked several times. No rudeness was intended. The Vietnamese are a polite but also inquisitive people and "How old are you?" may be one of the few English phrases many of them have picked up.

Edward gladly obliged and revealed his age.

"You look younger," she said. "You have beautiful skin."

With some language difficulty Edward managed to order a supper of noodles which he could dip into a soup containing beef and various vegetables. He tried, with little success, to use chopsticks, but eventually gave in and instead employed the spoon which was also helpfully provided.

As he ate Edward took in his surroundings and the sounds of noisy chatter from the many customers sitting both inside and outside the beer house.

Outside, three young men were sitting around a barbecue which appeared to be the source of the meat for the establishment. Near the entrance to the main hall was the corpse of an animal turning on a spit. The sign beside it said

"Thit Cho". Edward was to learn later that this referred to dog meat. Westerners receive a culture shock when they see dog and cat meat on sale, especially in north Vietnam. Although, of course, there is no logical reason for people to avoid eating dogs and cats, any more than, say, pigs and cows, the practice never ceases to jar on British sensibilities.

***

It was late August and temperatures in Hanoi were soaring. Owing to the heat, the hubbub from nearby eating and drinking places, including several karaoke bars, the continuous roar of motor-cycle engines and the motor horns, and the incessant tapping by construction workers, Edward found it difficult to get to sleep. He managed two or three hours, only to be woken at around 4am by the loud crowing of a nearby cockerel, answered by other cockerels some distance away. Then a dog rent the air with a frightening high-pitched cry. This disturbed other canines from throughout the area, which joined in with barks of tones varying from the bass to the castrato.

At last the cock-a-doodle-doos won the day and Edward, despite his ardent wish for more sleep, was wide awake. To ensure he did not resume his intermittent slumbers the Vietnamese national anthem blared out from an unseen loudspeaker system, a female voice then providing an unwelcome reveille call. And the tip-tapping of the building workers started again.

Edward looked out of his window on the street scene below. The immediate view from his sixth floor room was of what appeared to be a scrapyard. It contained a wide range of metal objects, including numerous broken strips of corrugated iron and piles of what can only be described as assorted detritus.

But amongst all the squalor Edward could see signs of everyday living. There were lines of washing and garments just hung over a perimeter chain fence which had so many sections missing that it had ceased to provide any useful service as a fence.

In the entrance to an old concrete pipe was huddled a thin bitch, seemingly not too uncomfortably housed but on a chain tether.

Frolicking in front of this rather sad looking creature was an adorable beige-coloured puppy with a permanently wagging tail. Unlike its confined mother it had the freedom to explore the whole adventure playground provided by the scrapyard.

As Edward scanned the scene further he noticed a large corrugated iron shed, almost hidden amongst the piles of broken corrugated iron sheeting. A light was coming from the door and three figures emerged. One was a skinny, poorly dressed old man. He had light grey hair, unusual in Vietnam where most older men darken their hair artificially. His companions were two slim teenaged boys with bright white shirts and smart blue jeans.

The trio crouched on the floor silently and Edward assumed they were praying. One of the lads interrupted his vigil by walking over to the edge of the yard and urinating.

A large open tank of water stood nearby. On its rim were two orange safety helmets, which Edward conjectured would be used by workers on the scrap metal site. However, his guess was proven to be wrong. The lad picked up one of the helmets, scooped up some water from the tank and drank from it. He then rejoined the two others who had remained staring at the ground in front of them.

Having nothing else to do until breakfast-time, Edward continued to gaze with interest at the yard.

After a few minutes the men went inside the shed from which shortly afterwards emerged two women, smartly dressed in matching tops and well-fitted trousers. They were carrying large plastic buckets. One contained green vegetables, of what variety Edward could not discern from his sixth floor vantage point. The other bowl appeared to contain some kind of pale-coloured meat.

The women proceeded to use the safety helmets as ladles to fill the bowls with water and painstakingly wash the food.

Having achieved this, they went back inside the shed, soon returning with two more large bowls, this time containing clothes. They used the same method with the safety helmets to provide water for washing the garments.

Meanwhile the puppy tried to attract the women's attention by vigorously wagging its tail, running backwards and forwards in a pretend chase and occasionally barking. Its efforts were in vain as the women ignored it. Edward rather feared that this little creature was not so much a pet as destined for the pot.

After breakfast at the hotel's restaurant he asked at reception for directions to the address he was seeking, which turned out to be about half a mile away.

His walk took him through more narrow back streets teeming with shoppers and across a couple of busy main roads where he had to screw up his courage to walk into the morass of motor cycles.

He had been asked to look out for a sign for a coffee house specialising in egg coffee, which he later discovered was a delightful drink, comprising egg yolks, sugar, condensed milk and coffee, and best described as being like a liquid tiramisu.

Nearby was a very narrow alley, which even the most tenacious motorcyclists found it difficult to traverse. Along there he found the number of the apartment he was looking for. He walked through an under-cover motor-cycle park which led to the front door of the apartment and knocked on a black-painted door.

A beautiful girl of around 14 years old opened the door. She was slim and quite tall for a Vietnamese person and had lovely sparkling eyes and a ready smile.

"Xin chao," she said.

"Hello", said Edward. "I am looking for the family of Anthony Dunsill."

"My father."

"Oh, good."

"You know my father?"

"Yes, I believe so."

The girl beckoned him to go inside.

He was led into a sparsely furnished but clean and well decorated room where a woman in her thirties sat on the floor sewing. She got up when she saw Edward and also gave him the greeting "Xin chao."

She was an attractive woman who looked very much like an older version of her daughter, but with rather darker skin and some blackness and bagginess around the eyes. She had obviously been a considerable beauty in her younger days.

The daughter spoke to her mother in Vietnamese, explaining that their unexpected visitor knew her father.

The mother looked somewhat distressed by the news and turned to Edward: "You know Anthony?"

"I believe so."

"You believe so?" said the woman suspiciously. She was thinking either he

152

did know her husband, or he didn't.

"Yes."

Edward took a photo from his jacket pocket and showed it to the woman.

"Who is this?" she asked.

"Is it your husband?" replied Edward.

"This is not my husband. You have made some mistake," she said in clear well pronounced English.

"Excuse me a moment," said Edward.

He put the photo back into his pocket and produced a second one, the picture which Peter Wattam had taken at the churchyard.

When he showed this to the woman, she declared: "This is Anthony."

She hesitated for a couple of seconds as she gazed at the image and then said: "But I don't understand. Why did you show me the other photograph?"

"It is difficult for me to explain," said Edward. "But I believe that other man is pretending to be your husband."

"Pretending?" she said, as if grappling with the meaning of this word.

"Yes. He has told me he is your husband. But I thought this other one was him."

"Why would he... *pretend*... to be Anthony?"

"I don't know. I believe he is a fraud."

"A fraud?"

"Yes, a criminal of some kind."

The woman began to cry.

"That explains the money," she said.

"Money?"

"Yes. Anthony and I have a shared bank account which we still use to pay for things for the children. But there is no money left. I have been blaming Anthony for drawing it out. But he is not like that. He cheated on me but he is not a bad man. I am sure he would not cheat his children. Could this man, who is *pretending* (she had trouble with this word) to be Anthony have taken the money?"

"Possibly so," said Edward.

He felt in his pocket for another photograph – of Jordan.

"Do you know this man?" he asked.

She looked at the photograph and flung it back towards him.

"Yes. I know that man. He is evil. He led Anthony to that woman – the one he cheated with. Please sit down. I tell you about it."

She invited Edward to sit on a floral rug where her sewing work was laid out and asked the daughter to make some tea.

Fighting back tears, the woman recounted very slowly and in a mixture of broken English and some French the story of the marriage break-up. She had met Anthony in Hanoi when she was working as a waitress at a Western-style restaurant where he was the chef. He had been a gentleman, kind and caring, and they had quickly become attached. After their marriage he had been a good husband and a loving father.

Then Jordan had started to work at the restaurant and things had begun to change. Jordan persuaded Anthony to leave the restaurant and go into business with him as a partner in a bistro.

Anthony was a talented chef and the business flourished, to the extent that he had eventually opened six bistros and made a large amount of money. Jordan, however, was lazy and feckless and bowed out of the business before it had had chance to succeed.

He had left Hanoi and travelled the world, pursuing various dubious occupations before returning to Hanoi the previous year penniless. He had begged Anthony to give him a job as a bar manager and, being good-natured and naive in personal relationships, Anthony had agreed.

Jordan mixed in bad company, including some women who worked at a local massage parlour "with extras". He had introduced Anthony to Lan, the owner of the parlour, a seductive 25-year-old woman with a stunning figure.

Jordan took Anthony, Lan and other ladies from the massage parlour to various drinking dens in the Old Quarter of the city. The result had been that Anthony and Lan had an affair. This had been discovered by a sister of Anthony's wife Qui, and there was a big row.

Anthony told Qui he would give up Lan and revert to being a faithful husband. But he continued to meet his mistress secretly and was again found out by another member of Qui's family.

The result had been that Qui had ordered him out of the house. Despite Anthony's protestations that he had no romantic attachment to his mistress, she expected that he would go to live with Lan. But by then he had already discovered he was only one of three men his lover was regularly having sex with.

He had begged Qui to take him back. She told him she still loved him, and so did the children, but she was not ready to forgive him yet. She was hoping that time would be a healer and that she might eventually come to terms with his infidelity. She almost believed him when he told her that he had never stopped loving her and respecting her, but that carnal lust had got the better of him.

Anthony's next move had been a shock to Qui and the children. He said Jordan had moved to Scotland where he had got a job with a hotel chain and that he had asked Anthony to join him. Her husband had decided to make a clean break. He had sold all of his Hanoi bistros to a business associate and moved to the Isle of Skye, with a view to opening a restaurant there.

He told Qui that he had plenty of money in the bank to support her and the family. He hoped one day she would agree to take him back.

Edward found this story hard to understand. Why would a man with six thriving businesses in Hanoi suddenly leave his family and up sticks to a Scottish island to live with a sinister n'er-do-well?

He told Qui, who had been distressed throughout her telling of her story, that he had some difficulty comprehending what had happened.

"Why would such a successful businessman wish to leave the city where his business was so successful?" he asked her.

She hesitated while she wiped away her tears and thought of her answer.

"My family were very angry with him. They had never been very happy that I had married an Englishman. When they found out he had cheated on me they were very nasty to him. I think he was worried what they might do to him.

"And that Jordan – I think he had some hold over Anthony. They say Jordan had to leave Vietnam because he was in trouble with the police. Perhaps he was a drug dealer. I don't know. I know he is a bad man and that Anthony should never have taken him back to work for him."

Qui's daughter came back into the room with a tray of tea things, including delicate and beautifully decorated teacups. She offered Edward green tea and some milk chocolate fingers, which he accepted graciously.

Qui asked the girl to go to the kitchen and start preparing their lunchtime meal. When the girl had gone she turned to Edward and asked: "Why have

155

you come here? All this way."

"I am worried about your husband. I think Jordan and this other man, whose photo I showed you, are up to no good."

"I am sure of it," said Qui.

"Tell me," continued Edward. "Do you know some people from England called Odling, George and Edith?"

"Yes, George and Edith. They are lovely people. They came here to stay with us."

"Anthony was staying with them a few weeks ago."

"Really? I know he was fond of them. They were friends of his grandparents. He was very fond of them too. They were good to him after his father died."

"I have spoken to George on the telephone," said Edward. "They were worried that Anthony had not contacted them since he left them. He had visited his father's grave and left some flowers. I saw them on the grave. That was how I came to know about Anthony and his father. I am interested in the history of our family you see."

"I see."

Qui began to cry again and held Edward's arm.

"What has happened to my Anthony?"

"I don't know. I don't know," replied Edward, welling up himself.

His mind returned to his obsession.

"You have a son?"

"Yes, Hien. He's 12 years old."

"And one daughter?"

"Yes. You just met her – Binh. She's 14."

"She's a pretty and polite young lady."

"Yes."

"Is Hien here today?"

"No. It is the school holidays. He has gone to stay with his cousin so they can play together."

"I would like to meet him."

"He will be at home tomorrow. You can come back if you wish."

"I would like that. Tell me, is Hien called Dunsill.?"

"No. We didn't take Anthony's English family name."

Edward, the quick thinker, had a plan in mind. Qui and her family were obviously short of money now that Anthony's bank account had been emptied. Perhaps they would agree to Hien taking the name Dunsill in exchange for some financial support. He kept those thoughts to himself, as he realised all that Qui was worried about at present was the whereabouts and safety of her husband.

"Could I call tomorrow morning, at, say, ten o'clock?" he said.

"Yes. You can meet Hien then."

"If I can find out any more about Anthony I will tell you about it tomorrow," said Edward, who then took his leave.

For the remainder of that day Edward wandered the streets of Hanoi in a sort of daze. He was trying to take in all that he had heard and make some sense of it. He used a tourist map to find his way around and was able to visit some of the city's main Buddhist temples.

He spent several hours sitting in these peaceful edifices with their magnificent gaudy icons, the sweet smells of burning incense sticks and the pleasant orchards with trees heavy with various large fruits.

He smiled as he saw some of the offerings left for the enjoyment of the souls of dead ancestors – fruits and flowers but also cans of Heineken, bottles of Famous Grouse whisky, packets of biscuits and ubiquitous Choco Pies. Being a soul of a dead ancestor seemed like a cushy number, thought Edward. And being a monk or nun living at one of these temples must have had its attractions too!

He was struck by the seemingly incongruous mixture of an ancient and sacred mythology with the more mundane artefacts and images of modern Vietnamese culture.

Representations of Buddhas were displayed cheek by jowl with photographs of such North Vietnamese heroes as Ho Chi Minh and General Giap, and with pictures of people who had very recently passed away.

For a Westerner like Edward it was all very difficult to comprehend. But, then, were the goodies left for the ancestral souls any stranger than the offerings made at an English harvest festival, which in modern times can often include tins of baked beans?

Edward's mind wandered pleasantly as he observed the unusual things around him at the temples and a feeling of calm came over him, the sort of mind-numbing calm that Ulysses and his followers must have felt after eating the lotus fruits.

He eventually roused himself, conscious that his idle daydreaming was inimical to the purpose of his journey. He needed to decide what to do about the Anthonys. This time the decisive Edward was stumped.

He needed someone to turn to for a second opinion and the obvious person was again Josephine. He Skyped her through his mobile phone and told her all that he had learnt. They agreed that what they had discovered was a case of identity theft. The "new Anthony", no doubt in cahoots with Jordan, had stolen the identity of the "real Anthony". At the very least they had emptied his bank account. There were clear grounds for asking the police to investigate.

They decided the best course would be for Edward to return to Skye as soon as possible, bringing as much evidence with him as he could. Then he and Josephine would go to the local police station.

***

The next morning Edward was again awoken early by the cockerel and the National Anthem. He looked out of his window towards the scrapyard. The puppy was bounding around chasing its own shadow.

The door of the corrugated iron shack where the family lived was wide open and a dim light was shining from it. Edward was able to see far enough inside the building to notice that it was bereft of furniture. There were stone walls and what looked like several small sleeping areas partitioned off by curtains hanging in tatters. What appeared to be the main living area was dominated by two parked motor-cycles and a wide screen television.

As if on cue the three men emerged again from the building and took up their silent crouching positions in the yard.

They were obviously at prayer, thought Edward. But what was their religion?

Then, mysteriously, the two young men went to separate corners of the yard and knelt down, looking towards the ground. This behaviour went on for some time, with positions being swapped. Even the old man joined in with this strange performance.

As the light improved Edward could make out that each man was carrying a mobile phone. Then it dawned on him. They were not participating in some bizarre religious ritual. They were looking for Pokemon.

158

This particular mystery having been solved, Edward breakfasted and made his way to Qui's house. He had two missions now: to obtain as much information he could from Qui about the bank account and to meet the son of the house – the current favourite to carry on the Dunsill family line.

He knocked on the apartment door but this time he was greeted by two men, one in his sixties, the other in his late twenties. They were both of short stature, thin and dapper with fine black heads of hair, typical examples of Vietnamese manhood.

They greeted Edward politely and took him inside the living room, where Qui was waiting with her son and daughter.

"This is my father and my brother," said Qui, "and this is my son, Hien."

The three males each offered two hands to Edward to shake his outstretched palm as he told them his name. Qui instructed her daughter to fetch tea.

"My father would like to know why you are here in Vietnam and why you have come to see me."

Edward explained that he was worried that someone was pretending to be Qui's husband Anthony. Qui translated his words.

The father and the brother talked to each other earnestly for some minutes before addressing Qui again with a message for Edward. He could see that they were deeply suspicious of him.

"They wish to know what relation you are to Anthony," she said. "And do you have any identification?"

Without going into the finer points of the family tree he said he was a fairly distant cousin of Anthony's. He produced his passport, which the two men examined. There was an animated exchange between them, which Edward took to be an argument. After a few minutes Qui told him that they had found the passport to be acceptable.

"You will help my daughter get her money back?" asked her father in his stilted English.

"I can't promise, but I will try," said Edward.

Qui said she had telephoned a nephew who was a student living in London. He in turn had found a telephone number for George Odling and contacted him. George had been in touch with Edward's daughter, Julia, to verify that the man who had telephoned him was in fact her father. Julia had been shocked to learn that Edward was in Vietnam, something he had overlooked to tell her. He gathered from Qui that he would again be in hot water when he did eventually contact his daughter. He was expecting to receive a tongue lashing via email very soon.

Qui talked with her father, as the brother looked on silently but listening intently. Edward was given contact details such as addresses, telephone numbers and email addresses which could be passed on to the police. They declined to give him details of the bank account, saying they would provide them to the authorities if asked.

Edward was satisfied he had all the information he needed to pass on to the Skye police.

Tea was served and the mood lightened somewhat. Edward was mightily impressed by the politeness of the Vietnamese people and the sense of harmony which pervaded the atmosphere of Hanoi. Even in the midst of the roaring mass of motor cycles he had not seen anything approaching the road rage he had often witnessed in western cities. And Qui's family had a serenity which appealed to Edward's sensibilities and made him all the more interested in getting to know the youngest member of the clan.

Hien had stayed quietly in the background while the serious business had been discussed. Now he stepped forward to take tea and his mother introduced him formally to Edward.

"You have your school holidays today?" asked Edward as an opener.

"Yes," replied the boy.

"Do you like school?"

"Yes, very much, thank you," replied Hien, very clearly.

"You learn English at school?"

"Yes. It is my favourite subject. I would like to teach English when I get older."

"I think you will be able to do that. Your English is already good."

"Thank you," said Hien. "You are very kind."

The fresh-faced lad was already making an impact on the Englishman.

"Perhaps we could be pen pals," said Edward, who blushed slightly at suggesting such an outmoded form of communication and then added. "Are you on Facebook? We could become Facebook Friends."

"I like that very much," said Hien enthusiastically. "I am on Facebook. I

160

have two friends, my sister and my uncle."

Edward and his new friend got on famously and spent the next half hour in amiable, if limited, conversation. The cultural and generation gaps meant they had little in common, but Edward put on his best patrician airs to probe his young friend's experience of Vietnamese education. Being something of a swot Hien was glad to oblige. He could also have told Edward the name of every regular player in almost every club in the English Premier Football League, a skill seemingly shared by two-thirds of the male population of Vietnam. He was a Man Utd supporter and was actually wearing a Wayne Rooney shirt. But Edward was not interested in soccer.

He was impressed by his newly found young relative. As he had lain in bed the previous night the thought had occurred to him for the first time that something sinister may have happened to the real Anthony. In the light of day he had dismissed this idea as a fantasy. But now it crossed his mind that if his quest for Anthony went pear-shaped that in Hien he had a ready-made substitute for his generous attention.

He said goodbye to his hosts, whom he had found to be charming and refreshingly straightforward and innocent. He was determined to try to help Qui find her husband and to have her finances restored.

He could do no more in Vietnam to solve the developing mystery of the Anthonys so on returning to his hotel he used the internet to book the first available flight home.

That night he read his emails. Predictably there was a strongly worded one from Julia.

"What the hell are you up to? I had a phone call from a man called George Odling, asking about you. He told me you were in Hanoi. What the hell are you doing there? I am really worried about you. It seems you have got mixed up with some scam. This obsession of yours with family history will be the death of you. When are you going to give as much attention to your own proper family? You have changed. Please give this up. The girls and I need your support here.

"I have some bad news, I'm afraid. Clive has left me and is going to live with Rachel. I am devastated and the girls are too. They love their daddy. I don't know what I'm going to do."

Edward replied: "My dearest Julia, can I tell you how very very sad I am to learn your dreadful news? I just cannot understand Clive. You have been a wonderful wife to him and I don't know what more he could want. Don't worry about my being in Vietnam. I have met some lovely people here and I will be on my way home tomorrow. I do think there is some sort of scam going on and that the Anthony I have met on Skye is not quite what he seems. I think I will have to involve the police. But don't you worry about that. I will be home the day after tomorrow (Tuesday) and will come straight to see you. Sorry if I have let you down again, Love Dad."

He had one more job to do, though, before he left the impressive city of Hanoi. He asked the woman on the hotel reception about the scrapyard he could see from his bedroom. These people seemed to be living in very primitive conditions, he suggested to her.

The receptionist said she believed the residents of the shack were probably immigrants from the countryside. Thousands of them had recently come into the city looking for work. In the meantime they were living anywhere they could find to rent.

"I notice they have a small puppy running around," said Edward. "Would that be a pet, or will they kill it to eat?"

"Many people have pet dogs," said the receptionist. "But a family like that would probably kill the puppy when it is fully grown and sell the meat to a local butcher or restaurant."

She continued: "Mr Dunsill. I have a letter for you."

Edward took the brown envelope and sat down in a corner of the reception to open it and read the contents. There were two pieces of paper inside. The first one was a brief note from Hien. It read:

"Dear Mr Dunsill, My mother has written a letter to show to the police. It will help you. It is about my father. Please find him for us, Hien."

The other piece of paper consisted of a two-sided hand-written letter from Qui in Vietnamese. Edward was touched by their faith in him but perplexed as to whether he was getting out of his depth. The sooner he could hand over the information to the authorities the better.

Edward strolled over to the scrapyard where he found an attractive middle-aged woman crouched down near the water tank washing some vegetables. The puppy came bounding up to him vigorously wagging its tail and yelping with pleasure at finding some new company. Edward stroked it gently.

The woman smiled at him and he asked her if she could speak English.

She shook her head but then called out someone's name. A handsome 17-year-old boy emerged from the shed and the woman exchanged some words with him. The lad knew a little English and a tortuous conversation ensued with Edward.

Although he could not get a definite answer to his questions about the fate of the puppy, Edward was pretty sure that it was destined for the table. As they spoke, though, the woman was stroking it and talking to it in an affectionate tone of voice.

Edward took out his wallet and pulled out a wad of millions of dong notes – the equivalent of around £500 sterling. He passed it to the woman and told the young man that this was to look after the dog, but they had to promise to keep it as a pet and not have it chained up like its mother.

The two Vietnamese people could hardly believe what was happening. They each shook Edward's outstretched hand with two hands and thanked him.

"We keep the dog – as a pet," said the young man.

"Promise?" said Edward.

"Promise."

Chapter Fourteen

History Man

Julia was doing what she now spent most of her life doing – cleaning the house. Like Henry VIII, Edward was obsessed with finding a male heir. Like the Yorkshire Ripper's wife, Julia was obsessed with cleaning. It was her way of trying to eliminate tragic thoughts and to clear her mind.

As she mopped the bathroom floor she imagined she was washing away Clive and Rachel and all thoughts of their coupling. It didn't work, of course, but it filled in the time between preparing meals for the girls and going to her lonely bed.

She had never slept alone in a bed in all the happy days of her marriage. Clive had always been there for her at night. Even in the past few months, when his habits had become increasingly erratic and he had generally been so aloof, he had joined her at bedtime and cuddled her. At night-time any worries she had during the day had been allayed. Recently Clive had been unusually restless in bed but she had put this down to his more irregular eating patterns. He would often not have dinner until 9pm or even 10pm, a sure recipe for poor sleep.

Julia had finished her mopping and was about to turn her attention to cleaning the lavatory bowl when she heard the doorbell ring and then some footsteps in the hall. She walked through the kitchen door and saw her father walking towards her. She ran to him and flung her arms around him.

"Dad. I'm so pleased to see you."

Edward had never been very tactile with his daughter but on this occasion he hugged her warmly. He felt her trembling as in vain she tried to hold back tears.

She led him into the farmhouse's large drawing room and they sat next to each other on a comfortable velvet settee. They both had long stories to tell about their experiences of the previous three weeks. Edward let Julia tell hers first. It did her good to confide in another adult and Edward was a good listener. He was so empathetic to her situation and at the same time so incensed by Clive's behaviour that by the time it came to tell his story Julia was much more sympathetic than he had expected.

Edward said he would stay with Julia for a couple of days so that they could talk about her plight as much as she wanted to. He would also pay lots of attention to the girls. He suggested that the four of them went on an excursion to the Lapwings Country Park, an extensive and beautiful nature reserve which is a favourite family destination for a walk and a picnic.

But he told Julia that he needed to return to Skye soon to talk to the police about the Anthonys. She accepted that he needed to do that. She would not have been so acquiescent had she known that Edward was still determined to marry and have a child by Josephine.

***

Josephine had been giving Jordan and Anthony a wide berth since Edward had been away. Jordan and her mother had been spending most nights together and Anthony had paid the occasional visit to fill himself with the contents of Marilyn's drinks cabinet.

Keeping the Vietnam trip a secret, Josephine had told her mother that Edward had gone away for a few days to deal with some business in Lincolnshire. Now she announced that he would back on Skye the following day.

"More's the fucking pity," Jordan had commented in front of them both. "He's a bit creepy that guy. Nosying into people's business. And thinking he can marry you. He should know better at his age."

Josephine reacted to this angrily: "He's a good, kind man. What the hell

165

difference does age make? You're talking out of your arse."

She stormed off and tried to avoid any further conversations with Jordan until Edward's return.

It was early afternoon when she saw Edward's BMW draw up outside Meadow Cottage. She was quick to go out to meet him, giving him a warm welcoming kiss.

"He's in there – Jordan," she said.

"Right," said Edward. "Get in the car."

They drove a few hundred yards along the Tote road and pulled up on to the grass verge. Edward told Josephine everything that had happened in Vietnam and what he had found out.

"I knew it," she said. "Anthony's an imposter. He and Jordan have taken the real Anthony's money and his cottage. And if you're not careful they'll be planning to have your money too."

"Let's talk about this some more," said Edward. "There's something I have to do at Trumpan. Let's take a trip there and then get our heads together. Before we go to the police we have to be sure that we're being fair to Jordan and Anthony – that we're not barking up the wrong tree. We don't want to get caught here going through the details and the paperwork I brought back from Vietnam. We'll go to Trumpan."

When they arrived at the car park opposite the Trumpan graveyard, a popular site for tourists, several cars were going to and fro. After parking up, Edward went to the car boot and took out a large spray of lilies.

"What on earth are those for?" asked Josephine.

"Are they for me?" she asked, half jokingly.

"No, my love. They are for another lady. I'm sorry."

Josephine gave him a quizzical look.

"Come with me over to the churchyard and all will be explained," said Edward, smiling.

"This is an interesting place," said Josephine as they entered the churchyard through a metal gate. "Have you seen the remains of the church?"

"Yes, I have – fascinating."

Josephine made a beeline to the ruined church, the atmospheric site of a notorious clan massacre when the McDonalds set fire to the building and smoked out Macleods who were worshipping inside. She gazed inside the

166

roofless ruin with Edward at her side, telling him the horrific tale – a story which he already knew but was too polite to say so.

Then she went to the back of the building to read some of the inscriptions on the gravestones. Edward left her there, keen to revisit the grave of his new heroine, the notorious Lady Grange. He knelt down and gently replaced the old, now dead, lilies, with the fresh ones.

There were tears in his eyes as he recalled the tragic story of this troubled woman.

As he delicately arranged his display of flowers the silence was rent by a muffled but distinctive sound. Edward's immediate thought was that this was a gunshot, but that it could just as easily be a birdscarer, a sound he was well used to as a resident of Lincolnshire where these are used constantly to protect crops.

Curious then, but not unduly concerned, he walked to the rear of the church where the sound had come from. He was astonished and horrified by what he saw. Josephine was laid out on the grass, face downwards.

"Josephine," he shouted. "What's happened?"

"A man…. he shot at me."

Edward darted glances in all directions but there was no one to be seen.

Josephine swiftly turned over and lifted herself up to a sitting position.

"I think he went that way."

She pointed around the corner of the church in the direction of the car park.

"Are you all right?" said Edward.

"Yes. He missed me. Go after him."

Edward ran through the churchyard gate and towards the car park. Three cars were parked there but there was not a soul to be seen in any direction. He went up to the cars and looked inside them. But again there was no sign of life. Josephine came running up to him.

"Where is he?" she said.

"I can't see anybody."

"He couldn't have disappeared as quickly as that. We would see him – he was completely dressed in black, with a black hood."

"Did you see his face?"

"No. It was covered."

"Did you see a gun?"

"Yes, a pistol."

"We must phone the police," said Edward.

He took out his mobile phone and dialled 999.

"Damn," he said. "No signal."

"I'll try mine," said Josephine.

She took her mobile from her jeans pocket.

"Bloody hell. No signal."

"Let's get back in the car and drive until we can get a signal."

"Ok."

They went to the BMW and Edward stopped short. There was a piece of white lined notepaper placed on the windscreen. In large ill-written black letters were the words: "BACK OFF, FAMILY HISTORY MAN, OR YOUR FAMILY WILL BE HISTORY".

Edward's normally steady hand began to tremble.

Josephine, who had regained her composure, said: "It's them, isn't it?"

"Yes. It must be. Let's get out of here."

The car sped off and a few minutes later stopped outside the old inn where Edward and Josephine had previously had lunch.

Edward ran into the bar and said: "We need to phone the police quickly. There's been an attempted murder – a shooting."

The barmaid took him to the phone and he dialled 999.

After he had made his report Edward and Josephine sat down in the bar where they were served with stiff whiskies by the concerned barmaid while they waited for the police to arrive.

***

The next few hours saw frenetic activity. The police went to Meadow Cottage to look for Jordan. Marilyn said she hadn't seen him or Anthony all day. A search of the house produced nothing.

Then it was on to Tora Cottage. Again no one at home and no car outside.

An urgent call went to Lincolnshire Police to give protection to Julia and her family. "YOUR FAMILY WILL BE HISTORY."

Edward and Josephine told the police everything they knew and passed over the information collected from Vietnam, including Qui's letter. Marilyn was questioned but knew nothing which could help.

168

Edward and Josephine suggested to the police that it might be worth their while to talk to the old boat builder. They recalled that Fergus' behaviour had been rather odd at their last meeting.

When the detective spoke to him he was immediately forthcoming.

"My next door neighbour, the black fella, burst into my house about a week ago. He told me not to speak again to Mr Dunsill or his girlfriend about the man called Anthony. He said if I did he would kill me. I was scared. I thought he meant it. I should have told the police then, but I was scared. I am so sorry. I've never been afraid of anyone in my life before. But I'm getting old. I feel very old – and useless. I know people laugh about me – about never building a boat for a long time. But I did build boats, dozens of them."

He burst into tears.

"Now all I can do is drink sherry – and daydream about building a boat. The only boat I'll see is the one that will ferry me across the River Styx."

***

Edward was desperately worried about the implications of the note left on his car windscreen. While he was still at the inn he rang Julia and told her what had happened. He wished to warn her but at the same time assure her that she and the girls would receive police protection.

Julia vented her anger at her father, telling them that his foolish quest had put his grandchildren's lives at risk. When she finally calmed down she suggested that her safest course of action was to move out of the farmhouse with the girls until there was no longer a threat. She said she would contact a close girl friend of hers who lived about forty miles away, and beg for some temporary accommodation at her home. Edward felt ashamed at what he had done but was assured that his daughter's commonsense would keep the family safe. He promised to return to Lincolnshire as soon as the Skye police had finished with him.

Julia put her plan into action straightaway. Her friend was as supportive as she had expected and now Julia had to pack some bags, round up the girls and drive to the friend's house. It was just before teatime and Eve and Samantha were riding their ponies.

Julia was accustomed to driving very cautiously into the stable yard, taking great care not to alarm any horses that might be close by. This time her Audi saloon flew into the car parking area, sending gravel spitting out in all directions.

She jumped out of the car and ran to the schooling area (at this school this was always referred to as the menage, although purists would probably be appalled by this and insist that it should be the manege). Clive was hanging over the boundary fence, drooling over his mistress as she barked out her instructions to the two girls on their ponies.

"Change the rein," she called out, "and trot to 'A'."

Julia shouted: "Rachel, please stop the girls' lesson now. We have an emergency on our hands."

Clive was incensed by her interruption: "What's all this about Julia? You'll frighten the ponies."

"Change to walk and then halt at 'B'," Rachel called out. "What's the matter, Julia?"

"I can't explain," said Julia. "I just need the girls to dismount, collect their tack together and get into the car as quickly as possible."

This sort of thing was totally out of character for Julia, whose calm temperament she had inherited from her father. Clive realised this and his initial anger soon turned to concern.

As the girls dismounted and Rachel took control of the ponies, he approached Julia hoping to get to the bottom of her actions.

"I haven't got time to explain everything now," she told him. "But basically Dad has got himself involved with some criminals and now they're threatening to take it out on us. There was a shooting. Luckily no one was hurt. The police are involved. It's not Dad's fault, just bad circumstances. We're going to stay with Maddy for a few days until it blows over."

"I don't believe it. Your dad involved with criminals. Is he going round the twist?"

"I can't explain it now. We have to go. I'll ring you."

She bundled the girls into the car and sped off, leaving Clive totally bemused and anxious for his family's safety.

***

Meanwhile Peter Wattam's car drew up outside Julia's farmhouse crunching the deep gravel which covered the spacious driveway. It came to a halt and Harry Greensmith got out. With Peter's help he had dug up some interesting new family history which he hoped Julia would email to her father.

Harry noticed that a black estate car was already parked at the front of the house. As he approached the front door a rough looking man came from the side of the property.

"Afternoon," said the man to Harry.

"Good afternoon," said Harry.

"I don't think there's anyone at home," said the man. "I've been round the back but I can't see anyone or make anyone hear."

"Oh, I see," said Harry. "Are you looking for Mrs Jones?"

"Yes," said the other man. "But I've given up. I'm off now."

Harry looked at him intently.

"I think I know you from somewhere," he said.

"I don't think so, guv," the man replied. "I don't live around here."

"I do though," said Harry, staring at his face.

Harry continued: "You're Anthony Dunsill, aren't you? But are you? I've seen a photograph of you. There's a bit of a mystery going on. There's two of you."

"Don't know what you're talking about, mate. Now I have to go."

"Just a moment," said Harry.

He walked over to Peter's car and knocked on the window, beckoning to Peter. The younger man got out of the car and Harry said to him: "Is this the Anthony Dunsill you met at the churchyard."

"No, Mr Greensmith. This ain't him. Nothing like him."

The man grabbed hold of Harry by his jacket lapels and then pressed his fingers hard against his throat.

"If you know what's good for you, you'll forget you ever saw me here," he growled.

Harry grew red in the face owing to the pressure on his neck and suddenly his knees buckled and he fell to the floor.

The man ran off in the direction of his car, while Peter knelt down to attend to Harry.

Gravel showered them as the black car was driven off at dangerous speed.

"Mr Greensmith, are you okay? Are you okay?" said Peter desperately.

The old man lay motionless. He had breathed his last breath.

***

From Stein, Edward and Josephine had gone to Portree Police Station where they gave statements about what had happened at Trumpan and explained all their fears concerning the Anthonys.

It was 8pm now, the questioning by detectives who had arrived from the mainland and the taking and processing of statements having lasted for several hours.

They were about to leave the station reception, when a male detective sergeant hurried out from a back office.

"Do you know a Mr Harry Greensmith?" he said.

Edward confirmed that he did.

"I have news that Mr Greensmith has died in suspicious circumstances outside your daughter's home in Sanderholme. It would seem that he was involved in a struggle with a man who may have been claiming to be Anthony Dunsill. The description is very much the same as the photo you have shown us of your alleged imposter."

"Oh my god," said a shocked Edward. "Harry. Poor Harry. What was he doing at my daughter's home?"

"It seems as if he had gone to visit your daughter with another man, a Mr Peter Wattam, to pass on some information to your daughter so that she could relay it to you. He may have died of a heart attack after some rough handling by your imposter."

"Is Julia all right – and the girls?"

"It would certainly seem so. She had already taken the children and gone to stay with a friend. If you don't mind, sir, we just need to ask you a few more questions about Mr Greensmith and how he got involved in this business."

"Of course," said a visibly shaken Edward. "I can't believe poor Harry has got caught up in all this mess. He was such a kind old gentleman. This is all my fault. My stupid fault. Why couldn't I just have stayed at home and looked after my family? This terrible thing would never have happened to poor Harry."

Josephine took his arm: "You weren't to know things would end up like this. It's that disgusting pair that are at fault."

The detective led the couple into the back office for a further round of questions.

***

"I have to go home," said Edward to Josephine as they left the police station.

172

"Julia is in danger."

He paused.

"But you're in danger here too – they've had one go at you. What are we going to do? Will you come down to Lincolnshire with me?"

"I'll be all right," replied Josephine. "I have work to do. I have a business to run."

"This is such a terrible mess," said Edward. "I feel so guilty. I've put my whole family at risk and my future wife is in danger too. I want to be by the side of all of you."

Josephine put her arm around his shoulder: "You may be in some danger too, whether you are here or in Lincolnshire. You will be even more of a target than the rest of us.

"It must have been Jordan who shot at me and we know that the so-called Anthony is a threat to Julia and your granddaughters. So there's some danger in Skye and even more at Sanderholme. But I don't think we should worry too much now. They must know the police are on to them, so I think they'll be lying low. What would either of them gain by attacking anyone else – you, me, Julia?"

"You are so cool. So rational and businesslike. You're right, of course," said Edward.

His mobile phone rang. It was Julia in an agitated state. She had been trying to contact him for several hours. Edward explained that he had switched off his phone while he was answering questions in the police station.

Julia had been visited by the police who had told her about Harry Greensmith's death. They had also told her about the shooting in the Trumpan graveyard.

Julia begged her father to return home as she felt vulnerable and lonely. Clive had been supportive but she needed her dad by her side more than at any other time of her life.

This telephone call clinched it for Edward. He told Josephine he would have to drive home straightaway. If she was determined not to go with him he begged her at least to be ultra careful. She promised she would and kissed him on the lips.

***

As he made his twelve-hour journey back to Lincolnshire Edward pored over in his mind the whirlwind predicament which had swept through his life in the past few weeks. He was savvy enough to realise that his unhealthy obsession with extending the family line and name had led both himself and others into a nightmare world. As an intelligent and rational man he knew he had shown a complete lack of judgement and wisdom. He reflected sadly that had Elizabeth been alive she would have saved him from himself.

In particular he had overwhelming feelings of guilt and grief over the way he had treated his daughter and put her life in danger.

As he drove along the main roads his sense of helplessness and hopelessness grew, to such intensity that he occasionally loosened his grip on the steering wheel, half-hoping that the car would drift into the path of an oncoming juggernaut.

He had lately been reading Kafka's short story Metamorphosis, the frightening tale of a salesman whose mother, father and sister have become dependent on him to provide their livelihoods. Then he wakes up one day to find he has turned into a repulsive many-legged insect. His shocked family are at first frightened and embarrassed but still sympathetic and attentive to his needs. But as time goes by they find him a burden too great to bear and neglect him until he eventually dies. The family members then undergo their own metamorphoses, getting jobs of their own and gaining in self-confidence. They are better off without the son.

Edward believes he has become just such an insect. Up until now his family have benefited from his wealth and generosity. But his recent irresponsible and skittish behaviour had made him a liability to them. They would be better off if he were squashed.

His thoughts also wandered to those redoubtable fairies in the Water Babies, Mrs Doasyouwouldbedoneby and Mrs Bedonebyasyoudid. He recognised his recent neglect of his daughter and her family fell short of the requirements of the former old woman and was deserving of severe punishment from the latter.

Such random thoughts were uppermost in his mind on most stretches of his journey and they filled him with sadness and horror. But during other parts of his drive his mind strayed back to the obsession from which he could not break free. He still desired to have a son with Josephine. He also wished to embrace Hien, his young relative in Vietnam.

Not content, though, with these family obsessions, he now had another nascent obsession, with the story of Lady Grange, the badly used woman whose only fault was to suffer from an acute mental illness.

He had an inexplicable empathy with this strange, wild woman. His rationality, by which he set great store, warned him that he might be as mentally deranged as she had been. They were both people who had lived among society but whose essential inner self was apart from the conventional world around them. She had had a loving marriage for 25 years and brought up nine children but had started to behave so appallingly badly that her family banished her to the edges of the Atlantic and beyond. Would Edward's own daughter wish to do the same to him when she found out about his fantastical plan to marry and fertilise a 25-year-old woman?

Edward had a grasshopper mind, hopping from one obsession to another. He had not always been like that. He feared that perhaps senility was setting in early. So many thoughts were rushing in and out of his head that when he arrived in Lincolnshire in the early morning he had no conscious remembrance of his 530 mile journey. This scared him.

Chapter Fifteen

Revelations

On Edward's arrival it was a fine sunny day at Marshyard – literally a good day for making hay while the sun shone.

Peter Wattam and his father, John, had spent the morning scything the deep lush grass at the top of the drain bank which ran through their land. It was midday now and the hot sun was beating down on them as they toiled. Both men were wearing voluminous white shirts and jeans held up by bright red braces. They had flat check-patterned grey and white caps, which they occasionally raised so they could mop their sweating heads and brows with white handkerchieves.

Peter and John may have been similarly attired – unsurprisingly as Mrs Wattam bought all their clothes for them – but they nevertheless cut very different figures. The son was tall, slim and gangly with angular, rather pinched, features, a sallow complexion and a good head of dark brown hair, whereas the father was rotund with an ample beer belly, his round red head adorned with just a few wisps of hair above his ears.

Peter was very talkative as he worked. He had a broad Lincolnshire accent, but was well-mannered and, until something excited him, had a precise way of speaking. The father, on the other hand, was rough-tongued and spewed forth a variety of expletives. He had an aggressive demeanour despite being basically harmless and good natured.

Peter had lots to talk about that day. The events surrounding Harry's death were bearing heavily upon him and had to be described in great detail and with considerable passion.

Eventually his father tired of his constant repetition and banned him from talking about the subject for the rest of that day.

The young man obeyed him, but then proceeded to annoy his long-suffering parent by whinging about having to work when he would rather be listening to his CDs or photographing everything and everybody in sight.

"Daddy, is it all right if I take a couple of hours off this afternoon? I need to collect some photos from town?"

"No. You stupid bugger. We need to finish this bank today. If you get your arse into gear I might let you go tomorrow afternoon."

"But Daddy.... Daddy.... look down there."

"What?"

"There's an arm."

Peter was staring into the drain.

"Bloody hell, boy."

The two men scrambled down the bankside forcing their way through the long grass and reeds.

"It's an arm. Get your phone out, Peter, and dial 999."

At the edge of the water, covered in green algae and muddy slime, were the remains of a black bin bag, with a human hand and arm gruesomely protruding from it.

"Shall we pull it up onto the bank, Daddy?"

"No, son. Leave it where it is. The police won't want us to touch it."

Trembling, Peter managed to make his phone call. Then the two men stood in silence in front of their grisly discovery. The only sound came from two brown ducks, quacking and dabbling as they searched for food along the edge of the drain.

***

Standing on her doorstep, Harry Greensmith's friend Sally said goodbye to his cleaner, Helen, who had visited to give her the news of Harry's sudden death.

Sally closed the door and went into her living room where she slumped on the sofa face downwards and sobbed uncontrollably.

After a few minutes she struggled to pull herself up, steadying herself by holding on to the arm of the sofa.

She went over to a sideboard and opened a drawer. After shuffling through various papers she produced a photograph. It was a picture of a row of tennis players proudly holding club trophies. A handsome man with perfectly creased white short-sleeved shirt and shorts was standing next to a stunningly attractive tall lady with shining auburn hair tied into a pony tail. It was Harry and Sally themselves.

She stared at the photograph for a full ten minutes as if mesmerised. Her only conscious connection with the present was the sound of a loudly ticking clock on the mantelpiece.

All her attention was on Harry, her truest friend in the whole world and yet one who had never shown any amorous intent towards her, nor she to him. Sally loved Harry, but in a pure, non-sexual way. She hoped that she might have had a small place in his heart. She knew she would miss him terribly.

Harry was modest, self-effacing, ineffably polite and cautious. He was a good man.

The previous day Sally had been wracked with awful pain from the terminal cancer which had been diagnosed some six months earlier. The only thing which had kept her going during that traumatic period of her life was her weekly meeting with Harry.

Because he was a courteous man, he would always greet her by asking about her health. She would reply succinctly and then the matter would be spoken of no more. Harry had known that on this afternoon of the week at least she wished to forget about her illness and think of better times in the past.

Now that avenue of relief had been closed for ever, Sally knew that all she had left to look forward to was pain – and death.

A strange calm came over her as she placed the photograph back in the drawer. She went back to the sofa and sat serenely, as if waiting for death to come.

And come, of course, it did. Not that day, or the day after, but after a couple of months, under the care of Macmillan nurses. She finally fell asleep while listening to a CD track of the Trish Trash Polka.

178

Standing next to her kitchen sink which was full of dirty pots and cutlery, Kathleen Wattam swigged deeply from a bottle of brandy as if her life depended upon it. Then, clutching the empty bottle, she dashed outside to the bottle garden. She picked up a trowel and, crouching down, dug a hole in a vacant space between the hundreds of vessels already planted. Carefully she placed the brandy bottle, bottom up, into the hole before standing up and admiring her handiwork.

She scurried back into the house to fetch her handbag and, leaving the cottage door unlocked, walked swiftly, although a little unsteadily, along the muddy grass track alongside the drain.

As she walked towards the lane at the end of the track she saw the familiar figures of her father and brother circled by several police officers. Three police cars were parked on the lane.

She hurried towards them, but, having consumed a full bottle of brandy, added to the distance by swaying from one side of the track to the other.

"What's up?" she called out.

John Wattam ran towards her and, holding her arms, stopped her from getting close to the grisly scenes further along the drain bank.

"You stay there, duck," he said. "Don't go any farther. There's bin a murder."

"A murder?" she shouted, incredulously. "What do you mean, a murder?"

"Peter and I have just found a body - or bits of a body – in the drain. The police are dealing with it now. It's a rum do, duck."

A female police sergeant approached them. She asked Kathleen what she was doing there. Kathleen explained, as coherently as she was able, that she lived further along the drainside and she had been planning to walk into Hayfleet, a small ancient market town about two miles distant, to do some shopping at the Co-op.

The police officer asked Kathleen to go with her to sit in one of the police cars so that she could take some details about her and ask if she had seen anything untoward happening in the vicinity.

But, except to provide her name and address, Kathleen was unable to provide any useful information.

When she and the police officer got out of the car, John and Peter were waiting for them.

"Have you finished with her?" asked John.

"Yes, for now," said the officer. "But we will probably need to talk to her again – as the closest neighbour."

Kathleen was looking flustered and a little disorientated. John took her hand and said: "You must come home with us. We don't know who's about around here. It might not be safe for you to be on your own."

"Yes. You must come home with us, Kath," concurred Peter firmly. "There are murderers about. Did you hear about what happened to Mr Greensmith?"

"No, I didn't," said Kathleen. "Tell me on the way to Mum and Dad's. Thanks, Dad. I will come home with you. It's all really scary, ain't it?"

The police officer checked with a more senior officer that the Wattams were free to go. She was told that they would first have to go to Sanderholme police station to make some statements. Also the scythes they had been using on the bankside would be needed for forensic examination.

This threw Peter into a panic.

"They don't think we did the murder do they, Daddy?"

"I should bloody hope not," replied John. "I expect they have to be sure, though."

***

The Wattams were questioned separately, John taking everything in his stride but Peter and Kathleen both becoming agitated with the worry that they might be in the frame as suspects. Then came an important breakthrough, as John was shown a photograph of Anthony Dunsill's impersonator.

"Oh, god, I know that fella," said John. "He was our Kath's boyfriend. Sid he was called. Me and the wife thought he was a wrong 'un from the beginning. Left her in the lurch a few weeks ago. Do you think he could have done it?"

The male detective declined to give an opinion but passed the photograph to a female colleague, who in turn took it to the woman detective who was interviewing Kathleen in the next room.

The photo was shown to Kathleen, who screamed out: "Oh, Christ. It's Sid. What's he got to do with this?"

Quivering in a state of shock, Kathleen told the detective all she knew about Sid, whose surname he had told her was Stone. She had met him in a

Hayfleet pub one night about six weeks previously.

The couple had quickly got to know each other and after a few days were into a full-on relationship fuelled by a mutual interest in heavy drinking. Within three weeks of their first meeting Sid had moved into her cottage.

She and Sid had got on really well together, although Kathleen said he could be moody and quiet.

"Well, a bit boring, if I'm honest," she said.

Their relationship had cooled off after a new person arrived on the scene.

"This half-caste bloke, called Jason, came into the pub one night. I didn't like him. He was full of himself and rude to me. He just used to ignore me but Sid couldn't get enough of him. The two of them would be chatting away all night at the pub. I used to leave them and walk home. But Sid and him would be talking and drinking in the pub until the early hours of the morning.

"This went on for a few weeks. I was getting fed up with them. Sid wasn't interested in me any more. It was all Jason. Then one morning Sid just left and I haven't seen him since. I wasn't that bothered to tell you the truth. I was getting bored with him. But I can't think of him as a murderer. He was too bloody boring for that!"

The detective showed Kathleen a photograph of Jordan.

"That's him. That's him – Jason. I wouldn't be a bit surprised if he was a murderer. Nasty piece of work he was."

After several more hours of questioning, the Wattams were returned home late at night by police car. They were welcomed by a worried Mabel, who had been visited by the police herself earlier that day.

"Oh, Mum. We've had a dreadful day," said a tearful Kathleen.

"I know, duck. I know."

The mother hugged her daughter – for the first time in many years.

John took Mabel to one side and explained everything that had happened at the police station. Out of consideration for Kathleen they determined not to speak about their suspicions regarding Sid and his friend.

The good farmer's wife had a welcome supper of sausage and mash, followed by bread and butter pudding, waiting for her family and they sat down at the kitchen table to consume it. John, Mabel and Kathleen sat in silence, while Peter posed dozens of questions about what had happened – all rhetorical questions as it happened as no one could be troubled to reply to

181

them. Eventually Kathleen told him to shut up and he went off to his bedroom in a deep sulk.

The others finished their meals and went to their beds, wishing each other cursory "goodnights" as if in a daze.

***

It is 3pm, two days after the discovery of human remains in the drain at Marshyard. Edward is in the sitting room of his Marshlands house, having arrived there that morning with Julia and the girls. They have decided to stay together at Edward's home both for safety in numbers and because the farmhouse has become a crime scene following Harry Greensmith's death.

Julia has gone out to keep a doctor's appointment while the girls, who are taking time off school as a precaution, are in one of the bedrooms using their tablets.

A police car with two officers inside is stationed in the driveway.

There have been numerous press reports about Harry's death. The bogus Anthony and Jordan are Wanted Men and the photos of them taken by Josephine have been circulated.

Now the focus of press coverage has suddenly switched to the discovery of two bags of body parts found in the drain. Forensic examinations and evidence about clothing from Peter Wattam and George Odling and his wife Edith have established that the remains were those of Anthony Dunsill – the REAL Anthony Dunsill.

A murder inquiry is under way, the chief suspects being the bogus Anthony Dunsill, now identified from police records as a petty criminal called James Welbeck, and Jordan Clarkson, a convicted fraudster and drug dealer. It is likely that they met while serving prison sentences.

Vietnamese police have tracked down and interviewed Jordan's aged father, Bertie Clarkson, who now lives in Ho Chi Minh City. They have revealed to British police that Bertie was a close friend of Gabriel Dunsill and that is how the real Anthony Dunsill and Jordan Clarkson came to know each other. By an apparently amazing coincidence Bertie was the son of none other than the mysterious Albert Clarkson, the Nigerian lover of Edward's Great Aunt Olivia! (It later came to light that through a random conversation in a bar many years previously Gabriel and Bertie had surprisingly discovered they both had a link with Sanderholme. Looking through his late father's correspondence, including diaries, letters and various newspaper cuttings relating to the African Jungle fairground attraction, Bertie learnt about Albert's dishonourable tryst with Olivia.)

The police have relayed much of this information to Edward, whose initial frisson of shock has turned into utter incredulity that he and his family should be enmeshed in such a living nightmare. He has found it difficult to take in that three generations of two families have become inextricably linked in the most bizarre and sinister of circumstances. Despite the chilling horror of it all and the danger he feels himself in, Edward cannot escape the frivolous thought that dear Harry Greensmith would have revelled in this rich discovery of juicy family history. Not just a skeleton in a cupboard but body parts in a drain!

As Edward sits silently contemplating all that has happened the sitting room door opens and Julia walks in. She looks pale and has a pained expression which suggests she is worried about something. She sits down next to her father on the sofa.

"Are you all right, love?" asks Edward. "You look anxious."

"Oh, Dad. I have some shocking news. Thing is – I'm two months pregnant."

"Pregnant?"

Edward pauses for a few seconds then puts his arm around her shoulder and declares: "That's absolutely marvellous. Congratulations!"

Julia looks at him quizzically and replies: "Congratulations? But I don't have a husband any more. I will be a single mother, fending for myself. Will I be able to cope?"

"Of course you will. You are the world's greatest coper. You're not going to be short of money and I promise I will be here for you. I'll stop all my wandering about. I really will. Is the baby Clive's?"

"Of course it is. I've not been with anyone else. Not like him."

"I only asked because I thought you two might not have been getting on very well recently."

"We have and we haven't. Yes, Clive has been distant for several months now. But we have got together a few times, although in retrospect I think that was probably because Clive was trying to cover his tracks – trying to prove occasionally that he still loved me and that all was well."

"I suppose you're right," says Edward. "He really has been unfair to you.

But, as they say, life goes on. A new baby could be just the ticket for taking your mind off your troubles."

"You're more relaxed about this than I am, Dad. But you always were able to take things in your stride. I used to be like you – but I've changed just lately. It's just been one damned thing after another.

"I just don't know if I'll be able to cope with a baby and the girls all on my own."

"You won't be all on your own," said Edward. "I'll do everything I can to help. I'll pay for a nanny if you like. And even though Clive has let you down so badly I'm sure he won't just disappear. I think he'll realise he has responsibilities and take them seriously.

"I'm sure that when all this nasty business of the murder is over and done with everything will start to get better. I'm absolutely sure it will."

"You're so bloody optimistic. I could kill you," snaps Julia.

But then she at last breaks into a smile.

"Husbands – fathers: they're no good for anyone."

"Sorry, dear. I'll make it up to you one day."

***

Edward was in a melancholy state of mind as he thought about his predicament. He knew that life is like a very long hurdle race. Even though you might knock down a hurdle you know you have to carry on and meet more of the obstacles. You will knock some more down and successfully encounter others. The hurdles will always be there. The extent to which you enjoy the race will depend on your personality, much of which you will have inherited from your forefathers.

Julia was wrong. Edward was not by nature optimistic. Rather he was a realist who accepted life as a continuum and who understood that we never truly know any other human being. We are born, we eat, we sleep, we die and then our atoms morph into a million disparate new forms – animal, vegetable and mineral. We meet a multitude of people. Sometimes we love them. Sometimes we even marry them. But however close we become everyone is a passing ship. We might cross someone's path in the street, meet them for a few minutes and have a conversation in a bar, or be friends with them for eighty years. But we never really know them. People are like icebergs; we only see what is above the surface. The innermost workings of our minds are unseen and impenetrable.

Our conversations are meaningless. They are a form of dancing with words, sometimes beautifully choreographed but never more than a superficial performance designed to impress, or just satisfy, our partners or other audience.

And we tell lies continuously to get through the day – the continuum of a humdrum existence.

Speaker 1: "Hello. How are you?"

Speaker 2: "I'm fine, thank you. Nice weather today, isn't it?"

The truth:

Speaker 1: "I can't think of anything interesting to say to you, because I am not a very interesting person and I don't think you are very interesting either. And anyway even if you are the most interesting, attractive person in the world I am too busy with my own affairs to have a proper conversation with you. I don't really care how you are. As to the weather, I couldn't care a stuff what the weather's like. I've got a car down the road and a nice warm house to sit in. You know exactly what I'm doing anyway, so no offence will be taken. We are just dancing a conventional dance of words."

Speaker 2: "I'm feeling absolutely lousy and I'm just going to the doctors because I have this dull debilitating pain, constantly – continuum. But I'm not going to bore Speaker 1 by telling him about my misery, because I know he won't be interested. In fact he will probably be pleased to learn that I'm suffering. It will make him feel better because he's okay himself. On the other hand, he may be feeling totally sick. But do I care? No, I've got my own problems, thank you. The weather? I'll just say 'Yes, it is a nice day' – just to be agreeable, you understand, and to show that I'm a sociable sort of chap, even though I can't wait to finish this boring conversation with this boring person and get on my own much more important life."

The dance of lies will continue throughout our lives until the day we die. That's the truth.

Edward had told plenty of lies in the previous few weeks. Somehow, though, he didn't much care. He just had to keep on dancing until the final dance of death took him into oblivion.

***

Father and daughter continued in conversation for an hour or so, mulling over her pregnancy and talking about the horrific events of the previous few days. What they said to each other, though, was superficial compared with those things which were unsaid. Julia's thoughts were all on a future with a new baby but without Clive. Her sadness brought her close to tears. Edward, by contrast, was elated by the chance that his new grandchild might be a boy – a true heir to the Dunsill family line.

The doorbell rang. Edward opened the front door to Detective Inspector Bronwyn Lewis and a male detective constable and he invited them inside. The police officers brought the welcome news that both Jordan Clarkson and James Welbeck (alias Anthony Dunsill and Sid!) had been arrested, Clarkson at Gatwick airport where he was waiting for a plane bound for the Far-East, and Welbeck at an M1 service station.

When the officers left a wave of relief swept through Edward's house. He and Julia hugged each other and then Julia rushed upstairs to tell Eve and Samantha. The nightmare was over.

***

Not only was the nightmare over for Edward and his family. The Wattam family had also had their lives turned upside down in recent weeks.

Peter Wattam's naïve view of the world had been shaken up entirely. A man with a simple and unquestioning Christian faith, he had been confronted with evils which had shocked him to the core. He had seen a kind, gentle old man, Harry Greensmith, meet an untimely death. He had seen mutilated body parts emerging from the drain running through his father's land. His sister had been co-habiting with a murderer and, at least for a few hours, he had the terrifying experience of thinking that he and his father might be suspects.

He constantly turned over in his mind the circumstances which had led to Harry Greensmith and himself visiting Julia's home on the fateful day of Harry's death.

Earlier that day Peter had excitedly phoned Harry, saying that he would like to see him as soon as possible. He had made a discovery about the Anthony Dunsills which would be of great interest to Harry and particularly to Edward.

A meeting at Harry's apartment was arranged for the same morning, Peter managing to evade his father who was expecting him to do some serious farm work.

Peter thrust a copy of a photo into Harry's hands.

"Who's this?" asked Harry.

"This is the man who reckons he is Anthony Dunsill," replied Peter. "He's not the man I met at the churchyard."

Harry asked Peter how he had obtained the photograph.

"I saw George Odling and we were talking about this rum do about Anthony Dunsill. He gave me a copy of this photo. Mr Edward Dunsill had sent it to him. I thought you would like to see it."

"Oh, yes. Thank you, Peter. It's very interesting. He is clearly not the man in the photo you took. I never thought for a moment that you were mistaken."

"The thing is, though, that I thought I recognised this man," said Peter. "I thought I had seen him about in Hayfleet. Then, well you wouldn't believe it, I came across this."

Peter passed over another photograph.

"I took this photograph at the Marshyard Summer Fete. The Queen's Head at Hayfleet were doing the bar and this man was helping the barman by collecting glasses."

"It's the same man," said Harry. "The one who says *he* is Anthony Dunsill. It's extraordinary. I don't know what's going on."

"It's a rum do," said Peter.

The pair decided that Edward needed to know about their discovery. So they decided to make their fateful trip to Julia's house with a view to asking her to email the new photo to Edward.

The upshot of all this was that Peter unfairly blamed himself for leading Harry to his death and a feeling of guilt stayed with him for the rest of his life.

For Kathleen too the revelation that she had been so close to a murderer was life-changing.

She became subdued and depressed, even deciding to give up her cottage and her beloved bottle garden to live the quiet life of a spinster with her elderly parents.

As could be expected, those parents did all they could to provide the love and stability which their troubled children so badly needed.

***

During the next few weeks Edward decided he needed to stay with Julia, whose emotions were fluctuating. One day she was excited by the prospect of her new baby, while on another she went into a deep depression about the loss of her husband and life as a single parent.

She was particularly upset that Eve and Samantha seemed to be spending so much time now with Clive and his mistress Rachel. She felt as if they were abandoning her, but in truth she was being paranoid. It was their ponies and their riding they were attached to as much as their errant father.

Edward was extremely fond of his granddaughters — and they of him. To lure them away from the stables so that he and Julia could spend more time with them he arranged a series of excursions in Sanderholme and the surrounding area.

Sanderholme has lost nothing of its appeal to families over the decades. It has some of the longest, sandiest and cleanest beaches in the British Isles. It retains most of the attractions associated with a traditional English seaside resort — donkeys, funfairs and amusement arcades, bowling greens and sea front gardens, ice cream, hot dogs and candy floss, fish and chips and mushy peas, brash pubs and reasonably priced cafes.

The end-of-the-pier shows have disappeared but the town has a bright new theatre, several leisure centres and a multiplicity of amusement centres offering the high tech experiences which modern youngsters demand.

Many millions of pounds have been invested in the tourism industry in recent years, with more ambitious plans on the horizon. Hotels and guest houses still play their part in providing value-for-money holiday breaks but now by far the biggest providers of tourist accommodation are caravan and chalet sites, often beautifully landscaped with tree-lined avenues and well-stocked fishing lakes.

Many UK holiday resorts have not kept pace with modern trends and are desolate, depressing places. But Sanderholme is on the up and continues to attract millions of visitors every year.

So there was no lack of facilities to cater for Edward, Julia and the two girls when they went on their days out. They went swimming, played crazy golf and putting, visited an aquarium, went tenpin bowling, made sandcastles, visited a virtual reality cinema, watched performing seals at a marine zoo and ate as much as they could eat at a Pizza Hut. Further down the coast they visited a nature reserve with scores of varieties of birds and got close to the animals at a farm park.

For Julia these little trips not only gave her the chance to bond again with Eve and Samantha but also offered her a glimpse of the fun she could have with her new baby. Edward could sense she was slowly returning to her usual positive self.

***

Edward was deeply conscious that he had unfinished business with Josephine on the Isle of Skye and he kept in daily contact with her by phone and email. He promised to travel to the island as soon as he could "get away with it". He had still not broken the news to Julia about his engagement.

Josephine accepted the situation with great coolness and patience, telling him that his first duty was the health and wellbeing of his daughter. But she did keep pressing him on two other matters: his promise to pay for her new boat and their house hunting, both of which had been put on hold when Edward made his hastily arranged trip to Vietnam.

Josephine said she had been to look at the £200,000 boat which she had seen advertised and it would be absolutely ideal for her purposes. But there was another potential buyer and so she needed to act quickly. Also she had gone ahead with several house viewings while he was away and had found a lovely lochside house at Skeabost Bridge which she was longing for him to see.

She emailed photos to him of the boat and suggested he looked at Rightmove to see details and pictures of the house.

Edward acted quickly to secure the money she needed for the boat, transferring the funds to her bank account. He owned several houses in Sanderholme which he rented out. The tenants of one had recently left to return to their native Poland because they felt unsure of their future in the UK following Brexit. So Edward put this house on the market to help towards the £200,000.

Edward had never been one to splash his money around. He had come from a well-to-do family with a useful pile of "old money" and he had gradually increased his wealth through prudent investments in property. Now, though, he feared he was being reckless. Although he could afford to buy the boat, it worried him that he had not drawn up a proper business agreement with Josephine. He was reliant on her good faith to keep to her word and marry him.

The lochside house on Skye was priced at £400,000 – a substantial sum even for him.

However, Edward's greatest anxiety was not the money as such; it was the thought that he was betraying his daughter and her children by diminishing their inheritance. Such was his obsession with having a male heir that he had managed to put this thought to the back of his mind. Now, though, his fantasy was fast becoming a reality and posing an existential dilemma.

Julia's pregnancy had muddied the water. If she had a baby boy why would he need to produce a baby with Josephine? The brutal fact was that his young fiancée would be surplus to requirements.

This was Edward's quandary. Did he stay loyal to his daughter and her family and cynically ditch Josephine? Or did he betray Julia and become a Sugar Daddy with a sexy young wife?

Edward had never been a gambler, but he had always been Mr Decisive. This time, though, he chose a course of least resistance – he would play for time. He would buy the boat but procrastinate on the question of the Skye house until he found out whether Julia's baby was a boy or a girl.

The fact that he had allowed himself to get into this predicament disgusted him. The worry of it stopped him sleeping at night. His damned Conscience was troubling him.

An additional cause of his insomnia was that he knew he would have to tell Julia something about what was going on. A "For Sale" board would soon appear outside the house in Sanderholme he was selling as well as adverts on Rightmove and in the local newspaper. Julia would soon find out about this and want to know the reason for the sale.

So, like Macbeth, he knew he had to "screw his courage to the sticking place" and tell her something.

With the murderers safely behind bars, Julia and the girls had returned to the farmhouse. Julia was still suffering from anxiety, though, and so Edward visited them every day to give whatever support he could.

He arrived one evening to find her clearing up after dinner. The girls were up in their bedrooms. He asked his daughter to sit down with him at the kitchen table. This in itself alarmed Julia as the last time she had been invited to sit down at this table was when Clive had announced he was leaving her.

"I have something I need to discuss with you," he said.

Julia sat down, cupped her chin in her hands and look at him intently.

"I've told you about Marilyn and her daughter, Josephine. Well – this is going to surprise you – Josephine and I got on really well and I went on a couple of boat trips with her. I told you she ran a boat business, didn't I?"

Julia nodded.

"She really is a very enterprising young woman and extremely ambitious. And she certainly knows her stuff about the boat business. I was very impressed by her acumen."

"Well, the thing is, she asked me if I would consider investing in her business. She wants to expand it by buying a second trip boat. I know that her ultimate ambition is to have boats running from all the main Scottish islands.

"The long and the short of it is that she has asked me to invest £200,000 to buy a new boat – and I have agreed."

Julia sat bolt upright.

"Two hundred thousand pounds! That's a helluva lot of money, and risky too, I should think. Dad – I really am starting to worry about you. What will you get back from this investment and where will the money come from?"

"Oh, we have gone into the investment very thoroughly," lied Edward. "I am sure I'm on to a winner here. As for the money – well I've put a property on the market – 12 Candleshoe Place. It should raise more than enough."

"12 Candleshoe Place? You must be mad. That's part of the family's security gone up the swanny. Are you deliberately trying to be cruel to us?"

"Of course not, dear. I'm sure I won't be losing any money in the long term. In fact I fully expect to make a good profit."

As he said these words his heart sank as he realised he really had no idea whether he would get any money back at all. Under the present arrangements the only circumstances in which he would have any share of the profits was when he and Josephine became a married couple.

Julia was entirely unconvinced. She was cautious, as her father had always been until now, and liked the security which she believed only bricks and mortar could provide.

"Please think about this a little more before you make a decision, Dad. For instance, are you really sure that her business plan is up to scratch?"

"Yes. I'm sure it is."

Edward had seen no business plan and had not even asked Josephine if she had one. He dared not reveal that he had already paid the money over to his fiancee. He knew he was a fool. He could see that Julia was incandescent at his news and he was desperately thinking how he could sugar the pill.

"I knew you wouldn't be happy at what I had to say, and I don't blame you in the slightest. I know that my behaviour has been a little… erratic… since your mother died and I apologise for that. I promise it will stop now."

He had no intention of keeping this promise as he was still planning to take two steps which were infinitely more erratic than anything he had admitted to so far – marrying Josephine and having a child with her.

He could see that Julia was becoming emotional. He was thinking "on the hoof" now and he blurted out a scheme to which he had given no previous consideration.

"I'm not getting any younger. As you know, I've been saving up for a pension for more than 40 years and I can draw it at any time I choose to now. This will give me more than enough to live on for the rest of my life – however long or short that may be.

"I don't want you and the girls – and the new offspring - to be waiting for me to die before I can share any of my money with you. So I have decided. I am turning over Dunsill's Properties to you – all its business and all its property assets except for Marshlands."

"But, Dad! Are you sure you're not being too reckless?"

"I'm quite sure. Never been surer of anything. You're probably going to be a bit short of money after all this business with Clive is sorted out. So I don't want you to have to wait for years for me to die before you can get some advantage from the family business."

Julia smiled and took his hand. There were tears in her eyes as she said: "Thank you so much, Dad. I'm sorry I've been so horrible to you. I shouldn't be telling you what you should do with your own money. You go ahead and buy your boat and enjoy following your investment. But do be careful. That's all I ask."

"I will," said Edward.

As he lay awake in bed that night the magnitude of what he had just promised to Julia suddenly hit him. It was true that if he signed over Dunsill's Properties to his daughter he would still have enough money to live on. But when he married Josephine and they had a baby his pension income would be stretched. Of course, there was no guarantee that Julia's new baby would be a

192

boy. Or that any baby he had with Josephine would be a boy either. She might have to produce three or four girls before a boy came along – with all those extra mouths to feed.

His pipe dream of fathering a male heir could drive him to poverty, or at least to being dependent on Josephine's business for his livelihood. He was pretty sure that this was not what she had in mind.

It was seven o'clock in the morning before he finally managed to get to sleep. But half an hour later he was awakened by the insistent ringing of the phone at the side of his bed. It was Josephine.

"I've got some very bad news," she said. "The boat was sold a just a couple of hours before I went to buy it. I'll have to start looking for another one. And, I'm afraid it gets worse. The house at Skeabost has been taken off the market. The couple who own it have split up and the wife is going to carry on living there."

Chapter Sixteen

Decision Time

After three weeks at Sanderholme Edward judged that Julia's state of mind had significantly improved. She was beginning to envisage a viable future for herself and her family – one where she would be financially secure and be able to look the world in the face.

He had also been in correspondence with Anthony's distraught widow, Qui. She was now quite heavily in debt to her family and had asked Edward to arrange for the sale of the Glenbernisdale cottage as soon as possible to raise some money.

Edward decided the time was ripe for a visit to Skye. He had a longing to see Josephine to discuss boats and houses and he had had TWO IDEAS.

He set off on his car journey up north without telling Josephine he was on his way. He knew he had   surprises up his sleeve.

On his arrival on Skye he did not look for Josephine immediately. Instead he drove straight to Glebernisdale where he found that Tora Cottage was locked up. The front door was boarded up because the police had smashed a glass panel to gain entry.

Edward decided he would need to contact the police to make sure that they had completed their investigations at the property, before finding a handyman to fix the front door and put a new lock on it.

He walked along the road to Fergus's cottage and found that old boat builder was at home and much more welcoming and relaxed than he had been on Edward's last visit.

Fergus showed him into his cosy sitting room which had a stone floor and was dominated by an ancient gunmetal grey wood-burning stove. The walls were covered with paintings of boats and there was an array of nautically themed ornaments placed on every available surface.

Fergus immediately fetched his bottle of Talisker whisky and started to pour out a large measure.

"Whoa," interjected Edward. "I'm driving. I will take a very small whisky, with a dash of water."

Fergus's hand had already slipped a huge quantity of whisky into the glass. But he complied with Edward's instruction and carefully poured some of it back into the bottle.

"I have had an idea," said Edward.

***

Two hours later Edward's car pulled up on the road alongside Portree harbour next to the mooring for Josephine's boat.

It was a Saturday in mid-October and the harbourside was teeming with an eclectic mix of visitors, including several coach parties of excited Chinese and Japanese people. Even more excited bands of seagulls were swooping down to grab chips from unsuspecting visitors who had bought them from the harbour's busy fish and chip shop.

Edward spotted Josephine standing on the deck of her boat, chatting to a handsome chiselled-featured, young man, with luxuriant dyed blond hair and a fake tan. Their conversation seemed so intense that Edward was at first loth to intervene. Eventually he got out of the car and stood on the quayside.

"Edward!" Josephine called out enthusiastically, turning away from her companion. "Come aboard."

Edward climbed on the harbour wall and then clambered onto the boat. Josephine put her arms around him and kissed him tenderly.

"It's good to see you, Edward."

"And you," he replied, beaming at her.

Josephine then introduced the young man as Sebastian, whom she had

195

recently recruited as her crew.

"This is Edward, a very good friend of mine," she said.

The two men shook hands courteously. Edward, though, felt a little put out that he had been introduced as "a very good friend" rather than "fiancé", "husband-to-be", "partner", or even – stretching it a bit – "boyfriend".

In his mind's eye he formed a picture of Josephine and Sebastian on the isle of Isay and how they might spend their time together while they were waiting for their Castaway Day customers.

After exchanging a few words about the weather – exceptionally strong westerly winds were expected later that day – Edward said to Josephine: "I have someone with me in the car. Fergus the boat builder."

"Oh, Fergus," said Josephine. "I'll come and say hello."

She climbed out of the boat and over the wall to Edward's BMW.

Fergus got out of the car to greet her with a big kiss on the lips.

"I have had an idea – about your new boat," said Edward. "I remembered that Fergus had shown me some very impressive plans for a vessel which could, I believe, perfectly fit the bill for your new trip boat."

Josephine hesitated. She immediately thought about what the barman at the old inn had said about Fergus' not having built a boat within living memory.

"What did you have in mind?" she asked.

"With Fergus' help we could have a boat built from scratch, and for a reasonable price."

Josephine looked Fergus up and down, trying to figure out whether such an old, frail looking man would be physically capable of building a boat.

"Would you be able to build the boat yourself?" she asked.

"No, ma dear. But I ken a young fella who would be able to do the building. I would supervise the project."

"Can I look at your plans?" asked Josephine, sounding doubtful.

"Aye, of course. I have them in the car now."

Edward was conscious that his car was on a double yellow line so he suggested they repaired to the village's largest hotel to discuss the matter further there.

Edward, Josephine and Fergus went to sit at a table in the hotel's comfortable lounge bar. Fergus produced his large-scale plans for the boat. He also showed some old photographs of previous boats he had built.

Edward was brimming with enthusiasm for the scheme, particularly when Fergus estimated that the total cost might be around £80,000, a country mile less than the £200,000 price tag on the boat they had previously thought of buying.

Josephine took a great deal of persuading that Fergus was capable of overseeing such a project, as allegedly he would be coming out of retirement after a break of more than 50 years!

She did, though, have plenty of confidence in Edward's business acumen, even though some of his recent decisions struck her as being surprisingly rash.

"How long would it be before I could have this new boat in action, making money out of the tourists?"

"I'm sure we could have it shipshape by the beginning of next season. Aye, that should be no trouble at all," said Fergus.

Both Josephine and Edward shook hands with him. They had a deal.

"Let me buy you both a drink to celebrate," said Fergus. "What will you have? I'll not have a drink myself – just a small sherry."

***

After they had discussed more details of their plans, Edward drove Fergus home, Josephine joining them for the ride.

After the couple had said their goodbyes to the boat builder they sat for a while in the car outside his cottage.

"Before we drive off," said Edward. "I have another idea."

"Steady on," said Josephine, laughing. "Two ideas in one day! I'm only just getting used to your surprise about the boat. Are you sure your head's up to a second idea? I'm not sure mine is."

"Just get out of the car and come with me," said Edward, pretending to be offended.

He took her by the hand and led her to Tora Cottage.

"You know we are looking for a house to share. Well what's wrong with this one?"

Josephine surveyed the exterior of the cottage with an air of distaste.

"I thought we were looking for somewhere at the side of a loch," was her first reaction.

"Ideally, yes. But this has a great view of a deer forest – and there's a lovely

197

little river down there."

"Yes, I suppose so," said Josephine, unconvinced. "But it's so run down. I like the idea of a character cottage, but this one just seems to have a bad character."

Edward asked her to imagine what the house could look like with a lot of money spending on it. Just to begin with, some coats of white paint to replace the present dirty grey colour would make the exterior look more cheerful. They could install a modern new kitchen and bathroom and knock several small rooms together to make a spacious lounge. Some landscaping work outside could transform the extensive gardens and they could add a conservatory and patio and a double garage.

Edward said he could oversee the refurbishment project while Josephine and Fergus took charge of the boat building scheme.

"I would need to have a good look around inside," said Josephine. "But I suppose with a little imagination we *could* do something with it. In fact, yes. We could. Thinking about it. Yes."

She squeezed his hand: "You're a genius."

Edward inwardly smiled with satisfaction. Buying and refurbishing this cottage could probably be done at half the price of the lochside house they had looked at previously. Another bonus which caused him pleasure was that by purchasing the cottage quickly he would be helping out Anthony's distressed widow, Qui.

He had got his mojo back! Not only had he satisfied a beautiful young woman with a boat and a house, he had probably saved himself a few hundred thousand pounds at the same time.

The couple felt excited and were full of animated conversation as they drove from Bernisdale to Tote.

Before leaving Sanderholme, Edward had spoken to Marilyn on the telephone. They had talked for a long time about Anthony's murder and the fate of Jordan and his accomplice. Marilyn was in a state of shock, fearful for the safety of her daughter following the shooting incident at Trumpan graveyard, ashamed that she herself had been gullible enough to become involved with a criminal, and apologetic to Edward for the way she had treated him.

She had accepted the relationship between Edward and Josephine and had said that Edward was welcome to stay at Meadow Cottage at any time.

When they arrived that afternoon she welcomed Edward warmly and a little tearfully. She was much chastened by the experiences of recent weeks, even to the extent of resolving to give up men. "Flying pigs" had been her daughter's reaction on hearing that news!

***

The next morning Josephine left early for work, arranging to meet Edward at a Portree hotel at 4pm. She arrived with her crewman Sebastian.

After an exchange of pleasantries and the buying of drinks, they settled down to a wide ranging conversation. Edward was particularly interested in finding out more about Sebastian, particularly as he suspected an embryonic attachment between the crewman and Josephine.

The young man was loquacious and full of self-confidence, although displaying the irritating nervous tic of constantly running his fingers through his blond mane of hair. Josephine had met him on a sailing course on the Isle of Wight where his parents ran a hotel. After leaving school with good A' levels he had spent three years backpacking fairly aimlessly around the world, taking jobs along the way as a barman, a lifeguard and a skiing instructor.

Encouraged by his parents to "settle down and make something of your life" he then took a degree in sociology at Southampton University, gaining a 2.2. Being unable to find a suitable job, he teamed up with his friend Josephine to assist in her business.

Edward was underwhelmed by this CV, feckless being the word which came into his mind. A typical beach bum. Should have been Australian.

Then it was Sebastian's turn to quiz Edward on his credentials.

"I run a property business," he said.

"Property, eh," said Sebastian, winking. "Marx said 'property is theft' ".

Edward countered: "Actually Proudhon said it first."

"Sorry to contradict, mate. But I'm sure it was Marx."

"Proudhon," insisted Edward. "He also said 'property is liberty'. He actually favoured people owning property – to a degree."

"Well, I'm talking about Marx, mate," said Sebastian, cockily.

"Marx didn't really believe that either. I understand he owned several homes."

"That's as may be," said Sebastian. "But the only property people should

199

have is what they gain from their own labour."

"So that's not theft, then?" said Edward.

"No. I guess not. But capitalists just building up their property holdings and then passing them on to their sons and daughters - that's where the unfairness in society comes in."

After a lifetime in the property business, but also with a keen interest in philosophy, Edward was well versed in this subject and ready with several well rehearsed rejoinders.

"Walter Lippman, the famous American journalist, said: 'The only dependable foundation of personal liberty is the personal economic security of private property…. Private property was the original source of freedom. It is still its main bulwark.' "

"That's tosh," said Sebastian. "Possession of property just reinforces the inequalities in society."

Edward pulled his dog-eared little notebook from the pocket of his waterproof coat and quickly thumbed through it.

"I have quotations from lots of political thinkers and philosophers to combat what you are saying. Okay, what about David Hume, the remarkable Scottish philosopher? He says: 'No one can doubt, that the convention for the distinction of property, and for the stability of possession, is of all circumstances the most necessary to the establishment of human society, and that after the agreement for the fixing and observing of this rule, there remains little or nothing to be done towards settling a perfect harmony and concord.' That's what I believe."

Sebastian replied: "I see you are well prepared for this argument. Even if I accept what you have just said, it still doesn't solve the unfairness of some people inheriting property while others never have the chance to do that."

This comment struck at the very heart of Edward's view of life. Property had always been his livelihood. He considered it to be the glue which held society together, the institution which saved human beings from being in a state of constant warfare. He had thought about this long and hard and he made it his business to enunciate his views on the subject whenever given the opportunity.

He thumbed through the notebook again. Next he quoted the 17th century German philosopher Baron Samuel von Pudendorf: "Most peoples have adopted the custom which is in itself a kind of consolation for mortality that a man may make arrangements during his lifetime for the transfer of his property in the event of his death to the person he most loves."

Sebastian began to feel out of his depth. He began to wish he hadn't started this argument. But he soldiered on.

"Just because something is the custom doesn't make it right. I don't know the people you are quoting but I guess they died hundreds of years ago. Times have changed. People care more about equality these days. You're just defending the privilege of a few."

"That may be the case," said Edward. "But you are trying to overturn the natural order of things. Why would you want to do that? Equality is a chimera which will never be achieved. Those societies which have tried too hard to enforce it have finished up as poverty stricken and totalitarian – nightmare states where thousands are slaughtered or imprisoned. Socialism is the humane suffocating the human. A journalist called Anthony Lejeune said that a long time ago. But listen to this. Sorry to go back to Hume: 'Whoever is united to us by any connexion is always sure of a share of our love, proportion'd to the connexion, without enquiring into his other qualities. Thus the relation of blood produces the strong tie the mind is capable of in the love of parents to their children, and a lesser degree of the same affection, as the relation lessens.'"

Sebastian threw up his arms in despair.

"Okay, mate. So you know a lot about old philosophers. But we're in the 21st century now. Those ideas that you're coming up with are no longer relevant. Can't you understand that? We have to get over these ideas of blood and family ties being the most important thing. All they do is perpetuate inequality. A few benefit but the vast majority are left behind, feeling dissatisfied and ignored."

Edward was well aware that this argument was difficult to counter. He had heard it all before so many times. His strong instinct was that the answer was not to take away property from those who already had it but to do everything possible to spread the benefits of property ownership, so that an increasing number of people felt the pride and satisfaction of having a stake in the country.

To some extent he was arguing against his own interests as he gained most of his income from *renting* property to people. He was genuine, though, in his wish for others to emulate his own good fortune and own their own homes.

Sebastian and Edward continued arguing in this vein for half an hour, putting their views forward in a fervent but civilised manner.

They ended their discourse by shaking hands and then Sebastian left Edward and Josephine on their own.

"A headstrong young man, but I quite like him," said Edward to Josephine, who had been cheerfully trying to hold the ring between the two combatants.

"Yes. He's lovely really. I'm sure that between us we'll be able to knock him into shape – just get him involved in the real world of business."

"That's my girl," said Edward, clutching her hand.

***

The next few months were a time of frantic activity for Edward and Josephine. There was a boat to build and a cottage to refurbish and the couple made very good clerks of works.

Work on the cottage was spasmodic owing to mixed winter weather. However, the boat building carried on apace inside a large warehouse. Fergus had a new spring in his step as he instructed his assistant boat builder.

Edward took advantage of periods of hiatus in the cottage building project to travel to and from Sanderholme. He was delighted to find that Julia's pregnancy was going well and that she was in much better spirits.

There was still plenty of involvement with the police concerning Anthony's murder and a string of other offences with which Jordan Clarkson and James Welbeck had been charged. All the signs were that they were intending to plead guilty to everything and that they were resigned to serving life sentences.

The circumstances of Anthony's murder were gradually coming to light.

Jordan had arranged for James Welbeck to travel to Lincolnshire to keep close tabs on Anthony's movements. Anthony made occasional visits to the Queens Head pub at Hayfleet so Welbeck found that a useful and hospitable base for his surveillance.

Eventually Jordan, posing as Jason, had joined Welbeck to lay their final lethal plans.

Anthony had died from revolver shots to the head, apparently administered shortly after he left the Odlings' house at Marshyard bound for Skye. His body had then been cut into pieces and placed in bin bags before disposal in the drain at Marshyard. His burnt out Alfa Romeo was found in a disused farmyard in the Yorkshire Dales.

By having James Welbeck take over Anthony's identity Jordan planned to gain all Anthony's money and the cottage he had bought on Skye.

On the surface Edward's life seemed to be full of promise. He had a beautiful, sexy, ambitious and interesting young fiancée who had promised him a baby. And it could be a boy. After the trauma of her marriage break-up and the nightmare of the Anthony saga his daughter was back on an even keel and soon to produce a baby herself. And it could be a boy. The prospects for extending the Dunsill line had soared.

But a scintilla of doubt had gradually entered Edward's mind. It concerned Josephine's crew member Sebastian. Josephine and Edward were having great sex and she was as loving towards him as she had been from their first amorous encounter on Isay. She inevitably spent a great deal of time with Sebastian too and Edward observed a growing intimacy between them. On deck he felt they were more tactile than would be expected between employer and employee. There was a great deal of eye contact and constant exchanges of smiles and knowing looks. Edward was sensitive to signs of chemistry between individuals and he was aware that a strong sensuous chemistry had developed between the young couple.

During the winter, boat trips were confined to fine days at the weekends so Sebastian was employed part-time to help Fergus and his assistant William with the boat building and also to carry out some labouring tasks for the builders who were working on Tora Cottage,

All this meant that Josephine and Sebastian were spending an increasing amount of time together, often nipping to the bars of local hotels during their work breaks.

Edward's suspicions were growing. But he was too much of a gentleman to say anything. He knew that Josephine was a sexually active young woman and it had been accepted from the beginning of their arrangement that he would not expect her to be monogamous.

He was one of the least jealous of men but he did feel that Sebastian might become a threat to his project. The problem was that he had no idea how to combat the threat. He knew of nothing which he could use to discredit Sebastian, who appeared to be hard working and likeable, if a little too pleased with himself for Edward's taste. If he was to show any disapproval the most likely result would be to drive Josephine further towards the younger man.

He decided, therefore, to keep his own counsel for the time being and wait to see how matters developed.

When March came the meteorologists were forecasting a spell of high winds, which were likely to hold up the work on Tora Cottage. Sensing an opportunity to get away for a few days, Edward acted on a whim – and booked a plane flight to Hanoi.

So much had happened since his last trip to Vietnam that he felt he needed to see Qui and her family, both to express his condolences and to bring some sort of closure to the traumatic experience of the past year.

***

Arriving at Qui's house, Edward was greeted by a welcome party which she had gathered together to show her appreciation for all he had done for them, both in helping to bring her husband's killers to justice and for buying Anthony's cottage and transferring the funds to her.

As well as Qui herself, those who were keen to meet Edward were her daughter, Binh, and son, Hien, plus her father, three brothers and their wives and various nephews and nieces. Everyone took it in turn to shake his hands to say thank you. The atmosphere in the house was restrained and filled with sadness. Qui, Binh and Hien were close to tears with thoughts of Anthony. The other family members still harboured resentment at the way in which the husband had treated his wife and children but did their best not to dwell on this for the sake of family harmony.

Edward presented Qui with a flowering plant and gave small wrapped gifts to Binh and Hien.

Qui showed him, in the corner of the living room, a small shrine, comprising flowers in ornately decorated pots and burning candles. It was dedicated to Anthony. She passed an unlit candle to Edward and invited him to light it and place it on this memorial. The family applauded politely as he did so.

"We are so grateful to you, Edward," said Qui. "You have saved my family."

Edward replied: "I have done very little. I just happened to be around."

Qui's father added: "Thank you. You will eat?"

Edward smiled and nodded. He realised there was no opportunity to refuse the offer as the women were already bringing a wide variety of dishes into the room. He was treated to a six-course feast of various Vietnamese specialities, mainly rice, noodle or fish-based, but all brightly coloured and delicious. The meal was completed by sweet biscuits and the famous Vietnamese coffee.

He was also offered Hanoi beer, quite light and not strong in alcohol content, but with a very pleasant taste.

As he took his first sip both the men and women of the family clinked his glass with theirs and declared "Cheers". He soon realised it was the Vietnamese way to repeat this every time he lifted his glass to take another mouthful.

When the meal was over Edward had a tete-a-tete with Qui discussing, as much as language difficulties allowed, the horrific murder of her husband and all the other dramatic events that had taken place.

Edward also made a special effort to talk to Hien, the twelve-year-old boy who had made a big impression on him on his previous visit. In fact Hien had been earmarked as the main Dunsill benefactor when Edward had begun to have serious doubts about the man he had then believed to be Anthony. How quickly circumstances had changed. Hien might now be third in line for acknowledgement as a male Dunsill heir, depending, of course, on the sex of Julia's baby and Josephine's potential offspring.

"I have been improving my English," said Hien. "I am having special lessons from a private teacher. The money you sent us when you buy the house pays for my lessons. Thank you very much, Mr Dunsill."

Edward was touched by this and told Hien how good his English had become. They continued to converse about the boy's school progress, his hobbies and the fortunes of Manchester Utd. Edward had spent part of the plane journey mugging up on Man Utd through Google.

Hien wanted to know about the Queen, the Houses of Parliament and William Shakespeare and expressed a wish to visit the UK in the future. Edward logged that wish in his mind with a view to helping Hien to fulfil that ambition in the years to come.

It was mid-afternoon when Edward finally took his leave of his convivial hosts, promising to return in the future and inviting any of the family to stay with him in the UK whenever they wished.

He took a couple of hours to walk around Hanoi's Old Town, visit some

Buddhist temples and just drink in the electric atmosphere of this exciting city.

On his brief visit to Vietnam Edward had experienced some surprises which had challenged all his preconceptions. His biggest surprise was the strong present-day American influence on this Communist country so relatively soon after the bitter and destructive 20-year Vietnamese war.

Both at the airport and in the streets of the Old Town he had noticed scores of American tourists. There was a huge amount of American merchandise in the shops and he had seen children eagerly tucking into KFC meals. He found the lack of any overt anti-American feeling very heartwarming.

Although still nominally a Communist state with one-party rule, Vietnam has a burgeoning capitalist economy which is bringing prosperity to millions of native people. There is an optimistic feeling among the Vietnamese who are among the most hospitable, polite and charming people in the world.

Edward was certain he would return to this lovely country before his dying day to see how it progressed.

Walking through the busy streets en route to the same hotel where he stayed on his first visit to Hanoi, he felt a warm glow of satisfaction at having done the right thing by Qui and her family.

Turning the corner of a particularly narrow street within a few yards of reaching his destination he had to swerve to avoid bumping into a smartly dressed and quite attractive middle-aged woman. Edward apologised to her and she smiled.

He noticed she was leading a cute little dog of indeterminate breed which was wearing a spectacular mauve diamante collar.

Edward looked at the dog, then looked again at the woman as they passed him. He suddenly recognised them both from the scrapyard. It was the dog he had saved from being served up as thit cho!

Edward backtracked and walked alongside the woman.

"You remember me?" he said.

The woman looked at him and smiled again.

"Yes," she said. "You gave me money for dog. Thank you."

By now the dog was jumping up and down and wagging its tail fiercely.

Edward bent down and stroked it affectionately.

"Dog's name?" he asked.

"Hien".

Edward gave a little laugh. The dog had the same name as Qui's son.

"Nice name," he said.

"It means 'friendly', said the woman.

"Ah. He is friendly."

Edward looked towards the hotel, expecting to see the woman's scrapyard home on the opposite side of the road.

But to his surprise the site had been cleared. A hoarding had been put up with a large artist's impression of a new hotel which was to be developed on the site.

Edward pointed to it.

"Your home has gone," he said.

The woman smiled broadly and pointed to a high rise apartment block nearby.

"We have nice flat there now. We are happy.

"No more...." She tried to make the shape of an animal with her hands and then put two fingers at the side of her mouth to denote whiskers."

"No more rats?" said Edward.

"Yes, no more rats," she laughed.

"I am happy for you."

"Thank you."

She offered Edward her hand and he shook it. He patted the dog once more and said goodbye to the smart pair.

This day was getting better by the minute for Edward.

But his warm welcome by Qui and her family and the chance meeting with the dog whose life he had saved were as nothing compared with what was just about to come.

He returned to the hotel intending to have a long night's sleep. His plan was to take a coach trip the next day to the magnificent Ha Long Bay, which, with its thousands of limestone islands, has been acclaimed as one of the seven natural wonders of the world.

Before going to bed Edward checked his laptop for emails. He clicked on one from Julia.

It began: "Dad, my baby has come early. It's a boy. Eight pounds two ounces. I am leaving hospital now. We are both well. I am going to call him

John Edward Dunsill."

Dunsill!

Edward's dream had been fulfilled at last.

He cancelled the coach trip and took the first available flights back to the UK – and then took a taxi from Gatwick to Sanderholme.

He found Julia and John Edward Dunsill in rude health and promised to stay with them to help out for the next few weeks.

Meanwhile on Skye Fergus had been true to his word and Josephine's superb new boat was ready to take to the sea. Work on Tora Cottage had restarted in earnest following the strong March winds.

Between changing nappies, preparing meals and doing the shopping Edward kept in close touch with Josephine.

After he had been at Sanderholme for a month he thought he could spend a few days back on Skye. So off he set once more.

On the night of his arrival he met Josephine at Meadow Cottage. Marilyn was at work.

After a brief kiss, Josephine sat him down on the sofa.

"Edward. I have something to ask you – something serious. You wanted a baby boy to carry on the family name, didn't you?"

"Yes, I did."

"And now you have one."

"Yes. I do."

"So, tell me honestly, do you still want to have a baby with me?"

Edward was nonplussed and stuck for an immediate reply.

A torrent of ideas swirled around in his head.

Here was the sexiest, most attractive young woman who had ever been a part of his life: a woman who did not mock him or pity him for his age. She was bright, ambitious and wonderful company.

And yet he had this gnawing doubt as to whether this was a relationship which he could realistically expect to endure. There had never been any intention that he would restrict Josephine sexually. This would undoubtedly lead to complications.

Although she was thrilled by her new baby, fundamentally his daughter was still in a vulnerable emotional state. He knew she would be horrified when he told her about his intended marriage.

Beyond this there was another problem: his damned conscience. His moral core told him that marrying a woman so much younger than himself was just, well – wrong. He could not rationalise this feeling but neither could he dismiss it.

He wondered why Josephine had asked him her question. He figured that the only possible reason for it was that she was hoping to duck out of their deal. So he took the coward's way out. He tossed the question back to her.

"Do *you* still want to have a baby by *me*?

Josephine was too direct a person to mess about with word games.

"You have done so much for me that I would never let you down. If you still want to marry me and have a child with me, then that's what we'll do. But if you have any doubts at all, now's the time to tell me.

"I have to tell you, though, that I am having a relationship with Sebastian."

"I almost guessed it. That's it, I suppose. That's your answer – and my answer. No marriage – no baby."

A sense of relief swept over Edward.

Josephine embraced him.

"I still love you. You're a gorgeous, kind, sexy man. And I don't want to lose you."

"You won't. Friends and business partners at least?"

Josephine gave a thumbs up sign.

"One last favour?" she said. "Could I rent Tora Cottage from you?"

"Of course."

"Close business partners, landlord and tenant, and loving friends," she said. "Shall we go to bed?"

***

John Edward Dunsill was baptised on August 12th, 2017. The Glorious Twelfth.

His deliriously happy grandfather, Edward Dunsill, started to plan his biography of Lady Grange the following day. First he needed to track down some of her family history.

THE END

About the Author

John Pendleton is a former newspaper editor who lives in Skegness, Lincolnshire, England, with his wife Wendy. All for Blood is his second novel. His debut novel, Ill Winds, inspired by the beautiful Scottish Isle of Skye, is also available from Amazon Books as a paperback or on Kindle.

Printed in Poland
by Amazon Fulfillment
Poland Sp. z o.o., Wrocław